what looks like crazy
on an ordinary day . . .

what looks like crazy
on an ordinary day . . .

A NOVEL

pearl cleage

AVON BOOKS  NEW YORK

This is a work of fiction. Names, characters, places and incidents either are the product of the author's imagination or are used fictitiously. Any resemblance to actual events, locales, organizations, or persons, living or dead, is entirely coincidental and beyond the intent of either the author or the publisher.

Excerpt on page ix is from "Celebration," *A Dark and Splendid Mass,* Harlem River Press, 1992. Used by permission.

AVON BOOKS
A division of
The Hearst Corporation
1350 Avenue of the Americas
New York, New York 10019

Copyright © 1997 by Pearl Cleage
Interior design by Kellan Peck

ISBN: 0-7394-3160-9

All rights reserved, which includes the right to reproduce this book or portions thereof in any form whatsoever except as provided by the U.S. Copyright Law. For information address Avon Books.

AVON TRADEMARK REG. U.S. PAT. OFF. AND IN OTHER COUNTRIES, MARCA REGISTRADA, HECHO EN U.S.A.

Printed in the U.S.A.

•

For Bill Bagwell,
21st-century love warrior

• acknowledgments

This book could not have been written without the love and support of my daughter, Deignan Cleage Lomax, and my husband, Zaron W. Burnett, Jr. *Thank you, thank you, thank you.*

I also thank my family and friends, especially my sister, Kristin Cleage Williams, and my father, Jaramogi Abebe Agyman, Debbie Thomas-Bryan and Don Bryan, Jimmie Lee Tarver, Walter R. Huntley, Jr., Melanie Lomax, Woodie King, Jr., Andrea Hairston, Kenny Leon and Carol Mitchell Leon, Cecilia Corbin Hunter, Carolyn Monteilh, Valerie Boyd, A.B. and Karen Spellman, Brother Kefing, *The Mongo*, Ingrid Saunders Jones, and last but never least, Jondré Pryor, who brought the good news.

Thanks also to Pat Lottier and the *Atlanta Tribune*, Susan Taylor and *Essence* magazine, Denise Stinson, Howard Rosenstone, Johnnetta Cole and Spelman College, and Carrie Feron, for their support and assistance.

I will bring you a whole person
and you will bring me a whole person
and we will have us twice as much
of love and everything . . .

"Celebration," Mari Evans

june

i'm sitting at the bar in the airport, minding my own business, trying to get psyched up for my flight, and I made the mistake of listening to one of those TV talk shows. They were interviewing some women with what the host kept calling *full-blown AIDS*. As opposed to *half-blown AIDS*, I guess. There they were, weeping and wailing and wringing their hands, wearing their prissy little Laura Ashley dresses and telling their edited-for-TV life stories.

The audience was eating it up, but it got on my last nerve. The thing is, half these bitches are lying. *More* than half. They get diagnosed and all of a sudden they're Mother Teresa. *I can't be positive! It's impossible! I'm practically a virgin!* Bullshit. They got it just like I got it: fucking men.

That's not male bashing either. That's the truth. Most of us got it from the boys. Which is, when you think about it, a pretty good argument for cutting men loose, but if I could work up a strong physical reaction to women, I would already be having sex with them. I'm not knocking it. I'm just saying I can't be a witness. Too many titties in one place to suit me.

I try to tune out the *almost-a-virgins*, but they're going on and on and now one is really sobbing and all of a sudden *I get it*. They're just going through the purification ritual. This is how it goes: First, you have to confess that you did nasty, disgusting sex stuff with multiple partners who may even have been of your same gender. *Or* you have to confess that you like to shoot illegal drugs into your veins and sometimes you use other people's works when you want to get high and you came unprepared. Then you have to describe the sin you have confessed in as much detail as you can remember. Names, dates, places, faces. Specific sexual acts. Quantity and quality of orgasms. What kind of dope you shot. What park you bought it in. All the down and dirty. Then, once your listeners have been totally freaked out by what you've told them, they get to decide how much sympathy, attention, help, money, and understanding you're entitled to based on how disgusted they are.

I'm not buying into that shit. I don't think anything I did was bad enough for me to earn this as the payback, but it gets rough out here sometimes. If you're not a little kid, or a heterosexual movie star's doomed but devoted wife, or a hemophiliac who got it from a tainted transfusion, or a straight white woman who can prove she's a virgin with a dirty dentist, you're not eligible for any no-strings sympathy.

The truth is, people are usually relieved. It always makes them feel better when they know the specifics of your story. You can see their faces brighten up when your path is one they haven't traveled. That's why people keep asking me if I know who I got it from. Like all they'd have to do to ensure their safety is cross this specific guy's name off their list of acceptable sexual partners the same way you do when somebody starts smoking crack: *no future here.* But I always tell them the truth: *I have no idea.* That's when they frown and give me one last chance to redeem myself. If I don't know *who,* do I at least know *how many?*

By that time I can't decide if I'm supposed to be sorry about having had a lot of sex or sorry I got sick from it. And what difference does it make at this point anyway? It's like lying about how much you loved the rush of the nicotine just because now you have lung cancer.

I'm babbling. I must be higher than I thought. *Good.* I hate to fly. I used to dread it so much I'd have to be falling-down drunk to get on a plane. For years I started every vacation with a hangover. That's actually how I started drinking vodka, trying to get up the nerve to go to Jamaica for a reggae festival. Worked like a charm, too, and worth a little headache the first day out and the first day back.

I know I drink too much, but I'm trying to cut back.

When I first got diagnosed, I stayed drunk for about three months until I realized it was going to be a lot harder to drink myself to death then it might be to wait it out and see what happens. Some people live a long time with HIV. Maybe I'll be one of those, grinning like a maniac on the front of *Parade* magazine, talking about how I did it.

I never used to read those survivor testimonials, but now I do, for obvious reasons. The first thing they all say they had to do was learn how to calm the fuck down, which is exactly why I was drinking so much, trying to cool out. The problem was, after a while I couldn't tell if it was the vodka or the HIV making me sick, and I wanted to know the difference.

But I figure a little lightweight backsliding at thirty thousand feet doesn't really count, so by the time we boarded, I had polished off two doubles and was waiting for the flight attendant to smile that first-class-only smile and bring me two more. That's why I pay all that extra money to sit up here, so they'll bring me what I want before I have to ring the bell and ask for it.

The man sitting next to me is wearing a beautiful suit that cost him a couple of grand easy and he's spread out calculators, calendars, and legal pads across his tray table like the plane is now his personal office in the air. I think all that shit is for show. I don't believe anybody can really concentrate on business when they're hurtling through the air at six hundred miles an hour. Besides, ain't nobody that damn busy.

He was surprised as hell when I sat down next to him. White men in expensive suits are always a little pissed to find themselves seated next to me in first class, especially since I started wearing my hair so short. They seem to take it as some kind of personal affront that of all the seats on the airplane, the baldheaded black woman showed up next to them. It used to make me uncomfortable. Now I think of it as helping them take a small step toward higher consciousness. Discomfort is always a necessary part of the process of enlightenment.

For the first time in a long time, I didn't grip and pray during takeoff. It wasn't that I was drunk. I've been a lot drunker on a lot of other airplanes. It's just that at this point, a plane crash might be just what the doctor ordered.

• 2

i always forget how small the terminal is in Grand Rapids. Two or three shops, a newsstand, and a lounge with a big-screen TV, but barely enough vodka to make me another double while I wait for Joyce, who is, of course, a little late. I truly love my big sister, but I swear if she was ever on time for anything, I'd probably have a heart attack at the shock of it.

The bartender seemed surprised when the drink he poured for me emptied his only bottle of Absolut. He set the glass down in front of me on a cocktail napkin printed with a full-color map of Michigan.

"Sorry I don't have lime," he said. "Most people come through here just drink a beer or something."

"It's fine," I said, taking a long swallow to prove it. I knew that if he could think of something else to say, he would, but our brief exchange seemed to have exhausted his conversational skills. He headed back to the TV.

It feels strange to be sitting here writing all this down. The last time I kept a diary was when I first got to Atlanta in 1984. Things were happening so fast I started writing it all down to try and keep up. Just like now. I was nineteen. I had a brand-new cosmetology license, two years salon experience, and an absolute understanding of the fact that it was time for me to get the hell out of Detroit.

When I was growing up in Idlewild, my tiny hometown four hours north of the big city, the motor city had always seemed as close to paradise as I could probably stand. Two years of really being there showed me how truly wrong I could be.

I had heard that if you were young and black and had any sense, Atlanta was the place to be, and that was the damn truth. Those Negroes were living so good, they could hardly stand themselves. They had big dreams and big cars and good jobs and money in the bank. They had just elected another one of their own to the mayor's office, they were selling plenty of wolf tickets downtown, and they partied hard and continuously.

My first week in town, I hooked up with a sister who was going to work for the new mayor, and she invited me to a cocktail reception at one of the big downtown hotels. When we got there, I felt like I had walked into one of those ads in *Ebony* where the fine brother in the designer tux says to the beautiful sister in the gorgeous gown: *I assume you drink Martel?* Folks were standing around laughing and talking and pretending they had been doing this shit for years.

My friend was steadily working the crowd, and by the end of the evening, I had been introduced to everybody who was anybody among the new power people. My first impression was that they were the best-dressed, best-coifed, horniest crowd I had ever seen. I knew my salon was going to make a fortune, and it did. I'd still be making good money if I hadn't tried to do the right thing.

When I got the bad news, I sat down and wrote to all the men I'd had sex with in the last ten years. It's kind of depressing to make a list like that. Makes you remember how many times you had sex when you should have just said good night and gone home. Sometimes, at first, when I was really pissed off at the *injustice* of it all and some self-righteous anger seemed more appealing than another round of whining, I used to try and figure out who gave it to me in the first place, but I knew that line of thinking was bullshit. The question wasn't who gave it to me. The question was what was I going to do about it. Still, when I think about all the men I slept with that

I didn't even really care about, it drives me crazy to think I could be paying with my life for some damn sex that didn't even make the earth move.

When I called Joyce and told her what I was going to do, she told me I was crazy and to let sleeping dogs lie, but I felt like it was only fair. I didn't even know how long I had been carrying it and I sure didn't know who I got it from. Atlanta is always full of men with money to spend on you if you know how to have a good time, and I used to be a good-time somebody when I put my mind to it.

So I sat down and tried to figure out how to tell these guys what was up without freaking them out. *Hey, Bobby, long time no see! Have you been tested for HIV yet? Hey, Jerome, what's up, baby? Listen, it might be a good time for you to get tested for HIV.* I don't remember what all I finally said, except to tell them I was really sorry and that if they wanted to talk, to call me anytime.

To tell the truth, I was a little nervous. I'd heard a few stories about people going off on their ex-lovers when they found out, but nobody contacted me for a couple of weeks, so I figured they were all going to deal with it in their own way. Then one Saturday, the salon was full of people, and in walks this woman I've never seen before. She walked right past the receptionist and up to me like we were old friends, except her face didn't look too friendly.

"Are you Ava Johnson?" she said.

"Yes," I said. "What can I do for you?"

"You can tell me what you think you're doing sending my husband some shit like this through the mail." She reached into her purse, took out one of my letters, and waved it in my face, her voice suddenly rising to just short of a shriek.

As noisy as the salon always was on Saturday afternoon, it got so quiet so fast, all I could hear was the Anita Baker CD we'd been playing all morning. I tried to stay calm and ask her if she wanted to go into my office so we could talk. She didn't even let me finish.

"I don't want to go anywhere with you, you nasty heifer!"

I knew she was upset, but she was pushing it. I wondered if he'd given her the letter to read or if she'd discovered it on what was probably a routine wifely search through his pockets.

"All right then," I said. "What do you want?"

"I want you to take it back," she said.

"Take it back?" I was really confused now. What good was that going to do?

"You heard me, bitch!" She shouted over Anita's soothing admonitions about the importance of finding your own rhythms. "Take it back!"

I held up my hand to let her know she had gone too far, and she drew back and slapped me across the mouth. Two of my operators grabbed her and pushed her out the door, but all the time she's hollering at the top of her lungs, "This bitch got AIDS! This bitch got AIDS!"

I tried to play if off, but it really shook me up. I finally had to cancel the rest of my appointments and go home for the day. I was distracted, and that's when you run the risk of leaving the perm on too long, or cutting the bangs too short, or putting the crimp in sideways and your life isn't worth two cents. Sisters will forgive you a lot, but do not fuck up their hair.

The slap didn't do me any serious damage, but the rumors that scene started didn't help business any. I sent out a letter to our clients explaining the difference between HIV and AIDS, but they were scared. They started calling to cancel appointments or just not showing up at all. That's when I really started to understand how afraid people can be when they don't have any information.

All those folks who had been giving me those African-American Businesswoman of the Year awards and Mentor of the Month citations and invitations to speak from the pulpit on Women's Day stopped calling me. When people I'd known for ten years saw me out, they'd wave and smile and head off in the other direction. Everybody knew, but nobody mentioned it. They acted like it was too embarrassing to bring it up in polite company. I guess we were all still supposed to be virgins instead of just stupid.

When I got a good offer from a hotshot young developer for the downtown land the salon building was sitting on, I figured this was a good time to take the money and run. It was time for a change. I wanted to open another business that didn't require doing heads or frying chicken, and I was truly tired of living in a place where so many people still thought getting AIDS was proof that you were a child of Satan.

I know as well as anybody that being diagnosed HIV-positive changes everything about your life, but it's still *your life*, the only one you know for sure you got, so you better figure out how to live it as best you can, which is exactly what I intended to do. I wanted to move someplace where I didn't have to apologize for not disappearing because my presence made people nervous. I wanted a more enlightened pool of folks from which to draw potential lovers. I wanted to be someplace where I could be my black, female, sexual, HIV-positive self.

The salon sale gave me enough money to finance a big move without stress. Add to that the money I made when my house sold immediately and I was set for a couple of years without working at anything but living right. From where I was sitting, San Francisco looked like heaven, earthquakes notwithstanding. Natural disasters were no longer my main concern. That's one of the things about being positive. It focuses your fear. You don't have to worry about auto accidents, breast cancer, nerve gas on the subway. None of that shit. You already know your death by name.

When I called Joyce to tell her I had decided to move to the West Coast in the fall and ask her if she wanted some company for the summer, she did the big-sister thing, got all excited and started talking a mile a minute. She started some kind of youth group at her church, and now that Mitch's insurance settled out, she's quit her job as a caseworker with the Department of Family and Children's Services so she can work this thing full-time. She said all the young people in Idlewild are going to hell in a handbasket and if *we* don't do something pretty quick, the town is going to be just as violent and crazy as the cities are.

I tried to say, *What you mean we,* like that old joke about the Lone Ranger and Tonto, but she sounded so much like her old self again, all happy and optimistic, I didn't want to discourage her. After Mitch, her husband, died, I never thought I'd hear her sound like that again. She hardly talked at all for months after, but I should have known that was only temporary. Joyce always finds a way to make it better.

She's had some bad luck, too. In fact, until recently, I thought Joyce had been given our family's entire allotment. Two kids and a husband, all dead before she hit forty. One baby died in her sleep two weeks after they brought her home from the hospital. The other kid was walking home from the school bus and got hit by a drunk twelve-year-old who stole his mother's keys and then passed out behind the wheel of the family station wagon.

Mitch drowned two years ago this February, and in the dictionary under the words *freak accident,* there would be a picture of that shit. A couple of years ago the lake in front of their house got real popular with ice fishermen. These guys would come out early in the morning, drill a big hole in the ice, and sit there all day drinking beer, peeing in the hole, and wondering why the *'spose to be that stupid* fish didn't swim on up and commit suicide for a chance at a plastic cricket.

By evening, the fishermen were too drunk and disappointed to clearly mark the area with safety flags like they're supposed to do, so the lake was dotted with all these open holes. Once it got dark, they froze over with a thin sheet of ice, not enough to support your weight, but just enough to camouflage the hole.

Mitch and Joyce went walking beside the lake on this

particular night and he started sliding around on the ice, doing tricks, showing off for Joyce. They had been married twenty-three years and he still acted like she had just accepted his invitation to the senior prom. So he got up some speed, slid way out, opened his arms into the wind, hollered, "I love my wife!" and disappeared. By the time they pulled him out, he was gone. Mitch was the sweetest man I ever knew, and for a long time after he died, I kept thinking how unfair it was for him to die that way. I was still naive back then. I thought *fairness* had something to do with who gets to stay and who *gots to go.*

In the bad-luck department, there's also the fact that my mother chose Joyce's wedding night to mourn my father's death five years earlier by taking all the sleeping pills she'd been hoarding for this occasion and drinking herself to death with a fifth of Johnny Walker Red. She left a note for Joyce, who was almost eighteen, saying she was sorry and that maybe Joyce would understand if anything ever happened to Mitch. I was still a kid and didn't even have a boyfriend yet, so she didn't leave anything for me.

I don't know whether or not Joyce finally understood when Mitch fell through that ice, but my mother's choice made a lot of sense to me when my doctor gave me the bad news. It occurred to me for the first time that there might be circumstances where what you don't know is infinitely preferable to those things of which you are already certain.

I was glad me and Joyce were going to get a big dose of each other before I moved three thousand miles away. I waited for her to take a breath and then told her I'd be on the four-o'clock flight to Grand Rapids on Tuesday and for her to *swear* she wouldn't be late to pick me up. She swore, like she always does, but I knew she was still going to be late.

Before we hung up, Joyce asked me if I ever prayed. I told her I had tried to start up again when I got sick, but I quit because I knew I was just hedging my bets. I figured if I was smart enough to know that, God must know it, too, and would probably not only refuse to grant my selfish prayers, but might figure I needed to be taught a lesson for trying to bullshit him in the first place. I know once you repent, Jesus himself isn't big on punishment, but according to all the Old Testament stories I ever heard, his father was not above it.

• 3

joyce sent wild Eddie Jefferson to pick me up. I couldn't believe it. I'd been sitting there for an hour and a half, which is a long time to be waiting, even for Joyce, when I see this brother with a head full of beautiful dreadlocks, some kind of weird-looking Chinese jacket, and some Jesus sandals walk up to the gate and look around. Now, there is no reason for the look since everybody else on the plane has been picked up by their grand-parents or caught a cab to meet their boyfriend and ain't a soul in sight but me. The way he's looking, you'd have thought it was rush hour at Grand Central Station and he was trying not to miss somebody in the crowd. He takes his time like he's got no place to be but here and nothing to be doing but looking.

At first I thought I recognized him, but I didn't want to stare, so I looked away. The last thing I needed was some wanna-be Rastafarian thinking I wanted company for the evening. When he didn't move on, I took another look at him, just to be sure. He had one of those smooth, brown-skinned faces that could be any age from twenty-five to fifty. He had great big dark eyes and he was looking right at me in a way that you don't see much in the city anymore. Like he had nothing to prove.

When he caught me looking at him, he walked right up, stuck out his hand, and called my name like we were old friends.

"Ava?" he said. "You probably don't remember me. I'm Eddie Jefferson. Mitch's friend."

As soon as he smiled, I knew exactly who he was. Remember him? *Was he kidding?* The exploits of Wild Eddie Jefferson were *beyond* legendary. He had done everything from getting into a fistfight with the basketball coach to threatening his father with a shotgun for beating his mother. He drank, smoked reefer before I even understood that there was such a thing, and had two babies by two different women before he got out of high school. One of them graduated and moved away. The other one, a thirty-year-old divorcée, went back to her ex-husband, convinced him the baby was his, remarried immediately, and lived happily ever after.

Mitch was always so straight-arrow, nobody could believe they were friends, but they were so close, they might as well have been brothers. The last time I saw Eddie was at Joyce's wedding. He was Mitch's best man and he brought a date from Detroit who had on a red strapless dress and silver shoes at eleven o'clock in the morning. After that, he got sent to Vietnam, and by the time he came back, I had finished high school and headed up the road to Detroit.

I'm sure he was at Mitch's funeral, but I don't really remember. That whole thing is still a blur to me. Besides, he looked so different, I probably wouldn't have recognized him, although I'd sure have remembered that hair. I wanted to touch it to see if it was as soft as it looked.

"How ya doin', Wild Eddie?" I said before I thought about it.

He cringed a little like he'd just as soon I forgot the history that produced the nickname. "Just Eddie."

Joyce had sent him to pick me up because some woman had shown up on her doorstep in labor and had to be driven to the hospital in Big Rapids, more than an hour away. They left so quickly, Joyce didn't even have a chance to call Eddie until she got there, which is why he was so late.

That was typical. Anybody with trouble knew if they could get to Joyce, she'd take care of it. Her feeling was that all crises could be handled if someone would take responsibility and start *moving*. Joyce could get going faster in an emergency than anybody I ever saw. When I first called and told her I was sick, she was on a plane and at my door by nine-thirty the next morning. Once I explained everything the doctor had said, I think the hardest part for her was realizing that there was nothing she could start *doing* that would fix it.

Eddie's truck was so clean, I could see my reflection in the passenger door. The truck was old, but it's bright red exterior was polished to a high gloss and the inside was spotless. The old fabric on the seat was soft and smooth when I accepted Eddie's hand, hopped in, and slid over to pop the lock for him.

I'm sorry automatic door locks eliminated the necessity to lean over and open the door for your date after he helped you get seated. In my younger days, I liked that lean because you could arch your back a little and push your breasts up and out just enough to make sure your boyfriend noticed. I didn't do it this time, though. It's a little late for all that now.

"Do you always keep your truck this nice, or were you expecting company?"

He smiled to acknowledge the compliment. "Don't you recognize it? This is Mitch's truck."

I was amazed. That meant this was the truck I learned to drive a stick shift on the summer I graduated from high school. I was on my way to Detroit as fast as I could get there and I was honing my survival skills. I didn't want to ever find myself needing to make a quick exit from someplace I probably had no business being in the first place and find I couldn't because the getaway car wasn't an automatic. Mitch agreed to teach me and we spent a day lurching up and down the road until I finally got the hang of it.

"Joyce gave it to me after he died. She knew I wanted it and I think she likes the way I restored it."

I guess she does. To say he *restored* the truck implies that it once looked this good and had now been returned to its former glory. *No way.* Mitch ran this truck so hard it would rattle your teeth. Now it rode soundlessly over the bumpy road.

I was wondering what Eddie had been doing for the last couple of decades, but I couldn't figure out a polite way to ask without opening myself up for a lot of questions in return, so I just looked out the window as we rode. Things didn't seem to have changed much around here, despite Joyce's conviction that her church group was all that stood between Idlewild and the Apocalypse. I was always amazed that Joyce had chosen to make her life here. You can't help where you get born, but as soon as I was old enough to know there was a world outside the confines of Lake County, I started making plans to get there.

"How long since you been home?" Eddie said.

"Almost two years," I said. "How about you?"

"This is home," he said. "I moved back for good."

"That sounds pretty final," I said, but he just shrugged.

"It was time."

He didn't offer to tell me *why* it was time and I didn't ask him. Timing is truly a personal thing. It's not such a bad place, I guess. Some people really love it. Look at Joyce and Mitch, but they're probably not a good example since when you're in love like that it doesn't matter as much where else you are.

The two-lane highway into town still offered cheap motels for vacationers on a tight budget, fast-food joints, and bait shops with vending machines out front where you could put in a dollar's worth of quarters and pull out a small box of live crickets or a ventilated container full of fat night crawlers. The smell of sweet grass was blowing in the window and I was remembering what I wrote on page one of the diary I bought when I first moved away: *Good-bye, Idlewild! Hello, world!*

• 4

when you first come to Idlewild, there are two stories the old-timers will tell you. It's strange, too, since it's an all-black town and both the stories are about Indians, but the place has never been known for making much sense. The first story is about The Founder.

The Michigan history books were always full of stories about courageous Indians and wily fur traders and white guys who wore stiff uniforms and built forts and thought there could really be such a thing as Manifest Destiny. We still said *Indians* back then. Not out of any disrespect. We thought they were cool. It was the word we *knew*.

Pontiac was one of the most famous of the Indian chiefs, according to the books we read anyway. He was also one of the baddest, but he still got tricked. When it came down to the final moment, he negotiated with the stiff white guys from a position of as much strength as he could muster and did the best he could, but it was all downhill from there.

Once Pontiac signed the papers and got his picture painted for the history books, nobody seemed to need him anymore and gradually his people died off, or moved away and left the guys in the stiff uniforms to their own devices. Except for one. This one Indian stayed around because he had decided to try and figure out what happened. He wanted to understand how his people had been defeated so rapidly and displaced so completely. And he wanted to structure his life in such a way as to avoid as much future contact with his enemies as humanly possible.

A noble quest, and one that still engages great minds from Atlanta to Capetown, but this one remaining Indian was not concerned about all that. He was looking to understand some things a little closer to home as he settled in for a long period of intense contemplation in the section of the Great North Woods that is bounded by towns with names like White Cloud and Wolf Lake and Big Rapids. Places where the lakes freeze solid and the first big snow is already old news by the middle of November.

One early fall morning, he was walking along through the woods and the day was perfectly clear and absolutely quiet and every once in a while he would see deer melting off into the trees of either side of him, and suddenly *he understood*. He went back to his house and took out all the money he had saved doing all the things he had been doing and bought up as much land as he could and wrote into his covenant that no white folks would be allowed to live in this small but identifiable sector he was bringing under his control. He welcomed his own blood brothers and sisters and any black people who would promise not to act a fool. And then he went back and sat down on his porch and sighed a deep sigh because he was finally at peace. He had not only figured out *who* and *what* the problem was. He had figured out a solution.

By this time, most of the remaining Indians had been moved farther west or had walked on over into Canada, but there were a lot of black folks with new money in their pockets crowded up in Detroit and Chicago and Cleveland who didn't know anything about The Founder's vision of an all-colored paradise, but who were soothed by the beauty of the lakes and moved by the mystery of the pine trees. First came one-room cabins for men-only fishing trips. Then, maybe a little reluctantly, summer cottages for the whole family. Enterprising Negro entrepreneurs opened businesses and stayed on year-round to keep things ready for the summer folks who always came flocking the first of June with lungs full of city grit and fists full of factory dollars, ready to enjoy the all-black paradise in the middle of the Great North Woods.

No one is sure how The Rajah came to Idlewild, but people always talked about his arrival as if The Founder had passed things on like Carl Lewis leaning into the last leg of the relay even though he and The Founder weren't even the same kind of Indian. The Rajah was supposed to be a *Bombay* Indian, as opposed to an Iroquois, or a Lumbee, or a Sioux, so he didn't come from generations of people who had lived and hunted and wandered in these woods. One day he was just there, his big square head wrapped in a snow white turban, and shoes on his feet that seemed to turn up at the toes even if they really didn't. He bowed low when he talked and he was traveling with a not-so-young white lady who seemed to be his wife or his business partner or both, but ultimately it didn't matter. She was *white*. That was the critical thing about her.

Everybody knew right off The Rajah was a regular Negro and not an Indian. *Bombay by way of Hastings Street,* they used to say. Why would a *real* Bombay Indian bring a white woman all the way to Idlewild, Michigan, to open a restaurant? He wouldn't. But this brother was laying it on thick, with an accent and everything, and *what the hell?* He wasn't the first Negro to opt for exotica as the most viable protective coloration and he sure wouldn't be the last one.

Back then, the place more than lived up to its name with *idle men, wild women,* and unlimited night life featuring stars like Dinah Washington and Jackie Wilson and Sammy Davis, Jr., before he went solo. For his part, The Rajah was convinced that Idlewild could support his establishment in much the same way that the community sustained The Paradise Lounge, The Flamingo Club, The Purple Palace, and a boardinghouse called The Eagle's Nest, renting exclusively to young Negro women, looked after by a large, handsome matron who never knew that after she rolled her hair at ten o'clock and went to bed, the ones who were working as shake dancers in the big nightclubs sometimes went skinny-dipping in the moonlight.

The Rajah's place was too small for shake dancers and too intimate for live musicians. There was only room enough for eight couples at a time, a modest number, but one that allowed The Rajah to treat each customer like the royalty he seemed to believe they were. Obsessed with service, The Rajah was the kind of host who *hovered.*

The place did good business right from the very beginning. The lighting flattered sun-kissed faces. The food was delicious, and the service, exquisite. Even when the place was full, The Rajah made each patron feel pampered. The water glass was never empty. The napkin was always freshly laundered. The butter rested in individual pats on beds of crushed ice in fluted silver dishes. The Rajah had *class* and a clientele who recognized and appreciated it. From the carefully made-up doctors' wives who no longer had to do their own manicures, to the misplaced romantics who spent all their time and hard-earned vacation money trying to impress the unimpressible showgirls, The Rajah's place was *the* place to see and be seen.

Now, the white woman was pretty much out of sight during this time, so everybody just assumed she was the cook because somebody was back there cooking up a storm and it wasn't The Rajah, who was forever out front being *smooth*. But nobody can say for sure whether that had anything to do with what happened. Everybody said it was a shame, too, because the place was doing so well.

The story is that one night, long after closing time and cleanup, a big party of folks came strolling over, drunk and happy and wanting something good to eat. Although he was locking up for the night and the white woman was already standing at the foot of the porch steps, he couldn't say no. He graciously unlocked the door, turned on the lights, and ushered them inside to a table.

The woman didn't move. The Rajah went to the door and spoke to her firmly. The woman still didn't move. The Rajah spoke to her again, more sharply this time, and it is at this point that the two versions of the story diverge. In one version, she hisses *"nigger"* at him from outside so loudly that the patrons can hear the insult from where they sit. In another version, she comes back in and shouts it at him from across the room.

In any case, wherever she was when she said it, *she said it*, and The Rajah narrowed his eyes and turned away from the chair he was holding for a bronzed beauty in a calico sundress and leaped at the white woman like a *for-real* Bombay tiger. They fought all the way out the door and down the steps and disappeared into the Great North Woods with her hollering and him hollering and that turban and that accent and that shouted charge of secret negritude flying *every which-a-way*, and nobody ever saw either one of them again.

Which just goes to show you, the oldsters would say, leaving you alone to consider all this while they eased off to pour themselves another drink, *wherever you go, there you are.*

• 5

if i hadn't asked Eddie to stop at the liquor store, none of this shit would have happened. Well, it might have happened, but it would be somebody else's problem, which would have been fine with me. I got enough problems of my own. It's a good thing Eddie remembered to go back for the vodka after the confusion died down because I damn sure needed a drink.

When we first pulled into the parking lot, there wasn't another soul around. Eddie went in and I'm just sitting there being glad he offered so I wouldn't have to jump my tired ass out of this truck again before we got to Joyce's. All of a sudden a big old brown and white Cadillac screeches into the lot and brakes so hard it skids three feet before it rocks to a stop.

The passenger door opens up fast and a woman jumps out and drags a little boy out right behind her. He's about a year and a half old, maybe, and has on a sagging diaper and a filthy T-shirt. His mama, I guess she was his mama but she could have been his sister, is cussing up a storm at whoever is still in the car and she sort of tosses the baby off to one side over in the direction of the pay phone to keep him out of harm's way, then she turns toward the man who is sliding out from behind the wheel, headed in her direction.

She was little, plus she didn't have any shoes on, so he might have looked bigger than he really was. Either way, he was big enough and he was mad. He got around the car so quickly, she didn't have a chance to run. He grabbed her arm and shook her so hard her earrings flew off and her tiny little black skirt rode up over her behind and gathered around her waist like a wide belt. Her panties had a heart over the crotch and the lace was gone around one leg.

Then he slapped her, hard, and when her head jerked over to the side, he backhanded her the other way and slapped her again. He was screaming that he was going to kill her and she was screaming *stop, stop, stop* and the baby had fallen down and he was screaming, too.

Eddie must have heard all the commotion—everybody for a mile could hear it!—but I didn't see him come out. All of a sudden he was just there. He pulled the man away from the woman and flung him back so hard the guy staggered and almost fell. The woman was scrambling around in the car looking for her shoes and her purse. The man was much younger than I'd thought. So was the girl. They looked like high school kids. I hoped that wasn't their baby, but I knew it probably was.

The guy got up and ran at Eddie like he was going to knock him out of the way to get at the girl again. Eddie crouched down a little bit until the guy was almost up on him, then he sort of lunged forward, his arm shot out, and he hit the guy square in the Adam's apple. The guy went down like he'd been shot, gasping and gagging and trying to catch his breath.

I sat there with my mouth open. I had come all the way to Idlewild and landed in the middle of a damn kung fu movie. The girl had her shoes in her hand now. The baby had crawled over and was holding on to her leg. They were both quiet, watching Eddie. He asked her if she was okay and she nodded, so he picked up the keys where the guy had dropped them and handed them to her. She asked if the boy was going to die, and when Eddie said no, she said she didn't want to take the car then since she figured he would really kill her if he got himself together and she had left him stranded. Eddie nodded like that made any kind of sense. I'd have taken those keys and rolled that big old piece of car back and forth across that Negro until I got tired, but that's just me.

Next thing I know, Eddie's opening the door and she's squeezing in next to me so we can drop her off at home. Her face is pretty swollen and she's so out of it, her skirt is still bunched up around her waist. Eddie hands her the baby, who definitely needs a diaper change, and who takes one look at me and starts crying again. His mother doesn't seem to hear it for the first mile or so, but it must have had a cumulative effect on her nerves because when we were almost there, she reached down and pinched his leg so hard that he gasped and tried to holler, but he couldn't make another sound and didn't for the rest of the trip. Once he shut up, the girl started muttering to herself like we weren't even there.

"Muthafucka just lying. He know he my baby daddy. Look at his damn face. Look just like him. Nigga know I ain't been fuckin' nobody but him since his ass got here and he can't give me five dollars a week? What the fuck I'm 'spose to do for money? What the fuck I'm 'spose to do?"

We took her to a tiny cinder-block house at the bottom of an overgrown, unpaved road with no lake at the end to redeem it. The yard was full of trash and broken toys and an ancient Ford Mustang on its own set of cinder blocks. She mumbled a quick thanks and jumped out as soon as Eddie stopped the truck, dragging the baby out behind her and finally pulling her skirt down over her little narrow behind, which she had the nerve to be switching as she went on up the walk to the house.

"Sorry about that," Eddie said, turning the truck around and heading back toward Joyce's.

"I wasn't expecting to see anything like that up here," I said.

He looked at me and smiled. "Welcome home."

I remembered how fast he had moved back there. The kid never saw it coming. "Where'd you learn to do that?"

"Army," he said. "He'll be all right as soon as he

catches his breath. That was a move the MPs used to use on us, so it's just to slow you down, not kill you."

"An important distinction," I said, realizing my hands were shaking. I kept seeing that girl's head flopping around when the guy was slapping her.

"I know that kid," Eddie said.

I was surprised. "You do?"

He nodded. "He's trouble."

Seems the kid came up from Detroit a couple of years ago to stay with his sister, who, coincidentally, is the woman Joyce took to the hospital. Small world.

"There's another sister, too. Mattie," Eddie said. "They're supposed to be providing a more stable environment for the young brother, but whoever sent him didn't bother to check out the house."

"Bad?"

"Crack."

I couldn't believe it. "Where do they get crack way up here?"

"From the city," he said. "All these little towns are virgin markets for these young wanna-be gangsters. People sitting around here with nothing to do and a police force with two cops who share one squad car. They probably don't even know what crack looks like. It's easy money."

I shouldn't have been surprised. Crack is an epidemic with a life all its own, just like AIDS. Small-town living doesn't save you anymore.

"I didn't scare you, did I?" He turned sideways to peer over at me since it was almost dark now.

I shook my head. "No. He wanted to hurt that girl. I'm glad you knew how to handle it."

"The army teaches you a lot of stuff like that," he said, turning down the road to Joyce's house. "The problem is, most of it is stuff you wish you didn't need to know."

• 6

joyce's house, the house I grew up in, sits at the end of an oiled but unpaved road that opens out into Idlewild Lake. There are other houses scattered around the edges of the lake, but they're spaced wide enough so that you don't have to worry about people being all up in your business. A lot of the houses are empty now anyway. Once the white resorts started accepting Negroes, people stopped coming to Idlewild. The old-sters who put such stock in their summer cottages when this was a big-shot resort haven't been able to interest their children and grandchildren in a place they had never seen on a travel brochure and whose name nobody had ever heard outside Detroit and Chicago.

Our parents moved here at the very end of the place's heyday. I was five and Joyce was ready to start high school. Anybody with any practical sense could see the handwriting on the wall, but my father had a big dream about opening a new nightclub that would single-handedly bring back the glory days. My mother, as usual, never questioned a word he said, even though they lost all their savings when the place went belly-up in one short season. My father died in his sleep, drunk and disappointed, the winter right after, and my mother never got over it.

It wasn't a bad place to be a kid. Having a lake at the edge of the front yard beat walking across a freeway bridge to get to kindergarten. Joyce and Mitch hooked up as soon as he saw her sitting two rows in front of him in geometry class, and once they got married, and Mom made me an official orphan, it was like having real young, real hip parents.

I could see the darkness of the lake just a few hundred yards from where Eddie pulled the truck into the yard. I heard the whispering of the pine trees that surrounded the house and I realized I was truly glad to be home, even if the arrangement was only temporary.

Joyce wasn't there yet, but I probably wouldn't have gone to Eddie's for dinner if she hadn't redecorated my old room. Eddie carried my suitcases down the hall for me, and when I went ahead of him and turned on the light, I thought I'd walked into the wrong house. Joyce sent me a magazine article a couple of months ago that said blue is a *healing* color, and I guess it made a big impression on her because everything in here is now *seriously* blue. Dark blue, light blue, turquoise, midnight, robin's egg, blue plaid, blue prints, sky blue, and navy. It would be funny except it means she's still trying to *fix it*. Like if blue was the cure, I wouldn't be wearing blue panties, blue bra, blue blouse, blue jeans, blue socks, blue shoes, and blue contacts right now.

I knew part of the reason Joyce was glad I was coming for this visit was so she could see if I still looked okay, which is the really fucked-up part of all this. I don't *look* any different. I don't *feel* any different. But everything is different. *Every single thing.* And all the blue curtains in the world can't change that.

Suddenly the idea of sitting in that blue room all by myself, drinking too much vodka and waiting for Joyce to come home, seemed like the worst possible way to spend my first night back. Besides, I was hungry and Eddie assured me he was a good, fast cook who could feed me and have me back home in under an hour and a half. I left a note for Joyce and stuck the vodka in my purse on my way out the door. I still wanted a drink, and at this point I felt like I had earned it.

• 7

in eddie's whole house, there was not a scrap of anything blue, except some photographs of the lake where the water and the sky came together, but that doesn't really count. That's *real* blue. Everything was sort of a soothing wheat color, except for a pile of bright red pillows stacked on the floor. There were bamboo mats, a futon couch, and a small table with two chairs. He had a couple of bookcases full of record albums. An elaborate, old-fashioned stereo system sat in the corner looking well used and well kept.

The kitchen belonged in a small restaurant. Hanging pots, stacked steamers, juicers, blenders, knives, woks, and three well-stocked spice racks. After I fixed myself a drink, he told me dinner would be ready in twenty minutes and I could put on anything I wanted to hear.

I always like to look at people's music. It can alert you to the presence of things that you might not find out otherwise until much later. I remember going to a guy's apartment in Atlanta for the first time and discovering that he had a huge collection of heavy metal. The *bad* white boys. The ones who have to go to court all the time to prove their evil lyrics and demonic chord progressions didn't make somebody's child shoot himself in the head. He had the good sense to be a little embarrassed about it, but I never felt the same about him after that.

Eddie looked like a jazz fan, and those dreads definitely indicated reggae. He had hundreds of records, neatly filed in alphabetical order. The first one was one of my favorites: King Sunny Ade, *JuJu Music.* I pulled it out of the cover and held the edges, checking for cracks. People who have grown up on CDs don't understand the sensual appeal of a well-loved piece of vinyl. Joyce and Mitch *loved* their albums, even the ones that were so scratched up you could barely make out the vocals. Every scratch meant something. Every nick recalled a perfect party; every smudge, a teenage heartache.

From the condition of the cover, *JuJu Music* was well used, but inside, it was perfect. I placed it carefully on the turntable and lowered the dust cover. This was somebody who took his records seriously. I had been wrong about the jazz, except for two John Coltranes and a Miles Davis or two, but right on the reggae. Old school. He seemed to have every album Bob Marley and Gregory Isaacs ever recorded, but he also had a serious Motown library (heavy on the Temptations and Marvin Gaye), a fair number of funk classics by George Clinton, James Brown, and the Ohio Players, and the essential Sly and the Family Stone. There was also a lot of international stuff that I was curious about, but I was too exhausted to look any further.

When I complimented him on having his music so well organized, he looked embarrassed.

"Shows I've got too much time on my hands."

"Idlewild still the fun capital of the Great North Woods?" I said, wondering again why he was living here.

"Absolutely," he said. "That's half the reason these young people are acting such a big fool. Nothing else to do."

He was chopping vegetables rhythmically and I liked the kitcheny sound of the knife hitting the gleaming piece of butcher block. I took my drink back over to the counter. He checked the oil in a large wok he'd put on the stove.

"You know the thing I always remember about you?" he said.

I was surprised he remembered anything about me. Last time I saw him, I was eight years old and my sister was hoping he would get there in time to stand up with Mitch at their wedding. He did, even though his uniform looked like he'd slept in it. *Twice.*

"I have no idea," I said, dropping another ice cube into my already watery drink.

"You told me not to go to 'Nam."

"I did?"

"Yes, you did," he said, dumping the vegetables into the wok and tossing them in the air with a slotted bamboo paddle. He made it look easy, but I know if I had tried it, we'd be eating dinner off the kitchen floor. "You waited until my date went to the bathroom . . ."

"I loved what she had on. That was the first strapless dress I'd ever seen up close."

"Me, too," he said, spooning the vegetables onto two plates of steaming noodles. It looked and smelled wonderful and I realized I was starving. I'd been drinking all day, but I couldn't remember when I had eaten anything.

"When you saw me standing by myself, you came over and asked me if I was really going to go to Vietnam. When I said yes, you told me it was a terrible war and that it would be wrong and dangerous for me to fight in it. I liked the way you said that. *Wrong and dangerous.*"

The conversation was beginning to come back to me. Joyce and Mitch were both involved in antiwar activities, although there was never much of a peace movement in Idlewild. When people got drafted, they had a party, got drunk, tried to talk their girlfriend of the moment into having sex, and reported for duty.

Most of the local protesting consisted of sending indignant letters to Congress and driving to bigger cities to march or demonstrate or demand something from whoever was in charge at the moment. They used to take me with them whenever I wanted to go, and I was caught up in the righteous passion of the demonstrators and their cause. When Mitch first found out Eddie had been drafted, he tried to talk him out of going and even offered to drive him over into Canada to a community of black draft resisters holed up in Windsor, but Eddie just laughed and said somebody had to protect the women and children since all the wimps were getting married and couldn't be bothered to go.

"Did I offer to smuggle you into Canada?"

He laughed. "That's exactly what you did. You told me Mitch probably couldn't go right then since he had just gotten married, but you were sure he'd take me first thing in the morning."

I could hear myself saying it, too, like it was the only reasonable way to deal with the situation, so, of course, he was going to do it. I was always sure about things in those days. It wasn't until recently that I started second-guessing myself.

"You obviously didn't take my advice," I said.

"But I should have," he said. "You were right. Worst move I ever made."

"Well, at least you got it out of the way when you were young," I said. "I saved my worst moves until much later."

"I'll bet you wouldn't know a bad move if you saw one," he said.

"You'd be surprised."

"Maybe we can compare notes one day." He picked up both plates and headed for the kitchen.

"It's a deal," I said, feeling the weight of the day settling around my shoulders. It was time for me to crash, but I was going to help with the dishes first. I wanted to be sure he washed all the things I'd used in good hot, soapy water. I *know* that's not the way you get it, but this was no time to be careless.

• 8

when we pulled up into the yard, Joyce was standing at the door reading my note. She turned and ran down the back steps and grabbed me in a big hug. Joyce gained a lot of weight when Mitch died, and even though it's been two years, she's still carrying it. Worrying about me probably hasn't helped her diet much either. Her cheeks were so chubby that when she smiled, her eyes almost disappeared.

She reported that Eartha had a baby girl and thanked Eddie for picking me up. I thanked him for dinner and he asked Joyce if her car was still acting funny. When she said it was, he said he'd come by tomorrow and look under the hood before she went back to the hospital. I wondered suddenly if they were lovers, but it didn't feel like that. It felt like friends.

As soon as Eddie left and we got inside, Joyce threw her arms around me and started apologizing for being late and asking me if I'd eaten enough and apologizing some more until finally I said, "Hold it! This is the part where you get to ask me how I'm feeling and I get to say I'm feeling fine and you get to look at me hard to see if I'm lying and if I'm not, you get to hug me again and say, welcome home, little sister. You look great!"

She teared up when I said that, and her body felt soft and plump when she hugged me. I've had clients whose husbands died and they blew up like balloons in no time. It's a lot harder to take care of your body when nobody's going to see you naked.

"Welcome home, little sister," she said. "You look great."

"Thank you," I said. "Now tell me everything."

Turned out the seventeen-year-old new mother had been lying about keeping up with her appointments for prenatal care and hadn't seen the doctor since her second visit. The doctor said they had tried to contact her, but all the information she'd given them was bogus, which was really unfortunate since he had some bad news. Before she had stopped coming, she had tested positive for HIV. When the doctor told her after the delivery, she freaked out and started screaming that they were lying and she didn't have to stay and hear no more shit from them about what she had or didn't have and to just hand her back what she came with and she'd get the hell out of there.

The doctor finally gave her a sedative and Joyce sat with her until she calmed down and went to sleep. The baby's tests wouldn't be back until morning.

"What did he think her reaction would be?" Joyce said. "He just told her outright. No preparation or anything. She's lying there with a brand-new baby and he just tells her like that? He didn't even give a damn. He might as well have been talking to a chimpanzee."

Joyce looked like hell. Her hair needed rebraiding. Her sweats were working overtime to accommodate her new hips and thighs, and her sandals were tired Woodstock wanna-bes.

"How's your diet coming?" I said.

She tried to get her feelings hurt, but I wasn't going for it. "I'm working on it," she said. "

I just looked at her.

"I've lost fifteen pounds," she said.

I raised my eyebrows.

"*Okay*, ten."

I knew the best she could claim was holding steady, and she knew it, too.

"So sue me," she said. "I had a couple of months when all that stood between me and taking a tumble was a bowl of Jamoca Almond Fudge and some homemade Toll House cookies."

I should have known. *The dread tumble.* When my mother committed suicide, some religious group sent us a bunch of pamphlets they had put together for the bereaved loved ones struggling to understand. We were pretty desperate for some kind of straightforward way to talk about what had happened, but when we read these little booklets, they were mostly full of ways *not* to talk about it, or if you did, to be sure you put the weight on the dearly departed and not on yourself.

Coping with guilt seemed to be a major deal for these particular pamphleteers, and one of them suggested that even using the word *suicide* gave it too much guilt-producing power. The left-behind loved ones were encouraged to try out new

words or phrases to describe the indescribable. The author offered several suggestions, including the fairly generic "slipped
away," the slightly more judgmental "took a wrong turn,"
and, our all-time favorite, "tumbled into the abyss." After that,
whenever we talked about suicide, we talked about "taking
a tumble."

"I just couldn't believe he wasn't coming back," Joyce
said. "At first I kept thinking if I could make it through that
first year, I'd be okay. But I wasn't okay."

"It takes time," I said.

"I know." She took my hand. "This is terrible, but
sometimes I used to sit here and make lists in my head of all
the people who deserved to die more than Mitch."

"I know that game."

"Not one of my favorites." She shook her head as if to
make sure there was no part of her brain still secretly taking
names.

"Better now?" I said, remembering one night after the
funeral when I got up and found Joyce sitting in the dark by
herself holding Mitch's glasses and crying.

"Much better," she said. "Once I stopped feeling guilty
about living off the life insurance money and quit working for
the state, I got so busy with the Sewing Circus, I didn't have
time to be sitting around here driving myself crazy."

"Guilty?" I said. "Why?"

"When the check first came, it felt like blood money to
me. How much could they pay me to make up for Mitch?"

"Ain't that much money in the world," I said, and I
meant it. Mitch was one of a kind.

"You got that right. So I put it away and didn't touch
any of it for a long time. Then I realized how much I really
wanted to find a way to fix the things we'd been busy half
repairing with all the tired programs that don't work and the
exhausted people who don't care. Mitch's insurance let me buy
myself enough time to try."

It was almost funny. In the middle of all the bad things

that have come our way, we both emerged as sisters of independent means.

Joyce frowned and shook her head. "That's why this
stuff with Eartha really makes me mad. She's been coming
every week for the last four months, lying the whole time,
and for what? Because she'd rather smoke crack than have a
healthy baby?"

"What the hell is the Sewing Circus?" I said, but Joyce
just yawned, which made me yawn, too. We were both
pretty exhausted.

"That's too long a story to start on this late at night,"
she said, "but I'll tell you everything tomorrow. I promise."

Joyce's room was quiet and I had settled into my blue
heaven before realizing I hadn't told her about Eddie punching
out the guy in the parking lot. We both had some stories to
tell in the morning.

• 9

the hospital called to say the baby tested negative for HIV,
positive for cocaine, and that they were going to do some more
tests, so Joyce couldn't see the baby until tomorrow. The other
big news was that the mother had disappeared. Not disappeared as in, *now you see her, now you don't.* Disappeared as
in, got up, got dressed, put on her shoes, picked up her purse,
and walked out.

Joyce can't understand it, but I can. Homegirl's trying
to walk away from that HIV. She's trying to decide if she's
going to tell anybody or just keep living her life and see what
happens. I used to wish I hadn't taken the test so I still
wouldn't know.

Before I tested, I had been celibate for almost a year. I
had had enough of those Atlanta Negroes for a while. They
talk so much shit when they're looking for some sweetness,

but they got no heart for the long haul. I figured ten years of rolling around with them was plenty.

Besides, in spite of what people will try to tell you, Atlanta is still a very small town, and the way I'd been living, it was getting downright ridiculous. I'd walk into a reception and there'd be a room full of brothers, power-brokering their asses off, and I'd realize I'd seen them all naked. I'd watch them striding around, talking to each other in those phony-ass voices men use when they want to make it clear they got *juice,* and it was so depressing, all I'd want to do was go home and get drunk.

Then I started keeping company with a bearded saxophone player who wore two gold hoops in each ear and played regularly at a club downtown. We hadn't formalized anything yet, but we'd been hanging pretty tough for about three months and he was making me rethink this whole celibacy thing in a serious way. He wasn't much taller than me, and built kind of round, but he had a lot of style and he could make a sax sound so sweet you couldn't decide if you wanted to take him or the horn home to bed with you. He'd already been tested, so it was on me.

When I got the results and told him, he sat there and listened to me tell it all and then he picked up his coat and his horn case and walked out the door. No *good-bye.* No *damn, baby, what we gonna do?* Nothing. One minute he was there, then he was gone. That was it.

I went with Joyce to see Eartha's sister. I had told her about what happened at the liquor store yesterday and I figured, why not meet the rest of what seemed to be a supremely fucked-up family. The woman who came to the door let out a blast of that peppermint-smelling vapor that means *crack smoked here,* but Joyce didn't blink. Joyce was a state caseworker for fifteen years and she'd been in most of the houses around here investigating for or against more benefits, custody rights, food stamp eligibility—all the questions that drive poor people crazy. By this time she was kind of like the telephone man or the cable guy: *nothing shocked her.*

"Hey, Mattie. Is Eartha around?"

Mattie, who looked to be about forty but was probably much younger, frowned at Joyce, confused.

"You the one took her to the emergency room, right?"

Joyce said yes, but the hospital had just called to notify her that Eartha had walked out and taken all her things with her except the baby. This did not sit well with Mattie, who thought we were going to tell her she had to take the kid.

"Oh, no," she said. "Fuck that. I ain't raisin' no more kids, especially no screamin' crack baby."

Joyce tried to tell Mattie that's not what we came for, but the woman was having none of it.

"Call the daddy if somebody gotta take the little mutha-fucka," she said.

"Who is the father?" Joyce had her social worker voice on.

"How the hell do I know?" Mattie said. "One of them crack-head niggas she been fuckin' for some rock."

"Shut the damn door," somebody yelled from the other room. "You lettin' all the damn smoke out, fool!"

"Fuck you!" The woman laughed with a cackle that ended in a huge explosion of coughing and then another evil look in our direction. Joyce took a deep breath. She was trying to be cool.

"The hospital said the baby can come home on Friday—"

Mattie interrupted her. "And if she don't come home, they ain't gonna do nothin' but send her to foster care just like they do all the other crack-head babies, so what difference it make?"

"She's your niece," Joyce said, and I could hear her getting mad. "Don't you think Eartha would want you to keep the baby until she gets back?"

This really struck Mattie as funny. "Gets back? Eartha Lee ain't comin' back here till she runs out of other places to go, and that baby be long gone by then. That girl ain't cut out to be nobody mama, so just call them nice white folks at the hospital and tell them don't nobody over here want her, so they may as well bundle her little ass up and send her to somebody who do."

The kid Eddie punched out in the parking lot came and stood behind Mattie in the doorway. He was tall enough to look over the top of her head without straining. The brother of the house.

Joyce looked at him. "Hello, Frank."

"What the fuck our dumb-ass sister done now?" he said.

"She had that baby," Mattie said.

"No shit," he said, narrowing his eyes at me like I suddenly looked familiar. "Well, you see one crack baby, you seen 'em all."

He laughed, pushed Mattie back inside, and then turned and pointed at me.

"And you do me a favor, awright? You tell Kung Fu I said to *stay black*, okay?"

• 10

"tell me about the Sewing Circus," I asked Joyce as we sat on the back porch drinking apple cinnamon tea and trying to get the crack smell out of our nostrils.

Joyce grinned at me. *"TSC is you and me,"* she said. "It's the wave of the future and they don't even know it. Most of the people up here think it's still 1958 and we're dealing with some high-spirited youngsters who are just sowing their wild oats. They can't see that this is something new. This isn't a phase they're going through. This is how they *are*. They don't know anything. They don't care about anything. They're selfish and mean and mad all the time. Who do you think is breaking into these old people's houses?"

"What old people's houses?" I said. Joyce was getting excited, and when she gets excited, she talks *fast*.

"It's practically an epidemic up here," she said. "They used to only hit the summer cottages once they were empty, but now they don't care if anybody's home or not."

"So that's why you started a circus," I said, trying to bring Joyce back around to the question. "To break up a burglary ring?"

She laughed, and even with the extra weight she was carrying, Joyce looked good this morning. Her skin was smooth, she had parted her hair in the middle and braided it into two thick cornrows, and she was wearing a pair of silver hoop earrings I had given her three Christmases ago. I wondered again how close Joyce was to Eddie. She had sent him to pick me up at an airport over an hour from where he was, which is the kind of favor you ask of a man who has more than a passing interest in you.

I tried to remember the sound of Eddie's voice when he said Joyce's name. A man who is *just a friend* says a woman's name differently than the man who is her lover. I've seen men give away a perfectly successful clandestine affair by casually dropping their girlfriends' names into an innocuous story without realizing that their tone of voice is suddenly filled with so many memories of sex and secrecy that it immediately sets off alarm bells in the mind of any wife who is serious about monogamy. I used to tell my lovers not to say my name at all, no matter how tempted they were. I knew their lips and tongues and teeth had memories of me that needed to remain between the two of us.

I didn't remember hearing any of that in Eddie's voice. When he talked about Joyce, he sounded like he was talking about a favorite cousin.

"It's not a real circus," Joyce was saying. "The oldsters just started calling it that because we took over an activity slot at the church that used to be called the Sewing Circle. It was the only women's group that met regularly other than the deaconesses', and I knew I wasn't ready for that."

Joyce walked over to turn on the flame under the teakettle, and I watched her behind jiggling under the bright fabric of her gauzy skirt.

"It may have actually been a sewing circle a long time ago," Joyce said, "but when I started going, it wasn't much of anything. Sometimes they'd get together and take up money to put flowers on the altar, but that was about it."

Joyce started going to church again after Mitch died. It's the same church we grew up in, but I knew she hadn't been for years. I never asked her about it, but I think she wanted to pray and she was too self-conscious to do it at home alone. Talking to God can make you feel like you're going off the deep end if you're not used to it. It's not as weird if there are some other people around doing it too, but if Joyce was so deep into it she was going to Wednesday night prayer meetings, it's no wonder she was gaining weight.

"Stop looking at me like I'm crazy," Joyce said. "There is method to my madness."

"Always," I said. "That's one of your finer qualities."

Joyce said when she started going to church regularly, she realized that a lot of the teenage girls she knew slightly from watching them grow up were there every Sunday, too. They weren't really religious. It was just a place to hang around together after the service and show off their babies and gossip a little about the boys who never came unless they were forced. Joyce thought they might like a chance to do some more of the same, plus whatever other interesting experiences she could sneak in without scaring them away. They had enough social worker types in their lives already.

Joyce leaned across the table and touched my arm lightly like she wanted to be sure I was paying attention. "These girls haven't got a chance," she said. "There aren't any jobs and there aren't going to be any. They're stuck up here in the middle of the damn woods, watching talk shows, smoking crack, collecting welfare, and having babies. What kind of life is that?"

City life, I wanted to tell her, but Joyce had already

gone into action. She invited the girls to come to a special meeting of the Wednesday Sewing Circle to talk about starting a nursery on Sunday morning where they could leave their babies with somebody they trusted and enjoy the services in peace.

That idea brought out nine young women under the age of twenty who had between them a dozen children under the age of five. The discussion was brief and to the point, resulting in a nine-week schedule laying out who was going to staff the nursery room, what her responsibilities would be, what supplies she might need, and how many kids she could handle. Questions were raised and discussed regarding discipline (no hitting; if the kid is uncontrollable, send upstairs for the mother), feeding (bottles with milk and juice and dry Cheerios only), and money for diapers.

Joyce said she thought the Pastor's Special Fund would kick in a few bucks if they asked the committee, and she also volunteered to stay with the person who was staffing the nursery each week so there would be another set of hands and eyes on all those babies and because, she said to me, grinning like the cat who swallowed the canary, it gave her a chance to talk to the girls one on one in a setting where they were doing something responsible, *by choice,* and where they were surrounded by children.

Joyce is good at this kind of stuff. She went into social work in the first place because she really believes that people *want* to take care of themselves and their children, and if they're allowed to do that with some dignity, everything else will fall into place. When I used to ask her why she and Mitch didn't ever leave Idlewild, she said it was a perfect place for her because it was small enough so that if she did any little thing, she could really make a big difference in people's lives.

"I could work myself to death in Detroit and Chicago," she said, "and the problems are so big, nobody would even know the difference."

Joyce's plan worked like she knew it would, and more

young mothers started using the nursery, so they had to keep meeting on Wednesday to fold these new people into the schedule and to make sure everybody knew what was happening and what their particular job required. The old ladies found all of this less than fascinating, so pretty soon they just stopped coming. What was left was a loosely organized group of seventeen young women, meeting once a week and handling a successful Sunday morning nursery school. Joyce wrote a small grant application and they got some outside funding to offset their costs and buy some toys and supplies.

After a while, running the nursery program settled into a pleasant routine and they could finish all their business in half an hour, but they didn't want to be finished that quickly, so they started talking about other things, like men and sex and how they were supposed to raise their kids without any jobs. The meetings got longer and longer and louder and louder. Joyce did a lot of listening and the girls did a lot of talking. A lot of *loud* talking, which is what people tend to do when they finally find somebody who will listen.

One time they were making so much noise, the choir director stopped his rehearsal and sent one of the lesser sopranos down to remind them that there were other activities going on in the building. A couple of weeks after that, somebody brought in a magazine article and they started talking about man-sharing and things got pretty heated between two women who had been best friends but who had been unhappily sharing the same trifling brother for two years.

Each one was waiting for the other one to get tired of the hassle and bow out gracefully, but neither of them would break and now he was asking them to have three-way sex. They were tired of having their business whispered about in the street, but they knew everybody knew and the man-sharing discussion set them free. They confronted each other in the middle of the Sewing Circus, but after a few minutes of shouting, they realized they liked each other a lot more than either one of them liked him. They burst into tears and forgave each other everything. The resulting reconciliation got so rowdy that one of the altos told the first tenor that Joyce was running a *three-ring circus* over in the fellowship hall, and the name just stuck.

"The only problem," Joyce said, "is that we got a new pastor about six months ago. Reverend Smith was so old, he didn't care what we did as long as we didn't burn the place down, but he finally retired and now we've got Reverend Anderson and his wife, Miss Gerry, and I think she's going to be a royal pain. They came from a big church in Chicago where he had put together this giant youth program, but now they're here and even though *he* hasn't said anything to me, *she* keeps telling me how much they really want to channel the church resources into the more traditional areas of Christian education and missionary outreach. When I ask her about the youth program they had in the city and whether or not it could work here, she starts talking in tongues.

"That's one of the reasons I want to go independent and open my own center." Joyce leaned toward me again. "I know the Circus is helping these girls and I'm not about to let Gerry Anderson mess it up by making them read Bible stories about obedience and chastity when they want to talk about domestic violence and birth control."

I looked at Joyce with her eyes shining and her voice full of the urgency and passion of *the cause* and I remembered how much I liked growing up with her and Mitch. In most houses, when the kids wake up late at night and the grown folks are still up talking in low tones, the discussion is about money or trouble. In our house, it was about the design and distribution of a handbill, the best place to hold a meeting or stage a rally. I'd stand in the kitchen doorway and watch them until one or the other saw me and sent me back to bed. I remember feeling lucky because I lived in a house where people didn't just fuss about what was wrong with the world. They tried to *fix it*.

Joyce finished her tea and her story at the same time

and Eddie's truck pulled into the yard like he'd been out back listening for his cue. He had his hair tucked under one of those multicolored knit hats that the Rastas wear and he was bringing bad news. Last night, while he was dropping me off here after we ate, somebody broke out two windows in the front of his house. He wasn't here but a few minutes, so either somebody just happened to see us leaving or they had been watching the house. They didn't take anything, but he'd spent the morning cleaning up and replacing windows.

"Who do you think did it?" Joyce said. I was trying to imagine who would shatter the calm of such a perfectly peaceful place.

"Don't know," said Eddie with a graceful shrug. "But I will."

Something in the way he said it chilled me. He must have felt my reaction because he turned to me with a smile that successfully distracted me from anything but the whiteness of his teeth in the middle of that beard.

"How you doing?"

"I'm fine," I said, glad he couldn't read my mind.

"Good." He nodded and turned back to Joyce.

"So how's Eartha and the baby?" Eddie lifted the hood of her car and peered inside.

Our news wasn't much better than his. There was still no word from the missing mama and the hospital hadn't called yet with any more of the baby's test results. Joyce said she was giving them another hour and then she was just going to drive back over there and be a pest until they told her what was what.

We made a strange little threesome, standing there looking at each other, trying to figure out what else could go wrong with this day, then the phone rang and Joyce went to answer it. Eddie leaned back against the truck and smiled directly at me for the second time that morning.

"I have a message for you," I said, suddenly remembering.

He looked at me, still smiling. "A message? From who?"

"From that kid at the liquor store yesterday."

"Frank? *The bad man?* Where'd you see him?"

"Joyce took me by his house looking for Eartha. He said to tell you to *stay black*."

I didn't say the stuff about *Kung Fu* since I had been thinking that, too, and it made me feel guilty when Frank said it out loud. Eddie just shook his head.

"Youngblood always looking for some contact," he said. "Bumping through the world, looking for that contact."

Joyce came back out to say the hospital had finished with the baby's tests and she seemed all right except for the cocaine, which she would have to deal with through withdrawal just like any other junkie. A hell of a way to spend your first couple of days in the real world. They had told Joyce a lot of crack babies scream when anybody touches them, but this one seems to be comforted by it. That was all it took. She came to the door with her keys in her hand and her purse already slung over her shoulder. Joyce was big on comfort.

Eddie wasn't finished with the repairs, so at his suggestion and his assurance that he didn't mind walking home, Joyce agreed to take the truck. I told her I'd have something on the stove whenever she got back. She kissed me and half nodded like food was the last thing on her mind.

After Joyce pulled off, I sat down on the steps. I could hear at least four or five different birds, squawking or singing as the spirit moved them, and I closed my eyes to see if I could identify any of them like we used to do in school, but I couldn't. Living in the country, I'd learned to recognize bird calls. In the city, I learned to recognize sirens.

One bird was singing louder than all the others, almost as if to insist that I remember his name. I concentrated, but nothing came to me.

"Cardinal," Eddie said.

I opened my eyes and he pointed at the bright red bird swaying on a low-hanging branch above the porch.

"It's a cardinal," he said again, as if I had spoken the question out loud.

He slammed the hood and wiped the oil off his hands on a rag, reached up and pulled off his cap. His hair fell to his shoulders in a cascade of softly coiled locks. It was so pretty, I smiled, and he saw me.

"Did you grow your hair for religious reasons?" I said as he stuffed the cap into his pocket.

He hadn't wanted a drink last night and he told me he was a vegetarian. I was curious.

He shook his head. "It was Mitch. One night him and Joyce were watching a documentary about Bob Marley, and Joyce started talking about how much she liked his dreads and how she wondered what they felt like and how sexy they were. After a while, Mitch started worrying about what would happen if Joyce ever really met a man with dreadlocks and he told her since she liked them, he was going to grow her some. Then he said I had to do it, too, since he wasn't going to be the only dreadlock in Lake County, but he couldn't make it through the Buckwheat phase. Not enough patience."

I must have looked confused.

"That's when your hair is growing but hasn't really locked up yet, so it's just standing all over your head looking like Buckwheat. He kept getting mad because people would ask him if he'd forgotten to get a haircut or comb his hair or something. Joyce promised him she wasn't going to run off with a Rasta and told him to go on and cut it if he wanted to, which the brother did that very afternoon."

I think that's probably the reason dreads never caught on any more than they did. Sisters always like having enough hair to toss around, but we're rarely prepared to endure the indignities of the in-between stages. That's why extensions were born. Even my clients who decided to really lock up wanted some help getting started.

"Most people twist their hair to avoid all that," I said.

He shrugged and raked his hand through his hair. "Misses the point," he said. "Learning to have the patience to let nature take its course is half the lesson."

"Is that why you didn't cut yours?"

"I don't know." He smiled again. "Yes, I do. I didn't do it because everybody thought I was going to."

"Defiance," I said. "One of my favorite reasons for doing anything."

That was the damn truth. The problem is, Eddie's defiance got him a head full of beautiful dreadlocks. My rewards weren't always quite so spectacular, but I bet his weren't always that way either. There was something in his face that made me think he'd seen enough and done enough that there was nothing I could say that would shock him. Which is not to say he couldn't be surprised. I didn't have enough information to speculate on that yet.

• 11

i've been masturbating like a madwoman for two days. I feel like I haven't been touched by anybody but me in a hundred years. I woke up last night with my hand between my legs in the middle of a seriously scandalous dream involving me and two guys I had sex with once during a particularly heated political campaign. Not at the same time, of course. I had one on the night of the primary victory and one on election day. But in the dream, the three of us were all there together, rolling around on the couch in the candidate's inner sanctum.

That's probably what woke me up. I hate politics. Plus, even in my wild days, I had pretty strict rules about some things. I was never interested in groups or animals, most especially *snakes*, which had their fifteen minutes of freakish fame during one memorable summer when somebody had a girl-friend in from New Orleans with navy blue fingernails and a seven-foot boa constrictor she liked to wear around her neck. Needless to say, whenever she appeared, Negroes lost their minds.

It's hard to think about that stuff now without beating myself up for being so stupid, but I think I'd feel that way even if I hadn't gotten sick. I used to justify some of the things I did then by saying, well, at least I'm having a lot of great sex, but you know what? I wasn't having a lot of great sex. Some of it was fun and exciting, but a lot of it was just sweaty and boring and seemed like the quickest way to finish the evening without hurting anybody's feelings.

Once I took the test and admitted the results, every-thing changed, of course. Folks who used to spend whole eve-nings trying to look down the front of my blouse would now break out in a cold sweat at the very thought of having sex with me. Some gay friends who've been positive for a couple of years tried to tell me that it gets better once you complete the transition from what they called your *preplague* lovers to your new *postplague* relationships, but I have my doubts. Most straight brothers are still in such denial that when you fess up, their first reaction is to run in the opposite direction as fast as they can. That pretty much leaves a bunch of people you wouldn't fuck on a bet or who are already sicker than you are.

After the first couple of months of my involuntary celi-bacy, I was so crazed that I went to one of those Sunday sup-port group gatherings where a whole lot of HIV people who want to have sex get together and try to see if they can work something out. Everybody gets a glass of cheap wine or sweet tea and then you sit in a circle like group therapy and tell your name and indicate whether you're just HIV-positive or already diagnosed with *full-blown* AIDS. I hate that expression. Sounds like a typhoon moving through your body, but those distinctions are important. Some people who'll give you a shot if you're just positive won't have anything to do with you if you're already standing in the eye of the storm. You're also allowed to say something about your sexual preferences if you want to be specific.

The first two people to speak were men with AIDS who liked integrated country-and-western gay bars where they could do the Texas two-step without being hassled because they were black. They had lucked out and found each other, but their immediate bonding only depressed the rest of us, who should have had a glass of wine to toast their good fortune and gone home to our memories and our vibrators. But we didn't. We went on around the circle: teachers, waiters, a musician, trying to sound casual and knowing none of us were attracted to any of the rest of us, except the first two guys, who had already made a date for Friday night, excused themselves, and left.

When it was finally over, I skipped the postconfessional cocktails, went home, ran a hot bath full of the bubbles I used to save for *serious* seductions, made myself a good, strong drink, and sat in that water until it got stone-cold, thinking about all the fucking I had done and all the fucking I wasn't going to do, and I realized that the only thing I was sorry about was that I never had a chance to *make love*.

Joyce told me that she had been in love with Mitch since she was sixteen years old so that in addition to being the only man she had ever had sex with, he was the only man she'd ever even kissed. I envied her that. I still do. I remember looking at the words in Mama's suicide note in her neat little handwriting and thinking to myself, well, if that's the price, *fuck true love*. It's too scary and too complicated and way too much weight to carry as fast as I intend to be moving. Some people weren't cut out for it, I told myself, and I was one of those people. The problem was, once I started running, I never slowed down long enough to be sure.

• 12

it's almost noon and the day is as pretty as any I can remember. I spent the morning like a cat, moving from one patch of sunshine to the other, turning my face to the softness of the breeze off the lake, stretching the last city kinks out of my shoulders. I've been here a week and Joyce has been at the hospital more than she's been home. She invited me to come with her to see the baby, but hospitals are the best place to pick up something random and that's the last thing I need. I haven't had any problems, *knock on wood*, but I don't take chances. Besides, the truth is, I've been working so hard for so long, I was enjoying a chance to just do nothing.

Besides, this little interlude isn't going to last much longer. Joyce is trying to get Eartha's baby released from the hospital. She had to get Mattie to sign a form as the baby's aunt giving Joyce permission to check her out and bring her home until her mother resurfaces or some kind of permanent arrangement can be worked out. All Mattie wanted to know was whether or not what she was signing obligated her to the kid in any way, shape, or form. When Joyce swore to her that it didn't, literally *swore*, one hand raised and everything, right there on the front porch, Mattie signed it. Of course, she couldn't ask us in. Crack addicts never ask you in. They're afraid you'll want to get high.

Joyce is ecstatic, although I will confess, I am still less than enthusiastic about spending the summer with a newborn crack baby. But what can I say? When she asked me what I thought, I knew it was a trick. Grown people never ask you what they should do until they've already decided for themselves. They don't tell you that, of course, but they stand there and wait for you to either confirm their good judgment or reveal yourself as not as smart as they thought you were by advising them in the other direction.

So I avoided all that pressure by pausing as if to truly consider the question, then giving her a sisterly smile and telling her to *go for it.* She was so relieved, she hugged me and promised not to ask me to change any diapers. I probably should have asked her to put that in writing.

It turned out to be a pretty interesting morning, though. I had just finished making myself a serious screwdriver with some of Joyce's organic orange juice when the same big brown Cadillac that had been the start of so much high drama at the liquor store a few days ago pulled up into the yard and stopped. A tall, slender young man who looked to be about sixteen years old swung the door open slowly, unfolded his lanky frame a section at a time, and looked around. In spite of, or in defiance of, the warm weather, he was wearing a hooded black sweatshirt, amazingly low-slung blue jeans, spotless white designer sports shoes, unlaced, a Chicago Bulls cap, and a bored expression. He looked as out of place in Joyce's yard as a Siberian tiger.

He sauntered around the car and opened the door for the woman waiting patiently inside. The woman didn't move until he leaned down and extended his hand in a way that looked strange and old-fashioned, given the boy's urban-warrior outfit. She grasped his hand firmly and raised herself regally out of the car like Coretta Scott King arriving for the martyr's annual birthday celebration. Although I'll never forget that car, I had never seen either one of its occupants before in my life.

The woman looked to be in her late fifties and was a lot more dressed up than people usually get around here in the middle of the week. She was wearing a pale blue polyester pantsuit and white sandals with stockings. Her hair, which was pressed and hot-curled within an inch of its life, was elaborately styled and piled like Mahalia Jackson's when she sang her solo at the end of *Imitation of Life.* Hardly anybody asks for that kind of hard press anymore. Sister seems to have missed the moment when we decided it was okay for the hair to *move*.

A thin white scarf was loosely tied under her chin to protect this well-sprayed helmet of hair from even the possibility of a breeze. She smoothed the pants suit over her well-girdled hips and turned to the boy, who was leaning against the car with his hands in his pockets, dragging the jeans down even further. I could see and hear them clearly through the screen door, but neither one had noticed me.

"I'll just be a few minutes," the woman said, starting toward the back steps. Joyce's car was sitting in the yard waiting for Eddie to finish repairing its fuel pump, so they must have assumed she was home.

"How about I go and come back for you?" the boy said without looking in her direction.

She stopped, turned toward him, held out her hand. He didn't move.

"Tyrone Harris Anderson, what did you promise your grandfather?"

The boy mumbled something.

"I can't hear you, son," she said.

"To cooperate," he said, louder, sounding like a stubborn first grader.

"That's right. So hand me the keys."

He slouched over and dropped them in her hand.

"Thank you," she said. "And don't sit there in that hot car either. Go walk down to the lake and enjoy the sunshine."

He looked at her like she had completely lost her mind.

"Go on now!" Her voice carried the sharp edge of someone who was used to having her way.

"All right, all right," he said, pulling his cap down over his eyes and squeezing the bill until the break satisfied him. "Don't take all day," he muttered, strolling down to the dock, my favorite peaceful place, although I would be willing to bet

51

the tranquil beauty of the scene was lost on him. His misery was self-contained, able to bloom anywhere.

She didn't see me until she reached up to knock and there I was. She jumped back about a foot and gasped.

"I'm sorry," I said, opening the screen. "I didn't mean to startle you. I'm Joyce's sister, Ava."

"Oh," she said, smiling with everything but her eyes. "I didn't even know Joyce had a sister."

"I'm visiting from Atlanta for the summer," I said.

"How lovely. Family is so important, especially in these terrible times." She looked at me, still with that fishy, too bright smile, and then clapped her palm to her forehead the way people do on television when they've forgotten something. "Where are my manners?"

She held out her hand with the complete confidence of an incumbent politician ahead in the polls. "I'm Gerry Anderson," she said. "The pastor's wife."

Of course she was. I smiled and shook her hand.

"Didn't Joyce tell you I was coming by?"

I shook my head. *Of course she hadn't.*

The Reverend Mrs. Anderson smiled brightly, but she was clearly annoyed. When I started to explain that Joyce had been spending a lot of time trying to get things straight with Eartha's new baby, she nodded and clicked her tongue.

"I forgot all about that poor little fatherless child," she said. "Such a shame. Babies having babies without any thought to how they're going to care for them. I keep telling Joyce these girls need some old-fashioned lessons in how to say *no*. All that other just confuses them. We need to teach them how to cross their legs and keep their dresses down. It's a shame is what it is."

I agreed it was definitely a shame, but I kept getting distracted by the elaborate construction of her hair. I was wondering how much of it she had grown and how much was cash and carry. I probably should have invited her in, but I was looking forward to a quiet afternoon alone. Entertaining the preacher's wife was not on my agenda. She waited another beat to see if I'd break down and offer her a glass of iced tea, but I just couldn't do it.

I looked over her shoulder down to the dock where the kid I assumed to be her grandson was smoking what looked like a big, fat joint and tapping the ashes into the water. He took a final, deep drag, then pinched the fire out and put the roach back in his pocket. Wasn't he afraid she'd smell it on his clothes when he climbed back into the car beside her?

"Well, let me leave something for her then," she said finally, handing me a large envelope. It was addressed to Joyce, in care of the church, and it was open. Gerry wagged her finger, frowning. "You tell Joyce the Good Reverend is not happy about this. Your big sister's been a bad girl."

A bad girl? Joyce was forty-two years old. No wonder this woman got on her nerves. I wanted to say, *Don't you know opening mail that isn't addressed to you is a federal offense?* But I had a feeling that would make me a bad girl, too, and one per house is usually plenty.

I just smiled again. "I'll be sure and give it to her."

She looked at me hard for a minute and I had the feeling that she knew exactly what I was thinking because when she smiled her good-bye, this time it never got beyond the corners of her mouth.

"Tyrone!" She called his name just as he came up behind her and reached for the door. The boy was high, but he was definitely on his J.O.B. "That's a good boy," she said. "Tyrone, honey, this is Mrs. Mitchell's sister, Mrs. . . . ?" She looked at me.

"Ava Johnson," I said.

He mumbled something that I guessed was supposed to be a greeting of some sort and took his grandmother's elbow, half helping, half pushing her into the car. She jerked her arm free and her look drew him up sharp before she pretended to soften it with that cold smile. "Slow down, son. Grandmother's moving as fast as she can."

He slammed the door and she handed him the keys when he slid in beside her.

"We look forward to having you in church on Sunday," The Reverend Mrs. said. "Both you and your sister. The title of the Good Reverend's sermon will be *'No Hiding Place Down Here.'* "

I felt like I should say *amen* or something, but Tyrone's patience was at an end and he turned the car around quickly and was gone. It wasn't until later that I wondered what Frank had been doing driving the minister's car to the liquor store.

• 13

i was sitting on the dock with a drink in my hand and my toes in the water, enjoying the last of the sun, when Joyce finally pulled in, blowing the horn and waving out the window like there was any possible way I might miss her entrance. I knew that meant the hospital had agreed to let her bring the baby home and I mentally said good-bye to the hope of any more peace and quiet around here.

Joyce had always loved kids and she took it hard when both of hers died the way they did, but the idea never appealed to me. I'm too selfish to be somebody's mother. Joyce would say all that changes once you hold your own kid for the first time, but I figured, why risk it? There were plenty of people who wanted to have children and a lot who didn't but ended up having them anyway. I never felt like my small contribution to the overpopulation of the planet was critical to anybody's agenda, especially mine.

Joyce had stopped by the mall to pick up what she called "a few little things for the baby," who would be arriving via social worker on Wednesday morning. She had a bunch of tiny nightgowns and sunsuits, six receiving blankets, an infant seat, and twelve boxes of disposable diapers. She also got a small crib (assembly required) and a musical mobile to hang over the baby's head that had brightly colored stars and moons twirling slowly around to the theme from Doctor Zhivago.

We hauled everything into the kitchen, including the crib. I mixed another drink and lit the kettle for tea while Joyce gave me the details.

"What's her name?" I said.

Joyce shook her head. "She doesn't have one yet. Eartha didn't stay around long enough to name her, and you heard Mattie say she doesn't care."

"What she said was she didn't give a fuck."

"I stand corrected," Joyce said, and the way she said it made me feel like shit. I brought her a cup of tea and hugged her.

"I'm just being mean," I said. "I missed you today, so I did the wife thing and attacked you as soon as you came home. Sorry!"

"Hold it," Joyce said. "I was a wife and I never did that."

"So I was just doing the asshole thing, is that what you're telling me?"

She laughed and drank a long swallow of her tea. "I've been calling her Imani. It means 'faith' in Swahili. What do you think?"

I liked it. I was tired of calling her the baby. I was even starting to feel like it might be okay to have her here. It would mean a lot to Joyce, and this kid deserved a break if anybody ever did. Her mama's an HIV-positive crack addict, missing in action. Her aunt is a foul-mouthed fool and her uncle is a violent woman hater. She's batting a thousand and she's not even two weeks old yet. Besides, I was only going to be here a couple of months before I headed out for the coast. This was Joyce's real life. It was just a stopover on mine.

We had cooed and oohed over the impossibly tiny baby clothes, debated the relative merits of cloth diapers, and decided to put the crib in Joyce's room before I remembered Gerry's visit. I handed Joyce the envelope.

"She says you've been a bad girl. That's a quote."

"A *bad girl?*" Joyce shook her head. "As the young people would say, this woman is *trippin'*. Was this open when she gave it to you?"

"Mail tampering is not my style," I said.

She withdrew the contents of the envelope, which included a cover letter on some official-looking letterhead, a handwritten note, and about twenty or thirty pamphlets. While Joyce scanned the letter, I picked one up and read the cover: *Living with HIV: Power of Attitude.*

"What is all this?" I said.

"I'm trying to do some AIDS education with the Sewing Circus and I sent in an announcement for the Sunday bulletin. I also sent away for some pamphlets from the state health department's HIV clinic, which they were more than happy to send me."

She indicated the pile of brightly colored brochures filled with undeniably alarming statistics and photographs of bravely smiling people who always had that startled look of disbelief lurking right behind their eyes.

"The only problem is, the Good Reverend and Mrs. Anderson think the topic is inappropriate for—" she read aloud from the handwritten note "—'discussion within the confines of a Christian church.' So they declined to put the notice in the bulletin and canceled the meeting until they can 'clarify things' with me 'concerning areas of great importance to us all.' She signed it *'Yours in Christ,'* and was kind enough to return my pamphlets."

I shouldn't have been surprised, but I was. I spent a lot of years being ignorant about AIDS because it was new and the information was usually bad or nonexistent. In 1981 they were still calling it a gay cancer and I was still cutting a wide sexual path through a group of ne'er-do-wells whose specific sexual histories I hesitate to speculate about even now. But this plague is more than a decade old now. Claiming it's too nasty to talk about in front of God is hardly the most effective defense.

People like Gerry Anderson don't even understand that there's a plague going on. They're watching these dumb kids fucking around like it's 1965 and the worst that can happen is some kind of minor venereal infection that penicillin can knock out in a couple of days. By the time they figure it's okay to hand out a public health pamphlet, it'll be way too late. It's probably *already* too late.

I remember that guy's wife who came up to the shop after he got my note about being HIV-positive. All she wanted me to do was take it back. Like calling its name conjures it up and makes it real. Like if I just wouldn't talk about it, things could get back to normal. I wish I'd had time to tell her to forget all that what-you-don't-know-won't-hurt-you fantasy shit. Those wild people from ACT UP got it right: *Silence = Death.*

"I thought truth was the light," Joyce said, stuffing the brochures back in the envelope.

"Bad girl," I said.

Joyce tossed the letter down on the table. "I refuse to think about this anymore tonight. Let's go swimming."

"Now?" I hadn't been in the lake at night since I was a kid, but the mysterious freedom of floating around in the dark was one of my favorite memories. All three of us used to go; me, Joyce, and Mama. Daddy didn't like to swim at night, so he'd sit on the dock and name the constellations as the stars came out. "You want to go swimming *now*?"

"This very minute," she said, pulling me along behind her, tossing me a suit and struggling into one of her others that she hadn't had on since she gained all that weight. When she finally got it on, a sizeable portion of her butt was still hanging out. She frowned at her reflection in the full-length mirror.

"I've got to get back in shape," she said.

"Don't let me say *amen*," I said, smug and still size

seven. I hadn't been off the circuit so long I'd let things get out of hand yet.

Joyce turned toward me and raised an eyebrow. "I thought you said you were going to stop drinking so much."

"What's that got to do with it?" I sounded like a whiny child.

"Nothing," Joyce said, "except that neither one of us is taking such good care of herself, you know?"

I tried to get my feelings hurt then, but I knew she was right. If I wanted to be as healthy as I could be, even now, *especially* now, I had to cut back on all the vodka I was drinking and figure out some kind of exercise I could do that wouldn't drive me crazy. Speaking of which, a little mental health effort probably wouldn't hurt either.

"Well, you're the oldest," I said. "Tell me what to do."

"Will you do it?"

"Will *you*?"

"God, yes! I look terrible. We'll start a program."

"Okay."

"We'll eat more nutritious food."

"Who's cooking?"

"I am."

"Okay."

"We'll exercise regularly."

"What kind of exercise?"

"I don't know," Joyce said. "Anything but swimming until I get a new suit."

"Don't worry about it," I said. "It's already almost dark outside."

We picked our way down the gentle grassy slope that ran from Joyce's back steps down a couple of hundred yards to the thin strip of sandy, weedy beach and stuck our toes in the lake. It was as warm as bathwater. We didn't see anybody out, but when I whispered to Joyce that we ought to go skinny-dipping, she swatted me on the behind like I was five years old again.

We walked out up to our chins, feeling the murky bottom of the lake oozing up between our toes, and then lay out on our backs side by side. The water was so still, all we had to do was flutter our hands and feet a little bit to stay close and afloat.

"It's not just the physical stuff," Joyce said.

That *just* leaped out at me. The physical stuff is never *just* to me. Not anymore.

"What isn't?" I said.

"Things we have to work on. Remember all those books we bought that day?"

How could I forget them? When Joyce came to Atlanta right after I first diagnosed, we took a whole day and went to every spiritual bookstore in town. Joyce thought this might be a good time for us to start meditating, so we were ostensibly in search of books to guide us in that practice, but I was lying through my teeth. My quest was for the secret of what God really wants so I could do it, be forgiven, and get well. I wanted to live forever, of course, but at this point I was prepared to accept an ordinary African-American old age, full of high blood pressure and bad feet, but ultimately dying in my own bed in a nice clean nursing home with color TV.

Every place we went had books about dying and preparing for dying, but I avoided those like the plague, no pun intended. I was interested in L-I-V-I-N-G. The dying part would have to take care of itself.

So we bought:

2 books on Buddhism
1 book of daily prayers for positive people (the author meant *positive* in outlook, but I liked the unintentional double meaning)
1 book on yoga with photographs of blissed-out-looking people standing on one leg with their eyes closed
1 silver sea charm to ward off the evil eye

3 packs of Blue Pearl incense
1 brass incense holder
4 tapes promising to teach us how to meditate in a
    variety of ways, including one that guaran-
    teed the same results as the traditional meth-
    ods, but you only had to sit there for three
    minutes a day instead of an hour.

Joyce was going to wear the evil-eye charm, but she kept looking at the symbols and weird writing all over it and she got nervous that it could be a trick, that the thing might have the opposite power and conjure up the Devil instead of chasing him off. I told her we should have gotten wolfbane like they do in the vampire movies, but she didn't think that was funny.

Then I started trying to figure out who we could send the charm to. Somebody who deserved some bad luck for doing some evil shit they never had to pay for. But that made her even more nervous since if it was a Devil charm and we sent it to somebody and something bad happened, we would be sort of like agents of the Devil, right?

It was really pretty funny since we had bought all this stuff to help us calm down and we were working ourselves up into a frenzy just trying to figure out how to use it. It's like reading those magazine articles about reducing stress. I read those articles all the time and I look at the things they recommend and I usually am not doing one single thing on the list. I *consider* doing them all the time, but I rationalize not starting to work on them immediately by thinking how they'd be so *easy* to do if I ever really wanted to do them. This is bullshit, of course, since each one of them would require a major redirecting of energy and since I'm already so guilt-ridden about not having done this stuff a long time ago, I could never just take one at a time. I'd have to tackle the whole righteous group simultaneously, or not at all, which brings us back around to why all that stuff we bought that day is still almost untouched by human hands.

"Do you still have them?" Joyce said. I was sure I did. *Somewhere.*

"Well, I've still got mine," Joyce said. "Maybe we can find something in there."

"Something *spiritual*?" I said, remembering the movie in which Tina Turner converted to Buddhist chanting after Ike beat her with a shoe in the back of that great big limo. I didn't know if I was ready for all that yet.

Joyce laughed and started treading water, something I have never been able to do for longer than ten seconds without sinking like a stone. "Don't say it like that. I don't mean we have to start playing tambourines on the street. Maybe we could just try the meditation or something. Eddie swears by it."

"Eddie meditates?" I said, giving my treading water its best shot and failing miserably.

"Twice a day, he told me," Joyce said, splashing for the dock, with me and my pathetic dog paddle bringing up the rear. We hoisted ourselves up onto the dock and immediately collapsed from the intensity of our feeble efforts.

"We are in bad shape," Joyce said.

I was wondering if Eddie went all the way and sat cross-legged on a pillow and lit incense and shit. "What else does Eddie do?" I said.

"T'ai chi." Joyce closed her eyes. "It's sort of like yoga, but it all flows together when you do it right. It looks like a dance. He tried to teach it to me once, but I was too embarrassed to do it all by myself, and Mitch wasn't interested. Eddie said that in China, big groups of old people do it outside at dawn in the public parks. Maybe that's what I needed. Some other old folks to be out there creaking around with me."

"Don't look at me," I said. "I'm not that old, big sister. I ain't creaking nowhere yet. And don't you forget it!"

"I never forget anything," Joyce said, suddenly serious. She opened her eyes and turned toward me, propped up on one elbow. "When Mitch died, I thought I would never be able to swim in this lake again," she said. "I thought it would make me too sad or too mad or something. But it never did. It always makes me think about him and remember what a good man he was." She smiled at me. "I miss him every day," she said softly. "Every single day."

I reached over and took her hand and squeezed it and we lay there like that for a while, just looking at the moon and listening to the crickets.

"I'm glad you're going to be here when Imani comes home," Joyce said.

"Me, too," I said. And I was.

• 14

eddie showed up this afternoon with a bag of the reddest tomatoes I'd ever seen. He was dashing off to town for something or other, but promised to come back and have dinner with us. Joyce lined the tomatoes up on the windowsill where the sun made their red roundness look almost artificial, it was so perfect. I could practically feel the juice running down my chin.

"These will be great in the salad tonight," she said.

I must have looked disappointed because she relented and handed me one.

"Maybe you should make sure they're not poison."

"No chance," I said, passing it under the cold water and biting into it like an apple. Even without salt, this tomato was spectacular. Firm and sweet and juicy without a hint of green. It actually *tasted* like sunshine.

"*Jesus!*"

Joyce laughed. "Is the man a *tomato-growin' somethin'* or what?"

"If he actually grew these, he is *the tomato master*," I said, popping the last bit of it into my mouth.

"It's all organic, too," Joyce said. "No chemicals, no pesticides, no poison."

"I don't even see a garden," I said, eyeing another tomato greedily.

"He plants a little ways off from the house to get the best sun," she explained.

"What else does he grow?"

"Everything. Potatoes, collard greens, lettuce, turnips. He used to raise rabbits before he was a vegetarian."

"To *eat*?" I couldn't imagine Eddie slaughtering bunnies.

"He meant to raise them to eat, but he couldn't bring himself to do it," Joyce said. "Should we eat outside? The mosquitoes haven't been too bad this summer."

"Sure," I said, glad Eddie had a soft spot for small creatures in tight spots. I could definitely relate.

Joyce handed me a blue ceramic vase I recognized from a long time ago. My mother liked to fill it with wildflowers. "Remember this?"

"Not without Queen Anne's lace and some black-eyed Susans." I tucked it under my arm and headed outside, but those fresh tomatoes winked at me from the windowsill. "How about a tomato for the road?"

"How far are you going?" Joyce knew I could have stepped right out the front door and gathered more flowers than we needed. Sustenance was a poor excuse, so I switched gears quickly.

"*Ple-e-e-ase?*" I said, falling back effortlessly into the irritating whine all little sisters carry as a blood memory and a sacred trust. If you don't annoy your big sister for no good reason from time to time, she thinks you don't love her anymore, and I was crazy about Joyce. I shifted into overdrive. "*Puh-leeeez?*"

"Take it, take it!" She winced, tossing me the smallest of the remaining fruit. Joyce can't stand whining.

"You brought that on yourself," I said, washing my prize and turning to see Joyce smiling tearily at me. Brattiness didn't used to make Joyce feel sentimental, but these days it doesn't take much.

"Welcome home, little sister," she said softly. "You look great."

• 15

if everybody who claimed to be a vegetarian cooked like Joyce and Eddie, the world would be a much safer place for a whole lot of animals. By the time we got through with home-made pasta, homegrown vegetables, and Eddie's angelic toma-toes, we decided to wait a few minutes before tackling the peach cobbler. No wonder Joyce had a hard time dieting. The girl could *burn*.

She and Eddie exchanged news while I sat there watch-ing the stars come out. I was realizing how many more stars you see in the country than you ever see in the city when I heard Eddie say something about finishing a house in Grand Rapids.

"Is that what you do?" I said. "Build houses?"

"Houses, fences, furniture," he said. "I'm a carpenter."

"Just like Jesus." I was just being a smart aleck, but I realized that with his hair hanging down around his shoulders, the beard, the sandals, and his penchant for dashikis, he defi-nitely had a biblical sort of look going.

"Eddie's the best around," Joyce said, refilling iced tea glasses all around.

"Is that what you always did?" I said, sipping the icy lemon-peppermint mixture.

Eddie smiled slowly. "Not always."

I waited for him to continue, but he just looked at me. He had answered my question, but gone no further. I'd have to frame my questions in a less open-ended way unless I wanted to end the evening without any more details then I'd had when we started.

"I saw something funny yesterday," Joyce said. "This kid was visiting somebody in the hospital and he had on a T-shirt that said *'Jesus Was a Black Man.'* Period. I watched him walk down the hall and all these white folks were glaring at him like they were waiting for God to send a lightning bolt in defense of his whiteness. But when you think about where he was born, what are the chances he'd be a blue-eyed blonde?"

She was right about that. "The sunburn alone would have killed him," I said.

Eddie laughed at that so loud it startled me and I knocked over my iced tea, but it didn't matter. We were outside and I didn't break anything. I mopped up a little while Joyce went in to get the cobbler and then me and Eddie just sat there looking at the sky, which was dark enough now to reveal the thousands of stars that only show themselves without the presence of neon.

"Can you name them?" he said.

"Only the real obvious ones," I said.

"Which ones are those?"

I pointed. "The Big Dipper, The Little Dipper, and sometimes Cassiopeia's Chair, if I concentrate real hard. Can you?"

"I can do those three and Orion's Belt."

"My father knew them all," I said. "I almost went blind as a kid trying to make out bows and arrows and goats with fishtails."

"Your father was the one who showed me the ones I know."

"Really? I always forget that you knew him."

"That's because you weren't born yet," he said. "I was probably about eight or nine and I was running away."

"From home?" I was trying to imagine him as a wayward eight-year-old.

"From *here*," he said, laughing and shaking his head at

the memory. "Your father passed me on the road and figured it was a little late for me to be out by myself."

"So he showed you how to find the Milky Way?"

"He asked me if I needed a ride somewhere, and when I didn't answer, he said he was going home and sit on his dock and read the sky and if I wanted to come, he'd sure like some company."

"I'm surprised he didn't take you home to your mother."

"He probably figured that was the last place I wanted to go. We turned in right here and strolled on down to the lake like this is what we always did on Saturday night. We sat down on the dock and took off our shoes and he started reading the sky to me, just like he said he was going to."

Eddie stopped and looked down the slope at the dock as if he could still see my father and his *boy self* down there talking softly so they wouldn't wake up my mother. "In the morning I woke up in your front room on the couch. Your mom gave me some breakfast and told me she'd talked to my mother, who was glad to hear I was okay, even if she was going to have to beat my butt when I got home."

"Did she?"

"No. She said she was sorry things were such a mess and if I ever felt that way again, to let her know and we'd figure out another way to come at it."

"Did you?"

"I didn't have to. After that I figured she was doing the best she could and I ought to be helping her instead of driving her crazy."

Joyce came back out with the cobbler, some freshly whipped cream, and a pot of coffee. For a while nobody said anything and then the mosquitoes came out from wherever they had been hiding and chased us inside. Eddie helped us clean up and as we dried the last dish, Joyce invited him to come to church with us in the morning.

"I don't think so," he said.

"Just thought I'd ask," Joyce said, laughing. "I figured I could get extra points in heaven by bringing in two nonbelievers on the same first Sunday."

"Are you a lapsed Baptist, too?" I said.

"I'm not a Christian," he said, making me instantly curious.

"What are you?"

"Now, that's another question altogether." He shrugged, a gesture I was beginning to recognize as one of his favorites. "I don't really know yet. But I'm working on it."

Okay with me, I thought, watching him walk off into the darkness, heading for home via the path at the edge of the lake. I've always been a sucker for a work in progress.

• 16

when we got to the church, Joyce took me downstairs to show me the nursery. The room was clean and bright, and even though it was only ten o'clock, there were already two toddlers and an infant comfortably in residence. A young girl who looked about fourteen, but was probably a couple of years older from the way she was handling things when we walked in, was balancing the baby expertly on her right hip while bringing out a box of toys to entertain the other two children, who seemed to be twins.

"Do you want puzzles?" she asked, and they nodded slowly in unison without letting go of each other's hands.

"Let me do that." Joyce pulled out several colorful wooden puzzles with pieces big enough for little hands to grab on their own and made the introductions.

"Aretha Simmons, meet my sister, Ava."

Aretha smiled, shifted the baby to her left hip, and extended her hand. "Welcome," she said. "Or I guess I should say *welcome back*."

•

"Thanks," I said, as two more toddlers and their mothers arrived and Joyce went to greet them.

"How old is your baby?" Up close, Aretha didn't look quite so young, but she didn't look like she ought to be a mother yet either.

She laughed. "This little pumpkin?" she said, tickling the baby gently under its double chin, which resulted in a contented gurgle and a sleepy yawn. "This is Doetha's baby."

"Which one is yours?"

"I don't have one."

"Hey, Ree." A young woman with a sleeping bundle breezed by us and deposited her baby gently in one of several portable cribs.

"Hey, Tomika," Aretha said. "How long she been asleep?"

"About twenty minutes," Tomika replied. "She ought to be good for another hour, but I brought a bottle just in case." She handed over a frilly pink diaper bag.

"You better." Aretha slung it over her baby-free shoulder. "Otherwise, get ready, 'cause you know I'm bringin' her right up to you!"

"You gonna be the one answerin' to Old Lady Anderson if you let this chile mess up her solo!"

"Everybody know she ain't my baby," Aretha said. "How am I gonna be the one in trouble?"

" 'Cause everybody also know I ain't got no sense," Tomika said with a grin. "You got no excuse!"

Aretha laughed, put the now-sleeping baby she'd been carrying in the crib next to Tomika's daughter, and turned to collect another one, already awake and howling, from a harried-looking young woman who practically threw her child into Aretha's arms and ducked upstairs to the relative peace of the sanctuary.

Joyce was busy getting the toddlers settled in with their choice of toys, picture books, puzzles, and doll babies almost as big as they were. It looked like an appropriate time for me to make my exit upstairs, too. I told Joyce I'd meet her after the service, waved at Aretha, who waved back while reaching to wipe a nose that needed it, went upstairs, and took a seat in the back.

There were three or four older men in the front on the left-hand side who I took to be the Deacon Board and two solemn ushers in dark suits and white gloves when you first walked in, but the congregation was overwhelmingly female, from the young ones who had dropped off their babies downstairs to the ones who had been old for as long as I could remember them. There were flowers on the altar and, as always, a large painting of a sweetly blue-eyed Jesus kneeling in prayer. I remembered our conversation of the night before and I mentally substituted Eddie's face, but that brought on such a rush of feelings that didn't have anything to do with church that I blushed in spite of myself.

It was already warm in the sanctuary, and the lazy ceiling fans were being actively outclassed by the hand-held variety provided by Brown's Funeral Parlor up the road in Baldwin. I think they're probably the people who put us on the list to receive the suicide booklets, but I couldn't swear to it.

It wasn't long before the choir took their places at the back of the church, the organist nodded her readiness up front, and we all stood for the processional. Mama and Daddy weren't big on church, so we hardly ever went while I was growing up, but I always like the music and they were singing one of my favorites, "Great Gettin' Up Mornin'." The choir started as one voice:

In that great gettin' up mornin',
Fare you well, fare you well,
In that great gettin' up mornin',
Fare you well, fare you well.
Let me tell you 'bout the comin' of judgment,
Fare you well, fare you well,
Let me tell you 'bout the comin' of judgment,
Fare you well, fare you well.

They were right behind me, clapping and singing, and they sounded so good they made me shiver even in all that heat. They surrounded my less-than-stellar soprano with such a symphony of passionate praise that I felt like I could really sing. We all did. The pews were full of smiling, swaying black women, eyes closed, heads thrown back, voices loud without apology, all of us convinced we were singing our sanctified asses off.

Then, all of a sudden, I heard a female voice lifting up and swooping over our best efforts like Diana Ross assuming leadership of the Supremes. This was a voice that celebrated the delicate, death-defying balance between the secular and the sensual that makes Sunday morning service the sweet, sweat-drenched experience that it is.

God's gonna up and speak to Gabriel,
Fare you well, fare you well.
God's gonna up and speak to Gabriel,
Fare you well, fare you well . . .

The choir, rising to the challenge of this amazing voice, leaped even higher in pursuit of the same ecstasy, and those of us in the pews opened our eyes and glanced at each other to confirm the unexpected wonder of it.

Blow your trumpet, Gabriel,
Fare you well, fare you well.
Blow your trumpet, Gabriel,
Fare you well, fare you well.

The choir started walking now, swishing their robes as they walked down the center aisle and up to the choir loft. As they passed beside me, I waited to see which of these women who I passed at the grocery store or greeted at the gas station had been hiding a voice that made you want to believe whatever she believed just so you could sing that way. As I turned to look, Gerry Anderson caught my eye and returned my surprised, admiring smile without missing a beat, her voice running between us like a bright red ribbon.

> *In that great gettin' up mornin',*
> *Fare you well, fare you well.*
> *In that great gettin' up mornin',*
> *Fare you well, fare you well.*

• 17

if the good Reverend Mrs.' voice was a surprise, the Good Reverend himself was a revelation. Tall, white-haired, and sixtyish, the Rev looked like an aging Cab Calloway and preached like Jesse Jackson. He had a long, black robe with full sleeves that billowed out like wings when he raised his arms in praise or flung them wide in surrender. His voice was rich and more powerful than his slender frame would lead you to believe.

His sermon topic, as promised, was "No Hiding Place Down Here." It was a fairly weird mixture of traditional references and contemporary anecdotes. The Apostles, for example, became *the Jesus Posse*, which I thought was going just a little too far, but at the heart of things, it was still a depressingly old-fashioned message about an all-seeing, always-judgmental God the Father, who's got a lake of fire waiting for your sinful ass if you don't shape up.

I hate that kind of preaching. It scares the shit out of people for an hour on Sunday and hopes the threat of hellfire will keep them under control until they get back for another dose the following week. I've been reading one of Joyce's Buddhist books and it was a revelation to me that an entire spiritual practice could be constructed without all that guilt and punishment and damnation.

The Rev, of course, was a *Baptist*, not a *Buddhist*, but

71

our basic theological differences aside, I had to admit the threat of an angry God had never sounded so good.

The Good Reverend was charismatic and he knew how to work it. After painting a picture of all the terrible things in the world from which any sane person would want to hide, the Rev came slowly out from behind the pulpit and began to pass among his congregation.

"But the Lord has already told us that there is no hiding place down here. Down here among the sinners and the unsaved. There is no hiding place down here!"

"Yes, Lord!"

"So what do you say when that alcohol says it can hide you?"

"No," said a church full of people who had been drinking all week.

"And what do you say when that dope says it can hide you?"

"No," said a church full of people who couldn't wait to go home and get high.

"And what do you say when that Devil sends that snake, that pet of Satan, just like he sent to Eve, and tries to tell you that sex can hide you?"

"No," said a church full of people who started having sex with as many people as they could as soon as they hit puberty.

But the Rev was on a roll, touching this one's shoulder as he passed, smiling Christian encouragement at that one as she gazed up at him, building and blending the message and the feeling and the promise with such conviction and style and passion that suddenly a woman threw up her hands and wailed. It was a long, high, desperate-for-relief sound, and every woman in the room recognized it.

That was all it took. By the time the Rev was through, two women had shouted, one had flung herself at his neck, and three more had swooned in their seats and been fanned back to consciousness by two large deaconesses in white dresses who were standing by for that express purpose. When the choir came in right on time as he opened the doors of the church to new members, his wife's voice again promised sweet rewards for those who, like her, found their way to the feet of Jesus. Eyes closed, the Rev sat in his thronelike chair behind the pulpit, seemingly exhausted by the demands of his message.

I was impressed with the quality of their act, but confused. They were good at this. As a team, probably one of the best I'd ever seen. It was sort of like seeing Jessye Norman and Kathleen Battle singing Puccini in a community talent show. You're glad to be there, but you can't help but wonder, *What the hell are they doing in Idlewild?*

After service, Joyce set up a meeting with the Good Reverend and his Mrs. for tomorrow afternoon, and we found out that another house got robbed last night. Hattie McNeil has got to be eighty and she lives alone. They took her TV, her radio, and all the money she had in her purse. She was in her room asleep and she never heard a thing. She came downstairs this morning and freaked out when she started thinking about all the things that could have happened if they'd come upstairs and found an old woman home alone. Joyce dropped me off and went to check on Hattie.

I guess the Rev had it right. *No hiding place down here.*

• 18

i dreamed about walking in Eddie's garden. I'm wearing a long, white dress and I've got on this big-ass straw hat and I'm holding up my skirt so it won't get dirty. Eddie's walking right in front of me telling me what he planted and when it's coming up. Neither one of us has any shoes on and the dirt is soft and warm and moist without being squishy.

He stops to show me a new kind of tomato he's planted this year for the first time. I am surprised to see that it is perfectly golden and not red at all like the other tomatoes he grows. It is also small enough for him to hold four or five in his palm like candy. I take one and pop it into my mouth, savoring the warm sweetness, and I drop my skirt to reach for another and the wind catches it and lifts me up like wings and I hold his hand and his hair lifts him up like wings, too, and all I hear is the sound of the wind and the sound of our laughter and then he leans over and tells me the name of the golden tomatoes.

"Yellow Plum," he says into my ear. "They're Yellow Plum."

And then I woke up.

• 19

joyce figured she'd need as much help as she could get trying to outmaneuver the Good Reverend and his Mrs., so she drafted me into going to the meeting with her. I groaned all the way there, of course. That's a younger sister's job, no matter how old you get, but the truth of it is, I'm really curious about the dynamic duo. There's something just a little off center about them, but I haven't figured out what yet.

Their grandson was at church yesterday, along with Eartha's brother from hell, Frank, who seems to be his best friend. Joyce said the rumor is that Tyrone's mother left him with his grandparents for the weekend and never came back, but that's just a rumor. She also told me that Frank was there only because it is part of the condition of his long probation. The judge who sentenced him must have seen too many Andy Hardy movies. *Send the young man to the country! Get him some fresh air and sunshine! Make sure he goes to Sunday school! He's still young enough to turn his life around! Of course, he's practically illiterate, couldn't get a job if there were any around to be gotten,*

and has no idea how the world works, but hey! He'll probably get a
great tan out of it anyway!

When the announcement was made about the robbery,
Tyrone and Frank looked at each other and snickered like the
idea of a terrified old lady sleeping through what could have
been something really dangerous was the funniest thing they'd
heard in ages. After service, they circled the church yard like
lions waiting for a distracted antelope to separate itself from
the herd long enough to be vulnerable. A couple of girls giggled in their direction, but nobody made an approach.

I felt sorry for them. I'd seen boys in my Atlanta neigh-
borhood grow into swaggering young men who were suddenly scary until you looked into their still baby faces and
realized who they used to be, but I also knew how dangerous
they were. I'd seen Frank hit that girl like he didn't care if he
broke every bone in her face. I'd seen Tyrone smoking dope
right behind his grandmother's back. It was tempting but fool-
hardy to focus on their vulnerability instead of your own.

When we got there, the front door was unlocked and
we could hear the sound of some pretty tortured hunt-and-
peck typing coming from the church office. Gerry was sitting
behind an Underwood upright frowning at the keyboard as if
somebody had mysteriously rearranged it. When she looked
up and saw us, she smiled and held up her hands in mock
surrender to the ancient machine.

"I told the Good Reverend if he doesn't hurry up and
find us a new church secretary, *he better!*"

Joyce and I were still standing in the door, and for a
minute she just looked at us. The intensity of her smile's wish
to be believed always gave her face a brittle appearance, and
the complete coldness of her eyes didn't help matters.

"I'm here for the meeting," Joyce said. "This is my sister, Ava."

"We met the other day," Gerry said. "Such an unusual
name. Does it run in your family?"

I wanted to say, *Only if you believe my mother's tale that*

Ava Gardner was a mulatto second cousin of ours, once removed, who had managed to pass her way into the movies and was therefore worthy of having children named in her honor, but I just shook my head no.

"Well, come in, come in," Gerry said. "Our little group is going to be just the three of us, I'm afraid."

She motioned us toward two wobbly straight-back chairs and settled herself behind the pastor's desk as if she belonged there.

"Isn't Reverend Anderson coming?" Joyce said in a tone that carried just a whiff of warning. Joyce has calmed down a lot lately, but her reputation as a firebrand had probably preceded her. When she was in high school, she chained herself to the church front door to protest the war in Vietnam. Of course, that was long before the Andersons got here, but it was too good a story for somebody not to have shared it in the normal recitation of local *who's who.* Joyce even got her picture in the Lake County paper. *Idlewild Teen Protest Reflects National Mood.* I was so proud of her, I took it to school for show and tell.

Gerry smiled again. "As he and I prayed together earlier in preparation for this very meeting, he received a sign from the Lord, *praise him!* He rose and went immediately to work on his message for next Sunday morning, understanding, as he must, that divine inspiration is not under any obligation to petty cares and earthly schedules. He'll try to stick his head in later."

Sure he will. Joyce had been right about the Rev. He was a preaching somethin', but when it came to doing the dirty work, Gerry was definitely the Head Negro in Charge. Excuse me. *Negress.*

"All right." Joyce decided to be cool. "I'd like to know why the Sewing Circus meeting was canceled."

"Postponed," Gerry said. "The Good Reverend wanted me to make it clear that the meeting has only been postponed until we reach a meeting of the minds."

Joyce just looked at her.

"And I'm sure that such a meeting can be reached, aren't you?"

"I hope so," Joyce said. "I think we have to do more for our young people, not less."

"The Good Reverend couldn't agree more." Gerry nodded enthusiastically as if now convinced that they were on the same wavelength. "As you may know, at our last congregation, the Good Reverend created a youth program that became a model for churches all over the Midwest. We had over two hundred young men actively involved in a program of Christian education."

"Where were the young women?" Joyce said.

Gerry glanced sharply at Joyce and then modified her expression to convey her disappointment at the lack of understanding reflected in the question. "The Good Reverend saw our young men as a top priority, both as part of his calling and personally." She lowered her eyes briefly and her voice softened a little. "One of the reasons this congregation is such a blessing is that it allows us to remove our Tyrone from the evil influence of the city and bring him to a place where God's majesty is evident all around us."

Too bad, I thought. They came all this way so Tyrone and Frank could find each other.

"The Good Reverend is an expert on the kind of outreach work you're trying to do with the young women in this community—"

"I thought he was an expert on programs for young men," Joyce said sweetly.

Gerry ignored her. "And what the Good Reverend has found is that what these children need is a straightening of their overall Christian values. They are already overstimulated and confused by all the terrible *sex* material aimed at them."

She got that right.

"The last thing they need is more information about those kinds of things."

"What kinds of things?"

"The things those brochures were talking about."

"And what things were those?"

"I don't think we have to play games here, do we, Sister Mitchell? I think we both know what I'm talking about."

I felt like I was back in Atlanta listening to people talking in tongues, trying not to say *HIV*. Joyce took a deep breath and her voice was very calm.

"They are ignorant, *Sister* Anderson. They need information about everything, but especially about AIDS. Their generation is dying faster than anybody else because they don't know how to protect themselves."

"*Abstinence.*" Gerry's voice carried the righteous conviction of people who still think the best way to combat any galloping social ill—drug abuse, sexual irresponsibility, teenage pregnancy—is to simply advise those undisciplined few who are tempted to *just say no.*

"It doesn't work," Joyce said. "We've had four new babies born in the last six months to girls who are still not twenty years old."

Gerry's voice cut in like a hot knife through butter. "Weren't all of them active in the Sewing Circle?" I wanted Joyce to reach across the desk and slap her, but she didn't. Joyce is nonviolent.

"Yes."

"So I guess your method isn't so surefire either, is it, *Sister* Mitchell?"

They looked at each other across the desk and then Joyce said slowly, "No, I guess it isn't surefire at all, Sister Anderson. It's probably many things, but surefire is definitely not among them."

Gerry looked pleased. "Well, see there. We agree on a lot of things after all."

Joyce smiled suddenly and stood up, extending her hand. "I appreciate your time. I'm sorry Reverend Anderson couldn't join us, but I'm looking forward to his message on Sunday, so I can't really be disappointed, can I?"

"Praise God!" Gerry got to her feet and shook Joyce's hand.

"Maybe we can talk again after I've had a chance to think about some of the excellent points you brought out this morning."

I thought Joyce was laying it on pretty thick, but Gerry was eating it up.

"Of course we can, dear," she said, holding out her dry, smooth hand to me. "And it was so good to have you in our little congregation on Sunday, too."

"You have a wonderful voice," I said, following Joyce's lead with some flattery of my own. I wasn't lying either. The woman could blow.

"He blessed me with an instrument to glorify his name!" she said as we headed for the door, then Joyce turned around with the phoniest innocent look on her face you could ever imagine.

"Sister Anderson? When shall I bring you the bulletin announcement for next Wednesday? It's only our regular nursery school scheduling session. Not very exciting, but if it helps free up these young mothers so they can concentrate more fully on the word of God, it's worth it, isn't it?"

Gerry peered closely at Joyce, but Joyce was totally cool.

"Of course, dear," Gerry said. "Just be sure it gets here by Thursday noon. I'm not as good at this typing business as I used to be."

When we got outside, I started fussing immediately, but Joyce stopped me.

"Wait until we pull out," she said. "I'm sure she's still watching us."

"You're not going along with all that, are you?" I said as we climbed into the car.

"Of course not, but now that she thinks I am, I've got some room to move around for a minute or two. She never comes to our meetings. I'll tell her we're going to be discussing the nursery from now until Christmas if that's what makes her happy. The woman's out of touch. She's worrying about them storing up points in heaven when what they need is some survival lessons."

As Joyce pulled the car out of the empty parking lot, I looked in the side mirror and saw Gerry standing in the window, watching.

• 20

i had finally convinced Joyce to let me pamper her a little bit with a hard wash, deep conditioner, and rebraiding. When I rubbed some warm oil on her scalp and snuck in a little neck massage, she sighed and closed her eyes like I had finally hit the exact spot that needed it.

"You were right," she said. "This feels great."

"I'm always right."

"I wouldn't go that far," she smiled. I rubbed a little oil in the kitchen where the hair is always so soft it feels like a baby's first growth. In beauty school, they told us to call the "kitchen" the "nape," but any black beautician worth the name knows you can't use a term that has the word "nap" in it. Joyce sighed again. "That feels wonderful."

"I'm good at this." I wasn't bragging. I always made good money, but I never really enjoyed it until I got into the psychology of the whole process. I knew sisters spent a lot of time and money and energy on our hair, but I figured it was all about looking good for whatever brother was on the home front or on the horizon. Then I started watching my clients and listening to them more closely. They all talk a mile a minute. I'm not required to talk much. My function is more to ask the right questions, praise whatever course of action they have already followed, show indignation or approval at appropriate intervals, and make sure I don't cut it too short on the sides or leave them under the dryer any longer than absolutely necessary.

I was good at it—the cutting and the listening—and

some of my clients came twice a week at thirty to fifty dollars a pop. Now, I like to look good, too, but I think it was only half about looking good and the other half about having somebody to actively listen, actively affirm, and actively *touch* without expecting sex or a home-cooked meal in exchange.

Most sisters lean into a good shampoo like it's as welcome as good sex. One of my operators used to say that's why black beauticians wash your hair so damn hard. *They know they're doing double duty.* I won't go that far, but I know Joyce had the most relaxed look on her face I'd seen there in a while. I worked both hands near her temples and was rewarded by another voluptuous sigh.

"Tell me about Aretha," I said. Her face had stayed in my mind ever since Sunday. There was something about her that made you notice, made you wonder, made you care. Even though she looked like most of the other girls around here— cheap clothes, too much makeup, and the worst haircuts I've seen in ages!—her eyes were bright and curious and she seemed aware that there was a bigger world available to her if she wanted it. Watching her at the nursery, I found myself hoping she was going to be one of the ones who survived.

"She's got a chance," Joyce said. "Her parents were movement people. Came up here hoping they could find a community of like-minded souls."

"An all-black paradise," I said.

"Well, maybe not a paradise, but at least someplace where black folks had figured out some things."

"We figured out some things, all right," I said. "How to get the hell on the bus to the city. Lean over."

"Why?" Joyce said.

"Get some blood flowing to that head," I said. "What do you think?"

"Who knows?" said Joyce, leaning over and shaking her head of thick, newly washed hair into a fluffy black cloud around her face.

"Were they at church Sunday?" I said, trying to decide

whether to make a continuous circle of braids or a pattern of angles. Joyce has really healthy hair, and once I get her to sit still, she doesn't mind letting me be creative.

"They got killed in a car accident. A big semi crossed the line. Aretha had just turned twelve."

"Jesus!" Poor people, I thought. What's that thing about if you want to make God laugh, start making plans? That's sure the damn truth.

"They were going to put her in foster care or send her back to Detroit to her grandmother, but then one of her mother's friends took her."

"Nice woman?"

Joyce shrugged. "She's all right. She's usually drunk, but she's very quiet about it, so nobody bothers her. I do what I can, but Aretha's independent and proud. She won't usually admit she needs any help from anybody. She just figures it out and takes care of things. She's pretty much raising herself."

"She seems to be doing a pretty good job of it," I said. "Is that too tight?" I patted the beginning of the braid lightly.

Joyce smiled. "It's perfect. Why'd you ask about Aretha?"

"I don't know. She just looked so *alive* when we saw her on Sunday."

"She's about the only sixteen-year-old who comes to the Sewing Circus who doesn't already have a kid."

"Good for her."

"She wants to go to Interlochen."

Interlochen was a boarding school for smart, artistic kids a couple of hours up the road. Tuition was steep and scholarships were scarce, even for white kids.

"Does she have a chance at it?"

"She's talented," Joyce said. "And she's determined. She applied for a special institute. A month in residence at the end of the summer. She ought to hear something in a couple of days."

"You think she'll get it?"

"I've got my fingers crossed."

"That's not a very scientific approach," I said, parting

Joyce's hair gently into small sections. The secret of good-look-ing braids is absolutely straight parts between them.

"And I've helped her with the application and drove her down for the interview."

"Okay," I said, tucking the end of one braid into the beginnings of the next one. "Just wanted to be sure you weren't falling down on the job."

Talking about Aretha made me see why Joyce is doing what she does. I liked the girl's energy. I guess she reminded me of myself a little bit at her age: alive and well and *on my way.*

• 21

eddie scared the shit out of me this morning. I was home by myself since Joyce went into town early to pick up a few last-minute things. She's bringing Imani home tomorrow and she's been spinning around like a top for the last twenty-four hours. I'm worn out just from watching her, so once I put the kettle on for tea (although I still prefer coffee even if it is bad for me!), I got out one of those meditation tapes Joyce had, and it sounded like something I might actually be able to do. In fact, it didn't sound like much more than sitting still for a little while and trying to calm down. The guy on the tape said to think of your mind as a monkey, swinging through the trees, chattering away a mile a minute, and the meditation was a way to catch hold of the monkey.

So there I was, sitting on the porch with my eyes closed, counting my breaths like the guy said to make sure I don't get distracted, and I'm feeling pretty silly about doing this at all, but it feels good just to be sitting out here. I almost never just sit anywhere. I'm always talking or working or reading or watching TV or on the phone or worrying.

So I'm trying to sit there and tell myself that everything feels silly the first few times you do it and not to give up and go make a pot of coffee when I felt a *presence*. I didn't hear anything, but you know how you can *feel* somebody looking at you? At first I figured maybe it was just the meditation kicking in, but it didn't feel like a spiritual presence. It felt like a *person* presence, so I opened my eyes and Eddie was standing there in the yard, just looking at me. I had expected to see somebody, but I still jumped. I couldn't believe he had gotten that close up on me and I hadn't even heard him break a twig.

"I didn't mean to startle you," he said.

"You don't make much noise when you move around, do you?" I said.

He smiled at me. "I didn't see you until I was already in the yard. You weren't making a whole bunch of noise yourself."

"I have my moments," I said.

"Joyce asked me to come over and put the crib together." I could see he had a small toolbox with him.

"She's gone to the grocery store," I said, "but it's sitting in a box in the middle of the living room floor if you want to get started."

"Good," he said. "I know she wants it ready for tomorrow."

"She's pretty excited," I said, glad to have an excuse for putting on that pot of coffee and joining Eddie in the living room where he was reading the instructions for the crib carefully and laying parts out methodically in a row so that once he got started he wouldn't have to be digging around in the bottom of the box like I always do, looking for the crucial four screws that I probably threw away an hour ago.

"You learn to walk that quiet in the army, too?" I said.

"Habit," he said, putting a weird little bracket down next to a set of weird little clamps.

He opened his toolbox and started looking at the various sizes of screwdrivers, matching them up quickly with the pieces of the baby bed where they would be required. One thing about Wild Eddie, he wasn't much of a talker. He never seemed to be uncomfortable. He just didn't talk to fill in empty space like most people do. I wondered if that was habit too.

I sat there and drank my coffee and he put that whole crib together and never said a word. And it was okay. There was something really *quiet* about Eddie. I don't mean just not talking. Something about him was *still*. When he got through with the crib's assembly and attached the mobile, we stood back to admire his handiwork.

"I figured out why I didn't recognize you at the airport," he said, like we'd been engaged in a discussion about it.

"Because I grew up," I said.

He gestured toward my almost-shaved head. "No. I thought you'd have more hair."

"I was in the hair business," I said, "but when it comes to my own, sometimes I go through periods where less is definitely more."

"What business are you in now?" he said.

I heard myself hesitate, but I played right past it. "I'm between engagements."

He looked at me. "I like it." He took his time before he said it, too, like he was really trying to decide.

"Thanks," I said, and picked up our cups to take back into the kitchen so he wouldn't catch me blushing.

"I like it a lot." And he smiled the smile that had been at the heart of most of the Wild Eddie Jefferson stories I'd ever heard involving women. I was beginning to understand why.

• 22

it was another pretty day. I'm making pasta for dinner tonight and I wanted to get some decent red wine to go with it, so I decided to drive to Big Rapids in search of Chianti. I borrowed Joyce's car, treated myself to lunch at a pretty little restaurant with outdoor café seating that looked like it had just dropped in from Paris for the afternoon, and found a liquor store with a huge, if dusty, selection of wine. I was poking around, to the complete disinterest of the bored owner, when the door opens and in walks Reverend Anderson. Well, he doesn't really just *walk* in. He kind of creeps in like he doesn't especially want anybody to see him in a liquor store in the middle of the afternoon. He didn't see me, so I just watched him.

"What'll it be?" said the owner, folding his newspaper and looking put upon.

"A fifth of Jack Daniel's and a pint of peach brandy," the Rev said, pulling out his wallet.

The owner rang up the sale and grimaced at the brandy as he bagged it up. "My wife likes this stuff, too," he said. "I don't see how they drink it. Too sweet for me."

"Thank you," said the Rev, folding the bills the man handed him and striding out quickly.

I took two bottles of passable Chianti to the cash register and looked out the window in time to see the Rev pulling away from the parking lot. His companion, a young man who looked about fifteen, sat as close to the door as he could without riding on the roof. He was probably on his way to a lecture from the Good Reverend about some sin or another, and he didn't seem to be looking forward to it one bit.

Well, I thought, *that's an interesting idea.* Combine some youth outreach work with a trip to the liquor store.

"You ever drink that sweet brandy?" said the owner, feeling more kindly now that I was actually buying something, I guess.

"No," I said. "Too sweet for me."

"Exactly," he said, double-bagging my wine and smiling now like he was pleased to see I shared his opinion. "That's it *exactly.*"

As I got back in the car and turned back toward Idlewild, I kept seeing that kid's shoulders hunched up around his neck like he was trying to retract his head like a human turtle. Too bad, I thought. If he'd been to church on Sunday, he'd know: *no hiding place down here.*

• 23

imani arrived this morning. She is the quietest baby I've ever seen. It's almost like she knows her family history and is just glad somebody cared enough to take her home. She isn't about to make any waves. When the social worker handed her to Joyce, she was wide-awake and looking at everything with this real serious expression on her face. The social worker, who turned out to be a former co-worker of Joyce's, said she didn't make a sound the whole drive down.

"Be great for you if she stays that quiet," the woman said. "Some of them scream bloody murder the whole time they're awake."

Them. The way she said it made me feel sorry for Imani. She was already part of a group nobody wanted to deal with: *crack babies.*

We looked at Imani, who looked back without blinking as if to say: *can you imagine me acting a fool like that? No way.*

When the social worker left, Joyce sat down on the couch and held Imani on her knees so we could look into her face. She was a thin, cocoa brown baby with long, skinny legs and big, dark, old-lady eyes.

"We have the same stylist," I said, running my hand lightly over her perfectly bald head. It was warm and smooth.

"Isn't she beautiful?" Joyce said, and leaned over to kiss the baby on both cheeks and smile into her face. Imani watched her intently without a trace of a smile back. She was also the most serious baby I had ever seen. The idea of chucking her under the chin or tickling her ribs was out of the question.

"I'll bet she has plenty to say," Joyce said. "Don't you? But you have to get someplace safe before you tell your secrets, isn't that right? I think that's right."

•

Imani's eyes never left Joyce's face.

"Do you want to hold her?"

I hadn't really thought about it, but when Joyce asked the question, Imani turned toward me like she was waiting for the answer, too. What could I say? Joyce put her in my arms and went into the kitchen to see what the social worker had brought from the hospital.

"Well," I said, wondering why there is such a strong urge to talk gibberish to babies. I resisted it. "You made it, huh? Got born anyway."

She looked at me with her old-lady eyes like it had already been quite a trip. I was glad that she had landed here with us and hadn't had to go with her angry aunt Mattie and her crazy uncle Frank. You don't get to pick your family, but sometimes it's good to have options.

I ran my hand over her little head again and she snuggled against me in a way that made me feel a surge of what I guess was maternal protectiveness. Imani had already kicked a drug habit cold turkey and outrun the HIV her mama was sending special delivery. She was stronger than she looked, and somehow that made me feel stronger, too.

"You go, girl," I said. "With your bad baby self."

All of a sudden I heard Joyce burst out laughing in the kitchen, but before she could explain, Eddie pulled up in the yard. Joyce stopped laughing long enough to introduce him to Imani. I handed her to him and he held her easily, like it was a perfectly natural thing to do. I liked that. It always pissed me off when men would go all thumbs if you asked them to hold a baby. Eddie even knew how to support the head. Imani gave him the same unblinking consideration she had bestowed on us while Joyce showed us what was so funny.

At the bottom of the bag the social worker had brought with bottles, diapers, bibs, and teething ring was a sort of harness thing that lets you pretend you're breast-feeding when you're really not. Supposedly some brother wanted to experience the joys of breast-feeding and invented this bib with tubes to simulate that. Eddie and I agreed this is *not* a brother that either one of us has any interest in getting to know. Bottle-feeding is one thing, but trying to fool the kid into thinking the milk is coming from inside you when it's really *cow's milk* seemed a little weird. Joyce said we're just scared to open up to new experiences and that when Imani gets older, she's going to tell her how we acted.

We all laughed, but in the middle of it, I realized I'm probably not going to be around for much of Imani's life. Two days ago I wasn't even sure I wanted to spend the summer with this kid, but now I'm starting to really feel sorry for myself, picturing Eddie and Joyce witnessing her first steps without me. Going to her dance recitals and softball games. Taking snaps at her high school graduation. My brain went through a fast-forward of Kodak moments where I was conspicuously absent. I almost started crying at how much I was going to miss, then I thought *fuck it.* I'm well *right now* and I'm not going to make myself sick worrying about what's going to happen next.

So I took a deep breath like they keep saying on this meditation tape and tried to focus on being *right in this room, right in this moment,* and I actually felt better! It was amazing. I dragged that scared part of myself kicking and screaming into *the present moment* and it was so good to be there. I started grinning like an idiot.

I hope I can remember this feeling next time I'm blubbering into my pillow because I can't count on the next thirty years. *One day at a time.* I ought to have that shit tattooed on my forehead. *One damn day at a time.*

• 24

i knew there was going to be trouble when Joyce came home with four packages of juicy jumbo hot dogs and six boxes of latex condoms, but I don't think any of us had any idea how *much* trouble until Gerry walked into the fellowship hall and saw Aretha unrolling a very slippery lubricated condom over a jumbo juicy that, to facilitate matters, had been mounted straight up on a chopstick like the hard-on from hell.

The evening started off calmly enough, considering that most of these girls had not only never *used* a condom, they had never seen one, except in drugstore displays with smiling white couples on the front and the mysterious thing itself well concealed within. The words *safe sex* were not a part of their erotic vocabularies any more than birth control entered into their family planning options.

When Joyce introduced the Wednesday night session, which she had assured Gerry would focus on nothing more controversial than scheduling nursery workers for Sunday morning, by saying they were going to talk about AIDS, one of the older women in the group, which put her at about eighteen, snickered and rolled her eyes. I thought she was the one who had told Aretha at the nursery everybody knew she *ain't got no sense*, but her hair and makeup were so different, it was hard to tell. Apparently the fairly ordinary upsweep she'd favored for Sunday morning was of no interest during the week. She had added badly braided extensions, which were gathered on top of her head in a tall, gold-toned comb and *still* hung well below her shoulders. The braids were clearly new and still pulled so tight her eyes now had a distinctly unnatural slant that wasn't being helped much by the frosty blue eye shadow she was wearing. Add the deep plum lipstick, and homegirl had a look that was uniquely, and *thankfully,* all her own.

"Ain't nobody in here fucking no faggots," she said. "Excuse my French."

Joyce didn't even blink. She just asked them what they thought was the number one killer of young black folks all over America. They guessed homicide, drug overdose, cancer, and car accidents, in that order. When Joyce said AIDS, they thought she was kidding.

"You just trying to scare us into reading this stuff, right?" said a thin, muddy brown girl who I recognized from the nursery, too. She was sitting alone, jiggling a sickly-looking baby across her knees and waving one of the health department pamphlets. The baby didn't look much happier than he had on Sunday, but at least he wasn't crying.

"You need to be scared," Joyce said calmly, "if you want to stay alive."

That sort of got their attention and they started asking questions. Sitting in the back, holding the peacefully sleeping Imani, my only job for the evening once I reminded Joyce that I was not here to do missionary work, *thank you,* I was amazed and frightened by how little information they had. A lot of us can chalk our HIV up to innocence or ignorance or Ronald Reagan's inability to say the word *AIDS* out loud, but this generation is supposed to know better. The information is *everywhere,* but it seems to wash right over them.

They wanted to know where it came from, how you could get it, could your kids get it, did you always die from it, and how could you tell who had it and who didn't.

"You can't tell," Joyce said. "That's why we have to use condoms every single time."

"My old man ain't havin' it," a woman with a long blond ponytail of somebody else's hair said, shaking her head. "He said he can't feel nothin' when he use 'em."

She hadn't even dyed the rest of her hair to match. The front was regular, dark brown, *need-a-touch-up* Negro woman's hair. The back was literally a horse of a different color. I wondered who was doing their hair. Probably the same person giving them birth control advice.

"My boyfriend say when we get it goin' good, he don't wanna stop and put no rubber on," somebody else said.

"That's part of what *we* have to do," Joyce said. That's when she reached into the shopping bag beside her and brought out the juicy jumbo. "We're going to learn how to put it on *for* him."

Aretha had been sitting in the back, but when Joyce said that, she looked at me and grinned conspiratorially. "Don't want to miss anything," she said, got up, and walked right up to the front. I laid Imani in her babyseat and moved up a little myself. As long as I was here, I didn't want to miss anything either. Joyce smiled and reached into the Baggie, took out the hot dog, held it up like she was demonstrating Tupperware, and then plunged it down on the chopstick so it seemed to stand at attention, awaiting her command. The women whooped with laughter.

"That look a little like Junebug!" one giggled.

"In your dreams," Blond Ponytail teased her.

Joyce reached into the bag again and brought out a box of condoms.

"Putting the condom on for your partner doesn't have to be a chore," Joyce said, and I mentally did the next sentence with her. "It can be part of your lovemaking."

This spiel assumes, of course, that *lovemaking* is the activity in which the parties are engaged. Safe sex is based on two people agreeing to plan ahead and prepare for their physical exchanges in advance of the moment where everybody is firmly in the grip of their hormones and whatever drugs or alcohol they use to enhance the moment. Looking around at the young women now crowded around Joyce's demonstration, I was willing to bet that making love is not any more a part of their sex lives than creative, mutually pleasurable foreplay.

First Joyce asked them to tear open a condom and look at it, touch it, roll it around in their fingers, smell it. This was all done with a maximum of giggling, signifying, and eye rolling, but I could see they were intrigued. Even the girl with the unhappy baby moved into the circle, too curious to hang back. By the time Joyce asked for a volunteer, six hands went up, but Aretha was standing right in front of the jumbo on a stick and she grabbed it.

The girl with the new extensions rolled her new eyes and snorted. "You better ask for a Vienna sausage to practice on, little girl. You know you can't handle nothin' like this."

Aretha was cool. She ripped open a packet containing a bright purple condom and smiled sweetly. "You know, Tomika, since I'm the only one in here who ain't got no baby, or about to have one—" she paused significantly, positioned the condom carefully, and slowly rolled it down the quivering jumbo"—I must be the only one who *is* handlin' it the way it's 'spose to be handled." She popped the condom securely in place and turned to Tomika. "Your turn."

Several of the girls applauded, but Tomika tossed her hair until it swirled around her head like Medusa. "I don't need no practice," she said.

"That's not what Roy say," the girl at her elbow said with a giggle, and moved quickly out of smacking range.

"We all could use some practice," Joyce said, handing a packet to the thin girl with the fussy baby. "You want to try, Patrice?"

Patrice looked at Joyce for a second or two like she was deciding whether to go along with the program or scoop up her baby and try to make it home in time to see *New York Undercover.*

"Go ahead, girl," said Tomika, glad to be off the spot. "You got it."

"Shit," said Patrice, taking the condom from Joyce defiantly and unrolling it, "you ain't said nothin' but the word." She looked at Joyce, who nodded approvingly. "Okay?"

"Okay."

"Now can I ask you one thing?"

"Go ahead," Joyce said.

"It ain't nothin' to it when it's sittin' still like that. But what you 'spose to do when it's wigglin' all over the place?"

This broke up the group, but Joyce didn't bat an eye. "Use two hands," she said, a technique that she proceeded to demonstrate to great and vocal delight, but which, from her reaction, the Reverend Mrs. didn't find at all amusing.

"What do you think you're doing?" Her voice, which was so beautifully spirit-filled on Sunday morning, sounded like the Devil speaking through that girl in *The Exorcist.* I turned toward the sound, fully expecting her head to be spinning around and pea soup to be spewing from her mouth. Clustered, guiltily now, around the table at the front of the room, we hadn't seen her come in. I wondered how long she had been standing there.

The power of her outrage brought an immediate silence. Even the children were suddenly quiet, waiting to see which one had provoked such a response from this woman who was now stalking toward the front of the room where the jumbo stood, safely hooded, in the center of a table scattered with condoms and replacement dogs in case this first one didn't hold up through the ministrations of all the sisters present.

The force of Gerry's outrage was so overpowering that the women fell back in her wake, groping behind them for their purses and their children, even while they hoped Joyce could save the situation.

Gerry stood across the table from Joyce now, pointing accusingly at the offending display. "What in the name of all that is holy do you think you are doing with these girls?"

Joyce didn't flinch. "I'm trying to save their lives."

"By exposing them to this . . . this filth?" Gerry spit out the words.

"By telling them the truth."

For a few seconds nobody moved and then Gerry stepped forward and swept her arm across the table, sending hot dogs, condoms, and pamphlets flying. It reminded me of that scene in *The Ten Commandments* where old Charlton Heston flings down the stone tablets to break up the decadent orgy in progress that greets his return from the wilderness, except I think Gerry was even madder than that. I could see her trembling even from the back of the room, struggling to regain control of her speech.

"This meeting is over," she said finally, looking sternly from one frightened woman to another. "All of you get your things and get out. Go home and pray to God that you have not marked your children for life by exposing them to such lewd and lascivious things."

They just looked at her, less in defiance than in confusion. *What the hell did lewd and lascivious mean?*

"Go NOW!" Gerry's voice was an angry bellow.

As the women headed for the door, Joyce's voice rose sweetly above the confusion. "You can pick up extra condoms from my sister at the door," she said, pointing at me. I remembered I had the other bag full of supplies in the back next to Imani, who was still sleeping, blissfully unaware. I scrambled to break them out and press them into the outstretched hands of the rapidly dispersing Sewing Circus members.

"Tell your sister to hang in there," Tomika whispered as she accepted a strip of condoms from me. "This was right on time no matter what Miz Anderson says."

"Thanks," I said.

When the last woman had grabbed a handful of condoms and gone, Joyce smiled at Gerry like they were neighbors exchanging gossip over the back fence and began cleaning up the mess on the floor. I went to help.

Gerry was staring at Joyce like she was trying to determine our specific degree of insanity before making her next move. Joyce picked up the chopstick, pulled the hooded hotdog off, and dropped it into the trash bag.

•

"I think it went well," she said to me as if we were alone in the room. I didn't know what to say, so I just nodded.

That was too much for Gerry, who turned on her heel and marched away. She turned at the door.

"This is the very last time you will have a chance to desecrate the house of God with such evil," she hissed. "I intend to see to it. *Immediately!*" She swept out with her threat still echoing behind her.

I braced myself for a bolt of lightning to strike me and Joyce down like the sinners we surely were, but apparently the Reverend Mrs. wasn't as tight with God as she thought or he was busy elsewhere because nothing happened.

Joyce grinned at me. "Did you see her face when she saw that hot dog with a condom on?"

I grinned back. "You have been a very bad girl." And we sat there in the middle of the remains of the evening and laughed until we cried. Imani looked at us like we were crazy, but what the hell? If you can't get hysterical in the face of the plague, when can you get hysterical?

july

dear sister mitchell:

It is with deep regret that I must inform you that the goals and purposes of the Women's Sewing Circle organization, which currently meets under your stewardship on Wednesday nights, here at the church fellowship hall, are no longer in line with the overall goals and Christian purpose of the New Light Baptist Church. The shocking display which was witnessed on Wednesday last by my wife, Mrs. Anderson, during your meeting, had no place within a building dedicated to the glory of God. She was alarmed and appalled, as I am sure any woman of good conscience and high moral character would be.

Both Mrs. Anderson and I are aware of your long history in this community and we value your continued active membership at New Light. However, due to your unwillingness to bring the Women's Sewing Circle back to its original purpose (and its original name, which more accurately reflected the pursuit of activities befitting Christian women), I am hereby suspending your right to use the church facilities for any gathering without my explicit approval in writing. I am disbanding the Wednesday night women's group until it can be reshaped more in line with our overall goals of building and strengthening Christian men, women, and children. Mrs. Anderson will assume the directorship of the Sunday morning nursery, which we do feel is a valuable service to the many young mothers within our congregation and should continue.

Let me say in closing, Sister Mitchell, how sorry I am that we have been unable to find common ground on which to meet. I feel that you may be going through some difficult times in your personal life that may have affected

*your judgment in this and other matters. Your spirit may
be tossed in turmoil from which you can find no solace. I
urge you to seek your answers in our Lord and Savior Jesus
Christ, not in the foul and deviant solutions suggested by
an evil and sinful world. The Lord can, and will, provide the
peace you are seeking if you humble yourself to him and ask
for his forgiveness. As your pastor, I would be happy, when
my schedule clears, to meet with you for further counseling
on the difficult matters which may have hardened your heart
toward the healing powers of being joyfully washed in the
blood of the lamb.*

Yours in Christ,
Rev. Jonathan Anderson
Pastor, New Light Baptist Church

• 2

it wasn't like Joyce had intended to keep the group connected
to the church forever, but this sudden parting of the ways
couldn't have come at a worse time. The Sewing Circus had
only been meeting regularly for six months and it was already
making a difference in these women's lives. Postponing meetings or trying to move to someplace new was bound to tamper
with the delicate balance of things and probably result in a
drop-off in active membership. Most of them didn't have cars
and there were no buses, so getting around up here was definitely a consideration.

Joyce wasn't having it. "It's working so well," she said,
ticking off a list of recent positive signs, including the fact that
Patrice had called after the session with the jumbos to say she
had finally gotten her boyfriend to use a condom and even
though he still didn't like it, she had felt so free knowing she
wasn't going to get pregnant that her enthusiasm had, he said,
more than made up for any decrease in sensation.

And just this morning, Aretha had come by with the news that she'd gotten her official letter of acceptance into the summer institute at Interlochen and that if she did well, there was a chance she might get the financial aid she needed to spend her whole senior year there. When she showed us the letter, her face was the sweetest mixture of triumph and terror. I knew what the look meant. She had just realized she didn't have to live and die in Lake County just because she was born there.

"I'll schedule a meeting, all right," Joyce said, folding the Rev's letter and putting it aside. "A meeting to tell them that me and the Sewing Circus are moving on."

I looked at her and the question in my mind must have been written all over my face because she laughed and shook her head.

"I don't know *where* we're moving on *to*," she said, "but we are definitely *on the move!*"

I told you. Joyce is that kind of a gal. Inertia is death. Forward motion is everything.

• 3

i was an asshole at the grocery store today. I didn't feel like going, but I didn't want to stay home alone with Imani either. She's going through a phase where she doesn't want you to put her down. She doesn't cry. She just sort of mews and whimpers like a kitten or some other sweet, helpless little animal.

Joyce put her in the baby seat while she picked through some strawberries that had seen better days. The cart with the seat in it was right up next to Joyce, so it wasn't like Imani couldn't *see* her, but she started that mewing anyway and it was working my last nerve, so I said:

"This damn baby just wants to be held all the time!"

"Don't you?" Joyce said, reached over, picked up

Imani, who was instantly quiet, and went on with what she was doing.

She's right. That's why I'm so evil. I had a brief flicker that she might have heard me masturbating downstairs, but that's crazy. The bed doesn't creak and I don't make much noise. I never was much of a screamer, even in my prime, and these days I mostly maintain a ladylike silence.

I'm just lonesome. I've even been thinking that when I get to San Francisco, I might be more open to the idea of having a woman lover. Wondering where do the titties go is only one small step from asking, *"Which one gets to be the man?"* one of the top ten most ignorant questions of all time. Besides, there is another possibility. *What if both of them get to be the woman?*

The funny thing is, the best sex I ever had was with a brother who really liked to *kiss it.* He wasn't like most of those Atlanta Negroes who act like oral sex means one way in their direction, period. This brother would start at the navel, kiss his way down, and then linger. He'd kiss up one side and down the other. And you know how sometimes men will make the supreme sacrifice and kiss it a few times like they're doing you a favor, but they hold their breath the whole time? This brother would *breathe.* Sometimes he'd just bury his nose and inhale like my stuff really did smell sweet as honeysuckle, a claim he made on more than one occasion.

I knew women who gave up on men after they hit thirty and the pickings were looking kind of slim and the few unmarried, straight men around were all acting like they were God's gift. Once they found a girlfriend, they never went back. When you tried to ease up on asking them about the *specifics,* they would smile mysteriously and suggest that if you've figured out a way to fuck *men* and get off, women will be a breeze and a blessing.

But, of course, Imani isn't interested in all that. She's busy living out her role as the flesh-and-blood proof of all those scary statistics about crack babies and drug addicts and the wages of sin. Joyce isn't interested either since she said she hasn't even thought about having sex since Mitch died. So it's on me.

Maybe I can reprogram my body to channel all this sexual energy into physical fitness. Maybe my disposition will improve if I start walking a couple of miles a day and do some sit-ups or something. I don't know, though. The way I've been feeling lately, I'll wind up looking like Arnold Schwarzenegger by Christmas.

When we got home, I apologized to Joyce and she hugged me and got all teary. She started saying how important it is that we love Imani as much as we can since her real family could come and get her any time they want to and we know what kind of life that would be. Joyce said we have to help her build up some good memories in case she's got some more bad times coming.

Now I really felt like shit. Gerry's messing with the Sewing Circus and Imani is still not tied to Joyce by anything but love. I told Joyce she should legally adopt Imani so they couldn't ever take her back and she said she wants to, but it's really complicated because they still can't find Eartha and nobody knows the father. In the meantime, just the possibility of losing Imani makes Joyce very, very nervous. She's only been with us three weeks and she's already family. I asked Joyce what she would do if Mattie and Frank came to claim Imani.

"Head for the hills," Joyce said calmly.

"Okay," I said. "Just so we've got a plan."

• 4

eddie took me into Ludington yesterday. It's only forty miles or so, but I haven't been there since we were kids. He had to go check on a job he'd done a month ago and when he asked me if I wanted to ride, I jumped at the chance. Maybe some of those stiff breezes coming in off Lake Michigan can blow away some of the bad vibes I've been carrying in spite of my best efforts.

"Joyce didn't put you up to this, did she?" I said, suddenly suspicious that this trip might be part of a coordinated effort.

Eddie shook his head. "No. Why would she?"

"I haven't been such good company lately."

"Really? What do you do when you're not being good company?"

I considered the question. "I snarl a lot."

He nodded. "Well, she hasn't mentioned it to me."

"I just didn't want you to feel like you had to do this."

"Do what?" He guided the truck easily around a patch of road construction.

"Take me for a Sunday drive."

"It's Tuesday," he said.

"Six of one, half a dozen of the other." *What was I talking about?*

"Was that a snarl?"

He was teasing me and I liked it. "I warned you."

"That's fair enough," he said. "I'll keep it in mind."

I waited while he went in to check the deck he'd built behind a little house tucked way off the main road in an acre or so of the most amazing pine trees. Of course, they wanted a deck. I'm surprised they weren't living in a tree house.

"Everything holding up?" I said when he jumped back in beside me.

"Yep," he said. "You hungry?"

Was I?

"I've got some fruit," he said. "We could go down and sit by the lake if you want. The beach shouldn't be crowded this time of day."

"Not on Tuesday," I said, and he laughed. I did, too. I didn't care if it was a plot to improve my disposition. It was working like a charm.

• 5

when eddie said he had fruit, that wasn't the whole story. He had a picnic basket full of green grapes and golden ripe bananas, two perfect mangoes, a carton of strawberries, a couple of different kinds of cheese, and the best loaf of homemade pumpernickel bread I'd ever tasted. He also had a blanket for us to sit on and a bottle of some blend of exotic juices that made you feel tropical even in the decidedly midwestern environs of Ludington, Michigan.

"What if I hadn't been home to accept your invitation?" I said, glad that I was, but never content to leave well enough alone.

"I'd still have to eat lunch," he said. "I just wouldn't be doing it in such good company."

"You eat this good all the time?"

He grinned and handed me a plump strawberry, which I popped into my mouth by way of thanks. "Don't you?"

I had an instant mental picture of my regular eating habits. I've been trying to eat better since I got diagnosed, but I spent years surviving on fast food and an occasional salad. I ate on the run so often, I had to consciously slow down when somebody took me out to dinner or I'd be ordering dessert before they finished the salad.

"No," I said. "I really don't."

"Why not?" He looked like he really wanted to know.

"Not enough time?" I said, sounding uncertain even to myself.

"Oh," he said, spreading some kind of soft cheese on a small piece of pumpernickel and passing it to me like I'd asked for it.

After we finished eating, we just sat there for a while,

looking at the lake, watching the gulls, talking a little bit, but mostly just sitting there together. It was a lovely afternoon, and by the time we started back, I felt like I'd found a friend for life. Better late than never.

• 6

aretha came by looking for Joyce, but had to settle for me and Imani. Joyce was trying to scout out a central place for the Sewing Circus to have their next meeting. Other than the church, there weren't many options.

"Do you want to wait for her?" I said. Imani was asleep and I was up for some company.

"Thanks," she said, and accepted my offer of a cup of peppermint tea.

"So are you ready for your trip to Interlochen?" I said, setting out the honey and two spoons.

"Yeah," she said, shaking her head *no* at the same time. "I can't believe it."

"Why? Joyce said your portfolio is really good."

Aretha ducked her head and blushed with pride. It made her look even younger. "She did?"

"She sure did."

"Well, that's what she keeps telling me and I know that's why they accepted me, but I guess I don't believe it yet." She sipped her tea and added another swirl of honey. "I wish my mom and dad could be here to see me," she said.

"They'd be proud of you," I said.

She nodded and stirred her tea.

"How soon do you have to go?"

"Ten days," she said, brightening again. "They said we don't have to bring anything except our clothes. They give you all the stuff you need when you get there."

"That's great," I said. "I'm sure it's going to be a great experience for you."

"Thanks," she said. "Are you really a hairdresser?"

"I used to be."

"What are you now?"

I loved the directness of the question. I wished my answer could have been more straightforward, but this was a kid. I didn't need to discuss my health with her.

"I'm in transition," I said. "I'm moving to San Francisco to consider my options."

She grinned. "That sounds real cool."

I laughed.

"How long have you been wearing your hair short like that?"

I ran my hand over my hair, glad I had learned to cut it myself without taking chunks out of the back. The secret is to get a mirror you can hang around your neck like harmonica players do so you have both hands free. "Five or six years," I said.

"For real?"

"Honest to God. Why does that surprise you?"

"I don't know," she said. "I just never saw anybody up close with their hair that short. You like it?"

"I love it," I said. "No fuss, no muss, no fuzz, no scuzz."

She giggled at that. "Well, you got the face for it, I guess."

"What does that mean?"

"You know. You got a nice face."

"Everybody's got a nice face," I said. "Most of the time you just can't see it under all that bad hair."

She considered this. "Weren't you scared? What if you did it and didn't like it?"

"What's the worst that can happen? It'll grow back."

"It'd be one less thing to worry about, that's for sure."

I looked at her smooth brown face. She had beautiful

skin and big dark eyes. If anybody had the face for this hair-
style, Aretha did. She'd probably never had a good haircut in
her life. A thought occurred to me.

"I'll tell you what," I said. "When you get ready to go
to school, I'll cut your hair for you."

"That short?" She looked intrigued, but a little doubtful.

"Doesn't have to be this short," I said. "I'll style it any
way you want. Something easy to keep so you won't be up
there worrying about your hair when you're supposed to be
contemplating the colors of the sunset."

"Would you really?" Her face begged me not to tease
her and I heard the sound of Joyce's car outside.

"You'd be doing me a favor," I said. "I don't want to
get rusty sitting around here all summer like a lady of leisure
and lose my skills."

"Okay," she said. "Thanks."

"You're welcome," I said. "And don't rule out cutting
it short. *You've got the face for it.*"

The smile she gave me was all the proof I needed.

• 7

one of the good things about meditating is that it helps you
spot your own bullshit much faster. The bad thing is, sometimes a little harmless bullshit is quite a pleasant diversion
from what are invariably the much harsher realities of a bull-
shit-free existence. Maybe *harsh* is too strong a word. How
about *barren?*

I figured out why I've been so evil. *I'm attracted to Eddie.*
Not *curious about.* Not *affectionate toward. Attracted to,* as in *sexually.* Talk about bad timing. I thought at first it was some kind
of residual crush left over from my girlhood or just a Pavlovian
response to a fine brother in close proximity, but it isn't. It's
him specifically for real. *Damn.*

Riding back from Ludington, I felt that thump of pulse between my legs that always alerts my sexual body to the presence of prey. I used to love that feeling. It announced the beginning of another round of first dates, late-night phone calls, slowly dawning (on his part) realizations of mutual interest, increasingly intense flirtation, and, finally, the sex. This process took a little time or a lot, depending on the brother's tolerance and ability to play the game—everybody is not amused by extended foreplay—and whether my own interest was cerebral *and* sexual, or pretty much focused solely on how he'd be in bed.

Men in whom I had no sexual interest were in another category altogether. I never allowed them to start the give-and-take everybody has to agree to if the seduction is to have some integrity to it. I think it's cruel to encourage men when you have no real interest in them, no matter how many dinners they pay for or how many long-stemmed roses they have delivered to the office for maximum impressing of your girlfriends. It's no crime not to lust after somebody just because they're lusting after you. It's only a crime when you use it against them.

So now that I've admitted the facts, what am I going to do? First of all, I have no intention of having sex with Eddie Jefferson. I'm only going to be here a couple of months and I don't need the complications sex always introduces. Sex changes everything between a man and a woman, and even though you say it won't, you know damn well it will. Great sex will make you overlook many a terrible weakness for the sake of all that *feel good*. It definitely adds something exciting to the mix, but whether or not it's worth the price you pay is the question to which I've never found an even halfway decent answer.

If you ask somebody who's hooked up with a man they love and the sex is good and he's not acting a fool, the sister will tell you the rewards are so sweet they are worth a little compromise. But ask somebody who just got her heart broken for the third time since Christmas and she'll tell you nothing beats curling up in bed alone with a magazine and a pint of Häagen-Dazs.

And that's not even counting all the safe-sex precautions

that are now a part of my life for damn ever. Have you ever tried to figure out how to have any kind of satisfactory oral exchange while holding a latex dental dam over your sweet spot?

I'm just not up for all that right now. Me and Wild Eddie seem to have the beginnings of a beautiful friendship. I'm going to leave it at that. Old habits are hard to break, but not impossible.

• 8

i had to have my doctor call from Atlanta to refill my damn prescriptions and the pharmacist in town didn't waste any time spreading the news that I had "caught the HIV." I went to the drugstore to pick it up and walked in on Gerry Anderson telling these two other old biddies how sad it was and how she just hoped I wasn't contagious since we had so many young people in town and all.

The druggist was standing there with the bottle of pills in his hand, showing it to them and holding it like it might explode if he jiggled it too hard. I was walking down a side aisle, so they didn't see me until I stopped right in front of them and they gasped and fell back like they had seen Dracula coming up the front walk. I wanted to grab the back of Gerry's head and give her a big, wet kiss, but I thought she might have a heart attack and I'd get prosecuted for murder, so I held out my hand to the pharmacist and said, "Don't you have to take some kind of oath to stay out of people's business when you fill their prescriptions?"

He dropped it in my hand like a hot potato and mumbled something about how he was going to send Tyrone, his delivery boy, out to the house with it, but first he wanted to be sure it was all right with his grandmother.

"Why wouldn't it be?" I said to him, and when he didn't answer, I turned to Gerry. "Why wouldn't it be?"

She looked flustered for a second, but she recovered quickly, offering me a sad smile. "Well, dear, my job is to err on the side of caution. Tyrone is our only grandchild . . ."

"That's not the way you get it," I said, handing the pharmacist the money, which he took carefully so there wouldn't be any possibility of him accidentally touching me.

"Well, they really don't know, now do they, dear?" Gerry said, pressing her luck.

I looked at her and all of a sudden I felt my eyes start burning. This is the reason I left Atlanta in the first damn place! Couldn't go anywhere without running into that wall of ignorance that can't stop pretending even when it's life and death to keep it up.

I took a deep breath. I sure didn't intend to cry in front of this crowd. I wouldn't give them the satisfaction.

"Keep the change," I said, walking right past Gerry and her friends and out the front door.

When I got outside, Tyrone and Frank and the girl he'd been slapping around at the liquor store were leaning on Gerry's car, which was parked right in front of mine. Looking at them made me feel tired. The games they were playing were so tired and they were playing them at such a rudimentary level that it was exhausting to watch.

Frank started a loud stage whisper as I searched my purse for the keys, cursing myself for not already having them in hand.

"I read about a bitch in Texas, man. Houston, I think it was Houston. When she found out she had that shit, she started giving away as much pussy as she could to pay back all the muthafuckas she thought might a give it to her."

I finally found my keys and clicked the locks open.

"That's some cold shit, man." Frank laughed and shook his head. "I'd have to ice a bitch tried to fuck me with some AIDS. That's some *death pussy* for sure. I don't need no part of that shit, you know what I'm sayin'?"

He looked at me as I got in and slammed the door.

Yeah, I thought. *I know exactly what you're saying.*

• 9

by the time I got home, the house was full of all twenty-six members of The Sewing Circus and their total of thirty-three children, including Imani, who was observing everything from the crook of Joyce's arm. The members always shared a pot-luck meal and the kitchen was now a beehive of female food activity as the women laid out the communal feast. Joyce hadn't found a new place, and the Rev was still ducking the meeting he had promised, but from the overflow crowd, it looked like being evicted from the fellowship hall was the best thing that had ever happened to TSC.

I could hear them talking and teasing, calling their children, asking for a pan or a platter. Patrice asked who bought the jumbo hot dogs and Tomika answered something I couldn't hear that made them all burst out laughing and start saying, "Hush, girl! Talking nasty in front of these kids! What's wrong with you?"

I had told Joyce I was going to run into town and pick up my prescription, and be back in time for the meeting, but the last thing I needed tonight was a house full of bad haircuts and fussy two-year-olds. What I really wanted was a chance to watch the sunset and have a good long cry, which is what I told Joyce, except about the crying, of course. There was nothing she could do, so what was the point in worrying her? I told her I was just tired, but that was the wrong thing to say.

"What is it?" Joyce has a way of looking at me real hard and asking me what's wrong that is guaranteed to make me start crying before I get the first sentence out.

"Nothing," I said quickly. "I just need some time to myself. Okay?"

She looked at me and nodded. "Okay," she said. "We'll be here."

I managed a smile at that. "That's what I'm afraid of," I said.

Joyce gave me a quick hug and headed back inside and I started walking. Frank's nasty mouth had upset me more than I wanted it to, and about halfway home I had to stop the car and get myself together with some deep breaths. I also indulged some really ugly wishes for bad stuff to happen to Frank, but I'm not proud of that, even though he deserves it.

I figured I'd walk down by the lake until it got too dark and then cut through somebody's yard and take the road back to Joyce's. If I knew anything about Gerry Anderson, I knew she'd find a way to use me being positive in her fight against Joyce, and I had no interest in letting that happen. I figured the simplest solution was for me to go on to San Francisco a little sooner than I had planned. Joyce and I already had a great visit. I'd had a chance to meet Imani and remeet Eddie. But now it was starting to get weird and I just didn't have the energy or the inclination for high drama. Maybe I'd come back Christmas when things settled down a little. I still hadn't given up trying to get Joyce to move to the coast with me. No reason Imani couldn't be a California girl.

My brain was clicking along a mile a minute. If the man on that meditation tape wants me to think of my mind as a monkey, that's cool, but now the one I have in residence had invited all her monkey friends over for the evening. I was trying to think about everything at the same time and all I could hear was Frank's voice talking about *death pussy* and how scared I was that he was right and that even in the progressive, AIDS-informed haven that was San Francisco, nobody was ever going to want to hold me again. *Not ever.*

That's when I saw Eddie. I came around a small path of pine trees that keeps you from being able to see his house until you're right up in front of it. He was standing on his dock in a pair of black pajama pants and no shirt, moving slowly from one position to another, placing and replacing his arms and legs in positions that should have looked strange with their weird postures and arms-akimbo transitions, but when he did them, they didn't look strange at all. In fact, it was one of the most beautiful things I'd ever seen another person do up close. I just stood there. It was pretty dark now, so he didn't even notice me and I relaxed into watching.

Eddie's body was more muscular than I had thought. He always wore loose clothes and I was surprised at the power in his chest and back. He leaned forward from the waist and his hair fell across his cheeks so I couldn't see his face. Then he turned his body slightly, leaned back, and turned his face more toward me. His eyes were closed, but he looked so perfectly peaceful that I never wanted him to stop and I never wanted to stop watching.

So I stood there at the edge of the trees until he finished. I don't know how long it was, but I was crying by the time he got through, although I can't tell you why. He stood for a minute, then slipped on one of those black dashiki-looking things he always wears and smiled in my direction like he had seen me there all along.

"Ava," he said, and it wasn't a question. I jumped and wondered suddenly if I had invaded his privacy in some terrible way.

I wiped my face quickly and tried to explain. "I'm sorry. I didn't mean to . . . The Sewing Circus is at our house and I was just out walking and . . ."

"Do you want to come in?" he said, walking toward me.

"Yes," I said, grateful for his outstretched hand. "I'd love to come in."

• 10

eddie's house was as soothing as it had been the first time I was there. He put on a record of what sounded like birds and bells and flutes.

"It's Brazilian," he said. "If you don't like it, let me know."

I was standing by the door watching him move around the room, tossing a couple of pillows down near the low futon couch, lighting large fat candles and a stick of Blue Pearl incense. The full moon rising over the lake was shining in the large windows that Eddie had just replaced, and I realized this wasn't a house. This was a haven.

"Do you need more light?" he said, turning up a flame under the teakettle. I shook my head.

"Do you have anything stronger than tea?" I said, knowing he probably didn't. Him and Joyce drink so much tea, they should be Chinese.

He smiled apologetically. "Let me put some shoes on. I'll go over to the liquor store and get whatever you want. Won't take me but a minute."

"That's okay," I said, figuring tea would probably be my best bet anyhow. I was still feeling weepy and a drink now would probably push me into crying and confessing more than Eddie wanted or needed to know. "Tea is fine."

He nodded and set out two cups, opened a cabinet and took out a box with a delicate white flower painted on the front.

"Chamomile," he said, dropping a bag in each cup. "The soothing effects of this tea are legendary."

"Do I look like I need to be soothed?"

"Everybody needs to be soothed," he said. "Have a seat." And he waited while I decided to settle on the couch. He sat down at the other end and put both cups on a low table in front of us. Almost everything he had done since we walked in the door should have felt like seduction, for which I was definitely not in the mood, but with Eddie, it felt natural. Not like we weren't a man and a woman, but like that wasn't all there was to it. I didn't feel like he was trying to help me relax so he could trick me into bed. I felt like he really wanted me to be comfortable.

We both just sipped our tea for a while. The Brazilian bird band was still cooing and strumming and chiming softly. The monkeys in my head were settling down for the night, at last. I sighed so loudly that Eddie grinned at me.

"Okay," I said. "So a little soothing doesn't have to be a bad thing."

He laughed out loud. "That's what my grandmother used to call a *left-handed* compliment."

His laugh lit up his face and crinkled his eyes at the corners. I was glad we weren't kids anymore. If you're living an interesting life, your face should get more interesting, too. Eddie's face was seasoned without being craggy and his eyes were as clear as Imani's. *Of course*, he saw me in the dark.

"Was that t'ai chi you were doing?"

He nodded.

"I didn't mean to bother you," I said.

"You didn't bother me at all."

I wanted to tell him how beautiful he looked out there, but I didn't want to tip the balance of things, so I settled for "How long have you been doing it?"

"A long time," he said. "Probably twenty years. I learned it in 'Nam. Helped me stay sane."

"Maybe I should take it up."

"I tried to teach Joyce," he said. "But she quit before she had a chance to get good at it."

"She told me. We were thinking of trying it together. Safety in numbers."

"First fifty lessons free," he said.

I was surprised. "How many lessons does it take to learn it?"

"About five."

Now I laughed. "It's a deal," I said.

The album finished and the tone arm lifted off with a click and returned to its rest. The sound was comfortingly old-fashioned and I sighed again.

"Do you have a preference?" he said, standing up in one long, graceful motion.

"Something soothing," I said.

"My specialty," he said, reaching for something around what looked to be the Js. He put on another album, lowered the dust cover, put a little more hot water in our tea, and sat back down next to me. The music was another dreamy blend of flutes and what seemed to be the sound of water bubbling over rocks.

"How can you have music like this *and* the collected works of George Clinton?" I said.

"Just lucky, I guess."

"Are you?"

"What? Lucky?" He considered his answer. "Hard to say. I'm alive. That's a big stroke of luck because I know none of that is promised. I lived through something that took out a lot of brothers smarter than me and had more heart than me, so I guess that's lucky." He stopped again, picking his works carefully. "But the stuff that landed me there in the first place wasn't so lucky, so I guess I'm about even. How about you?"

"*Lucky?*" Frank's taunting voice came back strong: *death pussy.* I took a sip of tea, but I felt my damn eyes fill up all of a sudden like I was going to start crying again. I tried to take a deep breath, but I hadn't been ready to hear that voice back in my head again. *Death pussy.* I felt a damn tear slide over the curve of my cheek on the side nearest to Eddie. He was turned toward me, so I know he saw it, but he didn't say anything. I felt a tear on the other side and then a couple of

117

more. I put the cup down and wiped my face without looking at him. *Damn!*

Eddie got up and picked up one of the red pillows and dropped it down near my feet.

"Can I sit here?" he said.

I nodded.

"Can I take your shoes off?"

I was a little surprised, but when I nodded again, he slipped off my sandals, picked up my left foot, and rubbed it lightly all over. Then he put it down and did the same thing with my right one. Then he picked up my left again and started massaging it gently. He kneaded the ball of my foot, stroked my arch, and pulled each toe out gently. His hands were large and warm. The palms were hard without being rough and his fingers were long and slender. He had put one foot down and picked up the other before he said anything else, which was okay with me. The more he rubbed my feet, the more I felt my face relax, my neck, my shoulders, the small of my back. I put my head against the soft pillows on the back of the couch and closed my eyes. I wasn't crying anymore, but I didn't trust my voice yet. I was not about to risk a quaver.

"I saw the worst things you can see human beings do to each other every day, the whole time I was in 'Nam," he said, curling my toes over softly and rubbing them slowly. "And I did my share. By the time I got back to the world, I was a *bad* man."

His hands on my feet never changed their pace or their pressure.

"I think maybe one of the reasons I had to go to jail was to make me think about 'Nam. On the outside, I could drink it away, or smoke it away, or snort it away, or sex it away, but in the joint, it was just me and my memories."

He was quiet for a minute, twisting each of my toes back and forth gently. I wanted to ask him what he'd been in jail for, but I didn't have the energy to ask the question.

"The thing about it is, thinking about 'Nam made me

think about everything. It was like doing LSD and looking at something so close that you see everything in it. All the good. All the bad. Everything."

He took both my feet in his hands and held them very gently. "First I got mad at them for sending me. Then I got mad at me for going. Then I got real mad at being a big enough fool to get myself locked up for ten years."

Ten years?

"Then I just got mad and stayed there. I got in so many fights, brothers were taking bets on how long it would be before somebody put me out of my misery. Then one day this old guy sat down next to me and said, 'You know what your problem is? You ain't slowed down long enough to see the lessons yet, youngblood. Lessons everywhere,' he said, 'flying around like birds, but you ain't even take a minute to check 'em out 'cause you movin' too fast cutting you a path. That's why you in here now,' he said. 'To slow your ass down.'

"He was starting to get on my nerves, but I was feeling too low to get him out of my face, so he kept talking. 'That's why there are so many geniuses in the joint,' he told me. 'They finally get time to slow down and look for the lesson. Problem is, then they get out and get goin' again and forget everything they learned and they end up right back where they started from.' "

He was holding my ankle, rotating my right foot slowly counterclockwise.

"That's when I started doing the t'ai chi again. Trying to learn my lessons. When I got out, I figured Idlewild was slow enough so I could hold on to what I'd learned longer here than in the city." He smiled at me. "And Mitch and Joyce were here."

He slipped my shoes back on my well-pampered feet and looked at me.

"And did you learn your lesson?" I said, liking the sound of my newly soothed self.

"I'm working on it," he said. "But the part that makes me lucky is that I know that's what I'm *supposed* to be doing. Trying to figure it out."

"Is that really why you came back?" I said.

I was used to the pause between the question and the answer, so I just waited.

"In 'Nam, the VC had miles of tunnels. They'd been building them for years, since way before we even got over there, and they were all over the place. They weren't always those little tunnels you had to crawl through, either. Some of them were big enough to walk around in standing straight up. They moved supplies through them. Hid in them. Lived in them when they had to."

He unfolded himself gracefully from the pillow and sat back down on the couch.

"They beat us for a lot of reasons, but I knew they were going to the first time I saw one of those tunnels. We were only there doing time, but they were in for the long haul. They were *home*. It made them stronger."

I wasn't sure what he was getting at and he must have seen the confusion on my face.

"If you have to take a stand, home's the best place to do it," he said, and his voice was as soothing as the music.

"Thanks for the tea." It was getting late and the Sewing Circus was probably winding down by now.

He looked right at me. "Are you okay?"

"Better now," I said, and meant it.

He offered me a ride, but I wanted to walk. The night was clear as a bell and the air around us was soft and sweet when we stepped outside. I could see the candles flickering through the window when I turned to say good night.

"Before you go," he said, "are you ready for your free, introductory t'ai chi lesson, so simple anybody can do it?"

"Even me?" I said.

"Especially you," he said. "Relax your arms." He turned me around, stood close without pressing against my behind, *thank God*, raised my arms up and opened them wide like kids always do when you first set them down in front of the ocean. Then he brought my hands around in front, and with his arms guiding mine, slowly softened my elbows and turned my palms to face me.

We stood there like that for just a moment and then he guided my arms back down to my sides and released them. This was not a moment for secrets and I felt mine burning between us. *Death pussy.*

"I have to tell you something," I said, and dammit, I *quavered.*

"Do you *want* to?"

"Yes," I said, but I felt myself tearing up again, scared that if I told him, he'd pull away. Scared of how much I didn't want that to happen.

"Do you want to tell me *now?*"

"I thought I did, but . . ." I stopped that one prequaver, but barely. *What the hell was the problem? We were only going to be friends, right?*

"Maybe you've had enough excitement for one day. Tell me another time. I'm not going anywhere." And he smiled that smile. "I'm home, remember?"

I nodded. "I better go."

"I'm glad you came," he said. "Don't be a stranger. My grandmother used to say that, too."

"Too late for me to be a stranger," I said, trying to keep it light as I headed back to Joyce's. "You saw me in my pigtails."

"But that was another life," he said. "All this stuff here is brand-new."

• 11

the last of the Sewing Circus finally straggled home around midnight, arms full of sleeping toddlers and hearts full of revolution. Joyce was ecstatic. She got no drop-off in membership moving the group to the house, and being under siege brought

121

out the best in them. Aretha, whose sociology class was study-
ing the sixties, suggested picketing Sunday morning service,
which Joyce thought was too confrontational. Tomika offered
to kick the Reverend Mrs.' ample ass, which Joyce confessed
did appeal to her, but which she rejected as inappropriate be-
havior between black women.

Finally Joyce suggested that each Sewing Circus member express her feelings individually to the Good Reverend
after church on Sunday. When they met next week, everybody
could report on what they had said and what he had said
before determining their next step. They thought that was a
great idea, even though they probably didn't suspect that it
was Joyce's way of getting them used to the idea of articulating
their outrage to the people they allowed to control so much of
their lives.

"If they can get in the Rev's face," Joyce said, "pretty
soon they'll be able to talk back at the food stamp office and
be indignant at the Welfare Department, and from there? Sky's
the limit!"

Joyce flopped down on the couch, exhilarated and exhausted, and looked at me to share the excitement, but the
truth was, I had hardly heard a word she said. I wanted to
know why Eddie had been in jail. I asked Joyce if she knew.

"Of course," she said.

"Why?"

"Ask him."

Typical Joyce. "It isn't anything really terrible, is it?"

"The worst," she said.

"I'm serious."

"Me, too." She looked at me. "He won't mind if you
ask him. He probably thinks I've already told you anyway."

"Then why don't you?"

Joyce took a minute before she answered me. "Sometimes I meet people who already know what happened to
Mitch because somebody told them about it. They've already
had a chance to hear it, and picture it, and have whatever

reaction they're going to have to it. So when we get introduced, they think they know something about *me*, when all they know is a bunch of details." She shrugged. "It's not the same."

I knew she would warn me if he was really dangerous or anything, so I wasn't scared, but she had said *the worst*. I figured he must have killed somebody, which isn't necessarily a problem for me. I think I'm capable of it. I knew a lawyer in Atlanta who said everybody can be a murderer under the right circumstances. More likely, under the *wrong* circumstances. Eddie was probably in the wrong place at the wrong time.

There were a lot of reasons why you might have to kill somebody. Maybe self-defense. I just hoped it wasn't a kid or a woman. I never really understood the reasons men kill each other, but the reasons they kill women and children are almost always about wanting to control things that don't belong to them or some weird sex stuff. Either way, that didn't sound like Eddie. At least, I *hoped* it didn't.

I'm not going to ask him about it yet, though. I think he'll tell me when he's ready to tell me. Like the Jamaicans always say when you start screaming because your flight home from Montego Bay is twenty-four hours late: *Patience, girl, patience. Soon come.*

• 12

the nice thing about Eddie living so close was that we saw him almost every day. The bad thing was, I never knew when he'd appear with a bag of collard greens or a loaf of fresh bread or some news for Joyce and smile for me that would set my mind racing along to its own conclusions. I can't deny that sometimes it was sort of exciting but sometimes it was just exhausting.

For example, when Eddie walked over this morning to tell Joyce some of the oldsters, mostly holdovers from the glory days who had wanted to end their lives here in peace, were really nervous about the break-ins. I wasn't ready to talk about last night yet, but Joyce wasn't here, so I knew it was only a matter of time.

"You doing okay today?" he said, looking at me while he waited for the tea I'd offered to cool off enough to drink.

"Doing fine," I said. "Thanks for being a port in a storm last night."

"My pleasure," he said.

I changed the subject and asked him who he thought was doing the break-ins. He said Frank and Tyrone without blinking. I told him Frank reminded me of the kid who killed the Koreans in *Menace II Society* and he had never heard of it. He doesn't have a television, and even though I gave Joyce and Mitch a VCR about five years ago, they never even hooked it up.

I convinced him that if he wanted to understand Frank and Tyrone, he needed to see at least two or three of these angry-young-black-man movies. He hadn't been to the city for a while and things have gotten a lot worse a lot faster than anybody thought they would. It's important to keep up, I told him, so you don't get careless and let your passport lapse or forget to keep a little getaway money stashed somewhere you can get to it without using your ATM card.

Of course, he doesn't have an ATM card, but the principle was the same and he agreed to hook up the VCR if I'd rent the videos. I said that sounded good and we made a date for Friday. Well, not a *date* date. A *friend* date. Joyce and Imani will be here to chaperone, and by that time, I hope he will have forgotten about last night.

He got all the way to the end of the driveway before he stopped and came back. I watched him walking and remembered how beautiful he looked in the moonlight.

"Can I ask you something?" he said, real serious, propping his foot on the bottom step.

"Ask away," I said.

"Why were you crying last night?"

"Which time?" I said, trying to play it off.

"Outside," he said, serious as hell. "When you were watching me."

I hesitated. *Because*, I thought, *I'm not going to be around long enough for us to fall in love.* "I don't know," is what I said.

"Would you tell me?"

I decided to lie. "Yes."

He smiled and nodded like that was the right answer. "Good enough."

And I nodded and said it back to him like it was my idea. "Good enough."

And it was.

• 13

"tonight?" i say.

"She just got the orientation packet from the school and she needs some help deciphering it," Joyce says, guiding a bottle into Imani's wide-open mouth. To be so skinny, that is the *eatingest* baby I've ever seen.

"You have to go tonight?" I say, and Joyce looked at me.

"You know Aretha. The longer she sits there staring at all that stuff she can't quite figure out, the more likely she is to figure it's a mistake for her to be going up there in the first place." Joyce wiped a little milk dribble off Imani's chin and cooed at the baby. *"Isn't that right, sweet girl? Isn't that exactly right?* Besides, she can't get over here and back at night by herself."

"But what about Eddie?" I said.

"What about him?"

I took a breath and tried to speak gently. Imani's eyes were already at half-mast, signaling sleep. The child can sleep anywhere. "He's coming over to watch a movie with us tonight, remember?"

"I'm sure you can handle it."

"That's not the point." I sounded petulant even to my own ears.

Joyce laid Imani over her shoulder and began to tap her back, gently encouraging a burp. "What is the point?"

"That we invited him," I said.

"*You* invited him," she said. "I wouldn't invite anybody to see those movies. They just depress me and I'm already so depressed about angry young brothers I can hardly stand it."

I couldn't argue that. These doomed homeboy movies are pretty intense. Joyce saw my surrender and she couldn't resist a parting shot as she got up to put Imani down for her nap.

"Don't worry," she said. "I think you're old enough to have company without a chaperone on the premises."

"It's not like that and you know it," I said.

Joyce just nodded, but I heard her chuckling all the way down the hall.

By six o'clock they were headed out and I felt pretty cool about Eddie coming. All we were going to do was watch a movie and talk about it. No big deal. No stress. Eddie and I were just friends. Joyce's chuckling was her problem, not mine.

So I kissed them both good-bye, sent regards to Aretha, watched Joyce buckle Imani into her car seat, and waved as they tooted the horn and turned out of sight. Then all of a sudden I got really nervous. It wasn't a date or anything, but standing in the empty house, it damn sure felt like one. I felt really weird and I couldn't figure out how to relax. Before I got here, I hadn't realized how much I was depending on vodka to calm my ass down in moments of stress and weirdness.

But since nobody here is a big drinker, I've cut way back and it's been cool, except right now I keep thinking about Eddie coming over and the more I try not to think about it like a date, the more it feels like a date until I actually dash upstairs at the last possible moment, take a shower, put on perfume and a black linen sundress that always makes me feel like my *cool* self, and dash back down as Eddie walked up in the yard and waved. He was wearing black drawstring pants and a black T-shirt that showed the muscles in his chest and his arms.

"You look great," he said, handing me a bunch of sweet purple grapes.

I felt that pulse between my legs again, but I ignored it, thanked him for the grapes, and made some tea while he hooked up the VCR. We settled in on the couch with a more than respectable distance between us and I cued up the video, *Menace II Society.* I hadn't seen the movie for a while and I had completely forgotten the opening scene where the father suddenly pulls out a gun and blows a man away for an insult during a card game. It is a very sudden and scary and violent moment and it happens in front of the young child who grows up to be the hero. Maybe *hero* is the wrong word. He's the one we get to watch as he careens full speed ahead toward the terrible, inevitable death we know he's going to die at the end of the movie.

When that first murder happened like five minutes into the movie, I felt Eddie's whole vibe change. We were sitting on the couch and it was like a blast of cold air came in the room. I looked over at him and his face looked like it was made of dusty brown rock. He was staring at the screen like he couldn't believe what he was seeing. I knew the double murder scene in the store was coming up, which is even more sudden, more senseless, and more random.

"I told you it was pretty bad," I said.

He just nodded. "You got that right."

I turned back to watch the two young black men change the course of their lives by shooting, and witnessing the shooting of, a frightened Korean grocer and his wife. Eddie's chill had become glacial and this sure didn't feel like a date anymore. It felt like a disaster. When the young killer proudly shows his friends the stolen security camera's videotape of the murders, Eddie got up and turned away. I reached for the remote, clicked off the VCR, and waited.

"They're training people to look at this for fun," he said so quietly it was like he was talking to himself. "They're going to make them love the shit, and once you learn to love it, it doesn't make any difference who it is. You just love it."

This was the first time I'd heard him curse. He heard it, too.

"I'm sorry," he said, looking at me. "I just . . . I had years around that kind of death energy. All those months in 'Nam. All those years on the street and in the joint, nothing moving through me but death energy, and I ate it up." He closed his eyes and took a slow breath. "I got good at it, too." He tried to smile at me, but I could feel him making up his mind. "This time I need to tell *you* something."

"But do you *want* to?" I said, giving him the same out he had given me the other night.

"Yes, I do."

"Then tell me."

"I want to tell you why I was in the joint."

"You don't have to," I said quickly, not sure if I was ready to hear it.

"I know," he said. "That's why I want to."

It was my turn to take a breath. "Then tell me."

He sat down on the couch again, but on the edge of the seat, back straight, at attention. "When I came back from 'Nam, I was crazy. I didn't care about anything or anybody. I had seen too much, done too much. I had learned to kill people with my hands so fast they didn't have a chance to holler. I knew how to make people give up information they never intended to tell a living soul. I was good at that. The best, they told me, because I never got anxious and killed somebody before they told me what I wanted to know. They thought I should be real proud of that.

"When I got back to Detroit, the union jobs had dried up, but there is always a place for somebody like me *in the life*. I was young and wild and didn't care about killing people for somebody else's reasons. That's what I was trained to do. I did a lot of coke, so I could stay up for days at a time. The kind of dreams I was having, I never wanted to go to sleep if I could help it."

Eddie stood up again and walked over to the window. "After a while I started working for some of the dealers. Collecting money. Scaring off people who wanted in without paying the dues. Taking care of people who got stupid and tried to steal the money or the drugs or the customers." He took another breath and stood there looking toward the lake, barely visible under the thin new moon.

"Just tell me," I said.

His hands were hanging at his sides like they didn't belong to him. "That's how I met Sela. She was working for a mean pimp and she thought I could help her move up to something better. She had already seen a little bit of everything, so she wasn't scared of me and my bad dreams and she didn't care how I made my money as long as I always had some. I hadn't been with a woman whose name I remembered since before I went to 'Nam and I was lonesome, I guess, so we hooked up and she moved in with me.

"She got tired of it fast, though, and started tricking again, so we broke up, but right after that I started dealing for myself and making a lot of money, so she came back, but it still wasn't right. It wasn't supposed to be right. It was just something we were doing until we could think of something else to do. When she moved in with the guy who was supplying me, I didn't give a damn.

"Then one day, I hadn't seen her for a couple of months, she called and asked if she could come over. Said she missed me and just wanted to say hello."

He shook his head, clenched and unclenched his fists slowly. I had said *tell me,* but now I wasn't sure if I was ready to hear it, whatever it was. He had said *death energy,* and I swear, I could feel it in the room.

"So she came over and started hugging me and asking me did I have any coke around since her old man didn't have anything coming through and she sure wanted to get high. That was music to my ears. I'd been hoarding big drugs for this drought, waiting for it. I intended to sell what I had for top dollar and move on. I didn't know where, but I figured if I brought out the coke I had now when people were crazy for it, I could buy myself a little time to figure things out. Now, without meaning to, Sela was letting me know this was the time for me to make my move.

"That's how stupid I was. I thought she just wanted to get high with me for old times' sake, so I let her see me take out the stuff from where I had it stashed and we did some of it together and then some more. We were flying . . . Then, all of a sudden, her old man busted up in my place and put a big gun in my face and told me I didn't work for him anymore. He asked her where the coke was and she hopped off my lap and went over to my stash and gave it all to him like I wasn't even there.

"He handed her the gun and dipped his finger in to test it, but she was too greedy and when I saw her look away from me toward what she really wanted, I knocked the gun out of her hand and ripped his throat open before it hit the floor."

I closed my eyes. My mind was saying *don't tell me/ don't tell me/don't tell me* so loud I thought he must hear it, but he didn't hear anything. He was back there in that room, fighting for his life.

"He dropped the bag of coke all over the floor and when I looked at Sela, she fell down and started pushing her face all up in it, trying to get as much into her nose as she could because she'd been on the street as long as I had and she knew the penalty for turning. She kept saying, *just let me get high first, baby, just let me get high first.*

"So I did."

• 14

when joyce got back, I was still sitting on the couch in the dark and Eddie had gone home. I tried to get him to stay, but he wouldn't. I don't even remember what all I said. I think I told him I was glad he had told me and then I got all hung up on apologizing for using the word *glad* because it seemed so wrong after what he had just said. *Glad* wasn't in it.

Then we just looked at each other for a minute and I opened my mouth to say I *understood*, but I didn't. Then I thought I'd say I was *sorry*, but for what? Or *it doesn't matter*, but of course, it mattered. People died. But he'd paid his debt to society, hadn't he? He'd learned his lesson and turned his life around and become a good neighbor and a good friend and a good man, hadn't he? Didn't people have a right to change, to grow, *to get better?*

All that was going through my head and I kept opening my mouth and closing it like a fish flopping on the dock, trying to catch a breath, until he said he thought he'd better go, thanked me, for what, I can't imagine, and walked out through the back door and was gone.

Joyce didn't even see me until she came in to turn on the lamp. Imani was sleeping against her shoulder and when Joyce saw me and jumped, Imani jumped, too, without waking up.

"What are you doing?" Joyce said. "Are you okay?"

"Eddie told me what he did," I said.

"He told you everything?"

I had a sinking feeling. What a terrible thought. *What if there was more?*

"Sela?" Joyce said, and I felt a flood of relief.

"Yes. Everything."

She sat down beside me.

"Pretty scary stuff," I said, earning myself the prize for best understatement of the week.

Joyce nodded, rubbing Imani's back slowly in one of those *comforting-to-the-bone* mother moves that you are too young to appreciate when you get them, and too old to ask for when you need them. "He was living a terrible life and he did some terrible things, but he's not that person anymore. I'd trust him with my life. With all of our lives."

"He killed a woman!"

"He killed a man, too."

"You know what I mean."

"Listen, little sister," Joyce said, shifting Imani to a more comfortable position and sighing like she couldn't understand what was the problem. "Ain't none of us sixteen years old anymore. We've done some good stuff and some bad stuff, but it's all our stuff at this point. I figure the best we can do for each other is try to understand and move on the best we can."

"I never killed anybody, Joyce."

"That makes you perfect?"

I hesitated. She had me there. "You know, if I wanted to be driven crazy by a bunch of complicated Negroes, I could have stayed in Atlanta," I said.

"You were crazy when you got here," Joyce said.

"So what am I supposed to do now?"

"About what?"

"About *Eddie!*"

"Why do you have to do anything about Eddie?" Joyce arched her eyebrows at me to announce a trick question, but I heard it, too, and I arched my eyebrow right back.

"I don't."

"Then don't." Joyce shrugged, and then grinned at me. "Guess what."

"What?"

"I've got a joke to tell you, but don't laugh out loud because you'll wake up Imani."

I wasn't in the mood for jokes. What was wrong with Joyce? A bad joke was hardly what I had on my mind.

"Ready?"

"Joyce, I don't—"

"Come on, now! Indulge me. Here goes . . . Why won't southern Baptists have sex standing up?"

"I don't know," I said, remembering all those Southern Baptist Conventions in Atlanta when downtown would fill up with grim-faced Christians notorious for their bad driving and worse tipping. "Why?"

"Because somebody might think they're dancing."

We looked at each other and started giggling like maniacs. Imani slept on, blissfully unaware of me and Joyce snickering our way into hysteria.

"You win," I said, gasping. "That was pretty funny. I'm amazed."

"Horizontal bop," Joyce said.

That set off another round of giggling until we were both wiping our eyes.

"Now," Joyce said, composing herself after we'd finally laughed ourselves silly. "What are you going to do about Eddie?"

"You told me I didn't have to do anything!"

"I lied," she said.

"No," I said. "You were right. I'm only going to be here for the summer. There's no reason to complicate things."

Joyce laughed so loud at that, Imani did wake up with a start. Her little tiny fingers grabbed Joyce's shirt and her eyes were huge.

"I'm sorry, sweetie," Joyce crooned, immediately maternal. "Auntie Ava is trippin' again, as the young folks say. Come on, darlin'. Let's put you to bed."

She stood up and Imani's eyelids drooped and closed.

"Why am I trippin'?" I said.

"Because, little sister," she said, kissing me good night on her way upstairs, "you're standing in the middle of the Great North Woods and you can't see the forest for the trees."

the phone rang just as we were sitting down to dinner. When Joyce answered and then brought me the receiver, I thought it was Eddie, but when I said hello, Aretha's voice answered, instantly apologetic.

"Are you all eating?"

"We haven't started yet," I said, relieved and disappointed at the same time. "How are you?"

"I'm fine." She sounded a little nervous. "I was thinking about what you said."

"What did I say?"

"About me having a good face."

A good face?

"Oh! For short hair!" I said, remembering my offer to give her a cut before she left for school.

"Yeah, well, I been thinking about it and I wondered if you could do it for me."

"Sure," I said. "How short do you want it?"

"Like yours," she said. "It looks good and if it's that short, I can go swimming every day. They've got a pool."

"Good for you," I said, and I meant it. Most of the black women I know can't swim a lick because in order to learn you had to get your hair wet. "How about Friday?"

"Okay," she said. "Do I need to bring scissors or anything?"

I smiled at that. She'd probably bring some of those little scissors with the black handles they give you in first grade. "Just bring yourself," I said. "And be yourself."

She giggled again and hung up. I couldn't wait to tell Joyce. Once you get that first glimpse of another way of looking at things, you can't get enough. Aretha was on her way.

• 10

i finally ran into Eddie in town today. He pulled right behind me at the gas station and came around to speak while the bored teenager at the pump earned his summer money lazily wiping my bug-spattered windshield. I was trying to be cool, but I wasn't cool. *Pulse city.* I hadn't seen him since he told me what he had done. I wasn't sure if he was waiting for a sign from me or I was waiting for one from him, but a week had gone by and that was too long to ignore.

I admit, it was still weird for me to think about what he had told me, but back then he was moving through a world where people knew the risks when they stepped up in it. From what he said, his ex would have shot him first if she'd been quick enough, so I guess they were about even. He had done the crime, and he had done the time, and being sorry can't change a thing about any of it. When you're young, there's a whole lot of stuff you say you'll *never* do. Once you get a little older, the list tends to get a lot shorter.

I had been doing my morning meditations on the porch, half hoping he'd come by and find me there, peaceful and composed, so we could talk. Instead, here I am in Joyce's un-air-conditioned heap, sweating like a hog with a backseat full of groceries and disposable diapers. He leaned down to smile a greeting and I didn't care whether I was acting cool or not. I was really glad to see him and I said so before I thought to censor it.

"I'm glad to see you, too," he said.

I handed the kid five dollars and looked at Eddie still standing there, leaning on the car, watching me. *Your move,* I thought.

"Maybe I'll come by later," he said.

I shook my head. "Sewing Circus executive committee

meeting at our house. They're plotting on the Reverend Mrs. and the last thing they want is witnesses."

"If you want a place to hide out, I'd love to have some company."

"Okay," I said. "Around seven?"

He hesitated for just a beat. "Do you want me to get anything for you?"

"I'm not drinking for a while," I said, not knowing that until I heard it come out of my mouth.

His expression didn't change, but he nodded. "All right," he said. "Tea it is."

I pulled away, but I did sneak a look at him bending over to pump his gas. It wasn't just when he was doing the t'ai chi. His movements were always effortless and complete, like a dancer.

I know I've got to tell him. I can't keep thinking about seducing him without letting him know what the deal is. If he's going to throw up his hands and run, the sooner I know it, the better.

• 17

by the time I got to Eddie's that evening, I had figured out how I was going to tell him. I was going to say it all at once and then leave, just like he did when he told me about his past, so he can have some time to think. *It's not a test.* That way, if the whole idea of us moving to the next level makes him nervous, he can just write me a note or something and I won't have to see it in his eyes. I can't take that again.

The house was full of candles even though it was just getting dark and the smell of incense was drifting out of the open door. Eddie was playing Marvin Gaye, "Wonderful One," and when he looked up and saw me standing there, he grinned and spread his arms wide and bowed low like he was greeting the queen.

He was teasing, but something in the way he did it made me know he'd been thinking about me these last three days, too. Then he walked up to me and stuck out his hand like the guys used to do at the dances where we'd be on one side of the room and they'd be on the other until some brave soul took that long walk and extended himself to one of us with enough courage to say *yes.*

I took his hand and listened to Marvin seducing every woman within the sound of his voice, no matter how long he's been gone:

> *Being near you,*
> *Is all that I'm living for . . .*

Eddie put his arm around me and started that slow, easy rock that begins a bop. I had grown up dancing with Joyce and Mitch, so even though my generation is not known for its bopping abilities, I'm good at it. I could see that Eddie was surprised at how easily I followed him. When he tried a fancy turn that doubled back on itself before ending in a slide, a mini dip, and that easy rock again, and I executed it flawlessly, he grinned at me like I'd been keeping a secret worth telling.

"You're too young to be bopping like that," he said.

"Mitch and Joyce used to dance all over the kitchen every time a Motown record came on the radio," I said. "I learned in self-defense."

The next song on the album was "Forever," a slow-down classic guaranteed to get you in trouble if you ended up dancing to it with somebody else's boyfriend. We looked at each other for a minute, but it was too soon for that kind of risk.

Eddie lifted the tone arm and indicated his collection. "What's your preference?"

"How about some more of those birds and bells you were playing last time?"

"You're not just trying to be nice, are you?"

"I'm not that nice," I said.

He put on the music and poured some hot water into a beautiful Chinese teapot, which he then deposited snugly into a basket whose brightly colored, upholstered interior had a hole cut in the center of it for that purpose.

When he closed the top and carried it over to the low table in front of where I sat, it looked like an ordinary basket, but when he opened it, the delicate, flowery smell of the chamomile tea he had brewed rose up in a cloud of fragrant steam that mixed perfectly with the incense. I had seen pictures of tea cozies, but I'd never known anybody who had one. Eddie poured us two cups and then sat down beside me.

"You know why they don't put handles on the cups?" he said.

I shook my head. I had always wondered.

"If it's too hot to pick up, it's too hot to drink."

That made a lot of sense to me. I guess when your culture's been around for five thousand years or so, you have time to figure out stuff like that.

I took a small sip of my tea and looked at Eddie. He smiled.

"I appreciate you telling me all that the other night," I said.

His smile faded quickly and I could see him waiting for my reaction.

"I didn't really know how to react to it," I said. "I probably still don't, but I think I understand."

He nodded and took a sip of tea.

"Now it's my turn," I said.

He smiled a little and waited for me to explain. The man didn't seem capable of rushing or trying to make me rush.

"I want to tell *you* something." I sounded serious as

hell and a flicker of something crossed Eddie's face. He put his cup down slowly and let the smile go its own way.

"All right."

I tried to remember my speech. All the stuff I was going to say to prepare him, to explain, to make sure he'd understand, but nothing came to me, so I sat there, looking at him, looking at me. He had paid his debt to society. It was my tab that was still running.

"I'm HIV-positive," I said. "I've known it for a year and I feel fine . . ."

His face hadn't registered any emotion at all and I was trying so hard to read his mind, I thought I was going to have a stroke.

"I just wanted to tell you because . . ." I couldn't say, *because I want to make love with you,* so I just stopped again.

Eddie was looking right at me and even though his expression didn't change, something in his eyes did. Then he reached over, picked up my hand, turned it over, and kissed my palm. His mouth felt warm and soft against my skin. His hair was brushing my wrist and I could hear my heart beating steadily in the room like the Wailers' original rhythm section when they'd been smoking serious ganja and Bob was in a good mood. It seemed as if all the nerve endings in my body had gathered together right there where his mouth was pressing against my hand.

His voice was very gentle. "Is that it?"

"Yes."

When he looked up at me, I felt like I could see every mistake I'd ever made in his eyes, but no judgment, no anger, no shame, no questions except one: "Do you want to be with me?" His voice was neutral.

"Yes." Mine was not.

"So that means we have to use a condom, right?"

He made it sound like the simplest thing in the world. I was so relieved, I wanted to fall into his arms and ask him if he would please kiss my palm like that for about three days, but we had to finish talking business first. I took a deep breath and tried to remain calm.

I told him *yes*, we always had to use a condom and there was some other stuff, too. The speech they give you at those *Living with HIV* workshops came back strong and I started reciting the rules like it was the first day of safe-sex summer camp.

"We can't exchange any body fluids. All noninvasive touching is okay . . ."

He was still holding my hand, but now he was moving his finger lightly around in the small circle where his mouth had been.

"What does that mean?" he said.

"It means you can't put your fingers inside me."

"Except for your mouth?" He leaned over and ran his index finger lightly around the outline of my lips.

"What makes you think I want your fingers in my mouth?"

"Do you?"

"Maybe," I said, then I thought *fuck it.* "Yes."

But I hadn't finished the rules, so I started up again with the *dos* and *don'ts* until he interrupted me.

"How about instead of telling me what I *can't* do, you tell me what I *can* do and I'll concentrate on that."

I hesitated. That sounded wonderful, but I didn't want to fool myself. I wanted to have it all on the table. There's nothing like pulling out some unexpected latex to ruin a romantic moment if you're not ready for it.

"I won't go anywhere you don't invite me," he said, and ran his fingertip over my eyebrows. I closed my eyes.

"Can I touch your face?" he said.

"Yes."

"Can I touch your eyes?"

"Yes."

"Can I touch your mouth?"

"Yes."

"Can I touch your shoulders?"

"Yes."

It was dark now and there were flickering shadows on the walls around us. He kissed my forehead, my cheeks, my chin.

"Can we take our clothes off?"

"Yes."

We slid out of our clothes and his body in the candle-light was as beautiful as it had been under the moon.

"Can I touch your breasts?"

"Yes."

"Your belly? Your beautiful soft behind? Your lovely legs?"

"Yes."

And he stroked and soothed and tickled and teased and looked and lingered and sighed and savored like he'd been waiting for this moment as long as I had. And when he saw that he was bringing me to the edge of someplace I truly wanted to be, he leaned over and asked me in the sweetest possible way if he could go with me, so I took him in my hands.

"Can I touch your penis?"

"Yes."

"Can I touch your balls?"

"Yes."

"Can I touch your nipples?"

"Yes."

By now, we were whispering the questions together into the darkness of each other's skin.

"Can I touch your heart? Your soul? Your spirit?"

And we sang the answers like a duet that we had practiced for a lifetime.

"Oh, yes! Oh, yes! Oh, baby, yes, yes, yes!"

• 18

eddie wanted me to spend the night, but I wasn't ready for that yet. If it was a dream, I wanted to wake up in my own bed when it was over. After we got dressed and I was ready to start back, he held me and kissed me for a long time and I had enough sense to let him. It felt so right to be there that, of course, I started second-guessing myself immediately.

What the hell was I thinking about? This man has spent a lot of time and a lot of mental and physical energy trying to find a place where he could tap into some peace and quiet and here I come with a shitload of problems nobody wants to deal with if they don't absolutely have to.

"Eddie?" I said.

"What, baby?"

I leaned back to look into his face and the memory of how good his body felt close to mine made me want to just shut up, and if this was a fairy tale, just keep believing, at least for another minute or two. But I couldn't. I took a deep breath.

"You're not pretending, are you?"

"Pretending what?"

"That this is the beginning of something."

"Isn't it?"

"You know what I mean."

"No, I don't," he said. "I really don't."

I took another breath. *"Pretending,"* I said, hating the whiny tone in my voice. "That now we'll get together and get married and have some kids and all the rest of it."

He always took his own time answering questions, but this time it seemed like we stood there looking at each other for an hour before he said anything.

"I don't need any of that," he said. "I had a wife who was willing to help some people kill me so she could get high.

142

I had two kids I wouldn't recognize if they walked in here right now because they were born when I was too young to raise them and too crazy to love them. I'm not planning anything and I'm not pretending anything and I'm not expecting you to do anything except love me as hard and as strong as I'm going to love you." He kissed me then for what felt like another hour and when we finally came up for air, he was grinning. "Fair enough?"

I just nodded and leaned into his arms again. It wasn't like I had to rush right home or anything . . .

• 19

when i got home, Joyce was still up. I tried to ease in and go straight to bed, but Joyce wasn't having it.

"What are you grinning about?"

"Me?" I said, feeling the grin grow wider while I tried to deny it.

Joyce just stared, and as hard as I was trying to compose myself, I must have looked guilty as hell because she raised her eyebrows at me like I was fifteen years old sneaking in after curfew.

"I went by Eddie's," I said, still trying to sound nonchalant.

"Just a friendly visit?" she said, enjoying the futility of my efforts to look like I hadn't just been doin' it to death.

"Exactly."

"Well, there's nothing like good neighbors, I always say."

"Is that what you always say?"

Joyce looked at me and folded her arms calmly. "Don't try to distract me," she said. "Are you going to tell me everything or do I have to start guessing?"

"Nothing happened," I said, sounding so unconvincing even to myself that I had to laugh.

"I'll bet Eddie would be disappointed to hear you say that."

"All right," I said. "You win." And I told her what happened.

She whooped so loud I thought she'd wake up Imani, then she grabbed me in one of her famous bone-crushing hugs and tried to break a couple of my ribs. She looked as happy as I was, but then she got all serious and took my hand.

"You were safe, right?"

I wanted to be indignant, but it was such a loving question all the way around, I told her yes and she hugged me again.

"Ouch!" I said. "If you wanted me to seduce Eddie, all you had to do was tell me."

"I don't care a *fig* about you seducing anybody."

Joyce says shit like that because she likes to read old British novels where the heroine is always described as *high-spirited.* She went through one phase when I was about twelve where if I asked her for money and she wasn't going to give it to me, she'd say, *not a brass farthing.*

"What I care about," she said, "is you sticking around here for a while."

"In *Idlewild?*"

"Don't say it like that," Joyce said. "You could do worse."

"I'm going to San Francisco at the end of August, Joyce. I can't stay here."

"Eddie going, too?"

I tried to act surprised at the question, but Joyce was doing what she always does—saying things out loud before I'm ready to fess up to them. The truth of the matter was, ever since we made love, my brain has been feeding me fantasies. Me and Eddie, driving across the country in a convertible that neither of us owns. Me and Eddie walking beside San Francisco Bay at sunset. Me and Eddie finding a place to live in one of those mixed-up San Francisco neighborhoods where everybody is a little bit of somebody else and nobody cares. Me and Eddie exploring just how sexy safe sex can be. Of course, none of these scenarios included me evolving into a person with *full-blown* AIDS, but that's why they call them *fantasies*, right?

"We haven't discussed it," I said, sounding prim.

Joyce grinned at me like she always does when I'm tap-dancing around the truth, but I didn't break. I was headed for San Francisco because I needed a new life and a new lover. The suggestion that maybe I was about to find all that in my own backyard was still just a little too *Candide* for me.

"Okay," Joyce said, shifting gears to throw me off. "If I've only got another six weeks, I better put you to work."

"I don't have to start tonight, do I?" I yawned. All I wanted to do was fall into bed and wait for my dreams to show up.

"No, sweetie." Joyce squeezed my shoulders and gave me a quick kiss on the cheek. She smelled like *home*. I hugged her.

"I'll start first thing tomorrow," I said. "Bright and early."

"It's a deal," she said. "Now, get some sleep."

"Thank you, ma'am," I said, heading for the hallway before I remembered how dangerous it is to give Joyce an open-ended agreement. "Joyce?"

"Yes?"

"What is it exactly that you want me to do?"

She grinned at me. "I'm sure I'll think of something."

Just before I fell asleep, I wondered how I'd feel the next time I saw Eddie. Well, that's not really true. I knew how I'd feel. I was worried about him. About whether or not he'd regret anything once he had a chance to think it through. I had been truly exhilarated by our first exchange. I was nervous at first, we both were, but we just kept trying this and touching that and we laughed a lot.

That was the best surprise. Most brothers are so worried about being the biggest or the baddest or the best you ever had that having fun ain't even in it. Not Eddie. He knew how to make me feel good and he knew how to let me make him feel good. That's the other thing a lot of brothers don't understand. When it comes to making love, *reciprocity is everything*.

I decided I was too exhausted and too satisfied to worry about what was going to happen next. I closed my eyes and whispered a thank-you to whatever spirits were hovering in the darkness, and for the first time in a long time, I didn't ask for a damn thing. I'm not greedy, and as of tonight, by any measure I can think of to apply, I'm already a little bit ahead.

• 20

even though i thought I'd sleep until noon, I woke up at six o'clock like an alarm had gone off inside my head. I tried to go back to sleep, but I couldn't. I had so much energy I felt like I could run the marathon. Nothing like some good lovin' to give you a new lease on life.

I didn't hear Joyce and Imani up yet, so I put on my sweats and my walking shoes quietly and I slipped out the back door. If Eddie was feeling anything like I was, I figured he'd be around sooner rather than later. My plan was to do my walk, take a quick shower, and be casually arranged on the back porch looking good by the time he pulled up.

The only problem was, when I rounded the first curve of the road, I saw Eddie coming my way. I guess we both had that energy surge.

"You're up early," I said, glad he greeted me with a kiss as warm and sweet as the one he'd said good-bye with last night.

"So are you."

He touched my cheek gently and smiled. I leaned into

his hand and loved the strength I felt there. "How did you sleep?" he asked.

I was amazed to feel myself blushing. "Like a baby," I said.

He laughed that laugh for me and I wanted to bury my face in the softness of all that hair. "Good. Want some company or are you walking solo this morning by choice?"

"I'd love some company," I said, and he fell in beside me like we'd planned it.

We walked for almost an hour, and every time I felt like I needed to say something, by the time I turned toward Eddie, I realized there was nothing to be said. It was the most comfortable kind of silence. All I heard was the birds waking up, the summer swish of the trees over our heads and the sound of the gravel road crunching under our feet.

By the time we wound our way back to Eddie's dock, the sun was up and sparkling on the placid surface of the lake and a cardinal was singing so loud it sounded like somebody paid him.

"I've been thinking about what you said last night," Eddie said after we'd been sitting there for a minute.

"I said a lot of stuff last night as I recall."

"About *this*," he said. "About knowing what *this* is."

"And what did you decide?"

He put his arm around me and pulled me over closer to him. I could feel the warmth of his skin beneath his T-shirt and his breath against my cheek.

"It's love," he whispered. "And you know what else?"

"What?" I said, whispering back.

"It ain't gonna get nothin' but better."

I truly wanted to believe him. "You promise?"

"Cross my heart."

I let myself relax against his arm.

"Okay," I said. "It's a deal."

• 21

when aretha came by Friday for her haircut, I thought she'd be nervous, but she was ready. I sat her down on a stool in the middle of the kitchen floor and draped her in a sheet. Imani and Joyce were an attentive audience and I gave Aretha the full treatment.

"Do you want to watch?" I said, handing her the mirror, but she shook her head.

"I trust you."

I laid the mirror facedown on the table and walked around to face Aretha. I put my hand under her chin and gently turned her head so I could see both profiles. I walked a complete circle around her. Joyce jiggled Imani gently against her shoulder and waited. So did Aretha.

"This is going to be the perfect haircut," I said, "to take you into the next phase of your life."

"Really?" she said, wide-eyed and delighted.

"Absolutely," I said. "Only free women can wear their hair this short."

"What about Joyce?" said Aretha, nodding at Joyce's braids.

"Only free women *can* wear their hair like this," I said, "but not *all* free women *do* wear their hair like this."

"Oh," said Aretha, and I was glad that was the right answer. We have such a mystical connection to our hair. Guilt and glory, pride and pain. I knew what it meant to be a sixteen-year-old black girl and cut your hair short. The sweet part was, Aretha knew it, too. She handed me the clippers.

Her hair had been pressed and permed and processed so many times, it didn't know if it was coming or going, but once I trimmed it down to about two inches of new growth, it was soft and fluffy as lamb's wool. I gave her a quick shampoo, including my world-famous *hard wash* and deep conditioner, cut it down to about a quarter of an inch, and shaped it into the prettiest little Afro you ever saw.

Now, Aretha may grow up to be a lovely woman. She may bloom in the glow of her first love. She may blossom with the birth of her children and wear her later years with full confidence in her glory, but I'll tell you this: she will never be more beautiful than she was when I picked up that mirror and held it for her. She gasped. Joyce applauded.

"Is it okay?" I said.

Aretha never took her eyes from the mirror. "It looks like me," she said softly.

"It *is* you," Joyce said, but I knew what Aretha meant. Sometimes you meet yourself on the road before you have a chance to learn the appropriate greeting. Faced with your own possibilities, the hard part is knowing a speech is not required. All you have to say is *yes*.

• 22

eddie swung back by this afternoon to give us a piece of bad news. Somebody broke into old Johnny Mack's house last night and found him asleep in his bedroom. They put a pillow over his face so he couldn't see them and then roughed him up a little. He wasn't badly hurt, but the other oldsters are all terrified.

Eddie still thinks Frank and Tyrone are the ones doing the burglaries, but Joyce said she can't see them doing something like this. She thinks it might be some of the migrant workers who stayed around after the last picking jobs finished up.

"The man is old enough to be their great-grandfather. Plus, he didn't hardly have anything to steal. They took a little old black-and-white TV with rabbit-ear antennae on the top and a bunch of change he had in a jar on the kitchen table.''

Joyce still doesn't understand that this is what crack addicts do. Eddie understands it, though. He told Joyce whoever it is, we ought to start keeping a shotgun in the house. Joyce is scared of guns, so that freaked her out big time.

"Think of it as living on the frontier," I said. "Peace-loving black women used to have shotguns around all the time as a way of keeping things peaceful."

Joyce knew we were right, but she didn't have to like it. Finally she just shook her head at Eddie like a disappointed Sunday school teacher.

"And you call yourself a Buddhist!"

We just looked at her for a minute and then we all started laughing. When we calmed down, Eddie said, "You know I love Brother Buddha, but until he reincarnates as a black man in America, I think we better go with what we know."

Joyce said she'd think about it, but I know she doesn't want to have a gun in here. I think she figures if it was Frank and Tyrone, she could talk them out of it. People always think that, but they're wrong. Crack changes everything. It's why Eartha could leave Imani and not look back. I'll be willing to bet all the money I got from selling the salon that the first thing she did when she left the hospital was go looking for the crack man. Her daughter was the last thing on her mind.

I remember when the stories started coming out about mothers on crack. A woman has a baby in the bathtub of the crack house, cuts the cord, and leaves it there to die while she goes back in the bedroom to get high. A woman gives her preadolescent daughter to the crack dealer in exchange for some rock. A woman shoots her grandmother who wouldn't keep her kids and give her money to buy crack.

I kept reading these stories and it was real clear to me that something basic was changing. What kind of life can you possibly conceive of when you're nine years old and your mama delivers you to the dope man because your virginity is all she's got left to trade?

I guess I was naive to think that Idlewild could escape all of that. It almost doesn't matter what black community you go in now, the problems are exactly the same. The kids are angry. The men are shell-shocked. The women are alone and the drugs are everywhere.

I sure picked a hell of a time to fall in love.

• 23

yesterday eddie started teaching us a little t'ai chi. Imani sat in her baby seat looking at us twisting around on the grass in our bare feet. I swear she must have thought we were crazed. Joyce is still pretty out of shape even though we've been walking two miles a day, so she quit after a few minutes, but I was liking it. I wanted to get good enough to do it like Eddie. His arms and legs just flow into the motions like water. It's almost a dance. He just smiles and *leans to the left*. Smiles and *leans to the right*.

Looks easy as pie, but don't believe it. I almost killed myself. When I woke up this morning, I couldn't hardly sit up. When I told Eddie, he just smiled and said the soreness would go away once I got back in shape. I liked that he said *back* in shape. Made it sound like I'd been there before and just stepped out for a minute.

Joyce wants to build an altar. She's been reading all these books about the Goddess. When she prays before we eat, now she says *Mother/Father God*. It's weird, but I like it. I never saw God as an old white guy anyway. In my mind he always looks sort of like my grandfather: tall and tan and like he's been working too hard.

I told her to be careful with that altar stuff, though. I don't want her to fool around and call up the wrong spirits.

august

• 1

now that her first meeting outside the church went so well, Joyce is busy trying to give a little more structure to the Sewing Circus so she can start formalizing the programs and raise some money. She wanted to start by changing the name, but the membership liked the old one. It reminded me of something a career campaign worker told me at the end of a long, drunken evening after his well-financed, well-spoken candidate crashed and burned at the polls.

"That's the problem with democracy," he said, pouring the last of his Jack Daniel's into a thimble full of Coca-Cola. "The damn *people* get to make all the decisions."

Of course, Joyce didn't feel that way about it. She was more concerned about goals and programs. It's like that old saying about being careful what you ask for because you just might get it. Joyce now had a group of young women who trusted her and were beginning to trust each other, enough money from Mitch's life insurance to pay herself to create an ongoing center for them, and a grant already coming from the state to pay some of the operating and program costs. The question was, *what kind of place was it going to be?* She kept trying out ideas on me and I'd tell her when I thought she was on to something real and when I thought she wasn't. I'd even add my two cents whenever she'd let me get a word in edgewise.

One morning she was up early, tapping something into the computer, so I strapped on the baby carrier and took Imani out with me for a walk. I loved walking early and Imani was good company. She'll be six weeks old on Friday and I can't remember what it felt like around here without her. I'm walking every morning now and I take Imani with me three or four days a week. She still doesn't have a lot to say, even for a six-week-old baby, but she sure is a good listener. She made you want to tell her stuff, and no matter what you were talking about, she'd look at you real hard like she didn't want to miss anything you had to say. Being a sucker for a good captive audience, I talked to her about whatever was on my mind. I figured even if she could understand, she couldn't talk yet, so who was she going to tell?

When I was little, I read *Mary Poppins*, who was a lot more interesting in the books than she was once Julie Andrews got ahold of her, but what I always remember is that in one chapter or another, a baby was born into the house where old Mary was working. One day somebody set the kid's bassinet down by an open window and a bluebird came by to say hello. This bird had a lot of sense, too, and was nothing like those cartoon bluebirds who show up *zippadeedoodah*ing around poor Uncle Remus' enslaved shoulders. This bird was *cool* and he had come there to hear the baby recite the story of its creation, which the baby did upon request in a paragraph or two that stays with me even now as one of the most beautiful birth stories I've ever heard. The bird thanked the baby, told her he had to take a little trip, and promised to come by immediately upon returning so he could hear the story again. The baby promised not to forget it before he got back.

The problem was, nobody in the baby's family could understand what she was saying. To them it sounded like a lot of meaningless gurgling, which meant nothing and usually generated a lot of cooing and clucking that distracted and distressed the baby, who, in the face of such ignorance, rapidly lost touch with her real roots.

By the time the bird came back to visit a few weeks later and asked the baby where she came from, she said something silly about her mother finding her under a cabbage leaf or the stork flying her in, and the heartbroken bird realized that another helpless human baby had been brainwashed out of her rightful magic. He knew that by the time he got back from his next trip, she would no longer hear his words, but only remember the music of his song.

I told Imani about that baby one morning and she looked at me so hard I almost expected her to start telling me about how she had traveled here on the winds of the universe, but she didn't.

By the time we got back from our walk, it was time for a bottle and a midmorning nap, so Joyce handed me a copy of what she'd been working on with instructions to read it while she fed Imani and tell her what I thought. I figured she was serious because she'd put on a pot of coffee so I could indulge my caffeine addiction while we talked.

At the bottom of the first page it said:

Statement of Purpose

To create and nurture women who are strong, mentally, physically, and spiritually; free of shackles, both internal and external; independent of the control of other human beings and dogma, religious or political; women who can take care of themselves and their children financially, choose their lovers based on mutual respect, emotional honesty, and sexual responsibility; women who raise their children to be contributors, not predators or parasites.

I had to smile. It just goes to show that if you give a sixties person an inch, they'll have you picketing the White House by dinnertime. I could imagine trying to get a working definition of *dogma* from the sisters of the Sewing Circus. I liked the idea, though, probably because the woman Joyce wanted to create and nurture sounded a lot like me, give or take a few points off for bad judgment.

But the thing definitely needed a little less Karl Marx and a little more Oprah. I sat down at the kitchen table, picked up a pen, and wrote in the margin: *to nurture free, independent women who can take care of themselves, choose their lovers wisely, and raise their children right.*

I crossed that last *t* as Joyce came back in and sat down across from me.

"What did you change?" she said, trying to read it up-side down.

I covered the note with my hand. "Just wait a second," I said. "I'm not through yet."

"You haven't even read it all and you're making changes?"

I put the pen down. "I was minding my own business," I reminded her. "You asked me to read it."

"Sorry," she said. "Go ahead."

Under the Statement of Purpose, Joyce had typed in all caps:

TEN THINGS EVERY FREE WOMAN SHOULD KNOW
1. How to grow food and flowers
2. How to prepare food nutritiously
3. Self-defense
4. Basic first aid/sex education and midwifery
5. Child care (prenatal/early childhood development)
6. Basic literacy/basic math/basic computer skills
7. Defensive driving/map reading/basic auto and home repairs
8. Household budget/money management
9. Spiritual practice
10. Physical fitness/health/hygiene

At the bottom she had written, *not necessarily in that order*, and underlined it twice.

I wondered if she can do all that stuff. I'd say I've got a grip—a loose grip—on about half. Maybe a third. But I had to admit, Joyce's list covered the waterfront. I'd never seen anything like it written down that way. It looked so sensible and orderly. I wished somebody had handed me a list like that when I was about twelve. It would have been nice, first of all, to know that what I was trying to become was a *free woman*, and it would have been great to have some specific suggestions about what skills I needed to qualify.

But that's not what we got when we came crashing into

puberty. What they gave us instead was a little pamphlet with a very repressed-looking young white girl on the cover entitled *What Every Young Girl Should Know*. Unlimited copies of this brochure were provided by one of the sanitary napkin companies, although I don't know why since the slender booklet accomplished the almost impossible feat of explaining our periods to us without once mentioning the word *blood*.

Joyce's list was grounded in the real world. I wondered what the women in the Sewing Circus would be like if they all achieved mastery of the Ten Things. I wondered what I'd be like. I looked at Joyce sitting across the table trying to read my mind.

"This is great," I said.

"Really?"

"Really."

Joyce smiled and reached over to take the list from my hands. Her eyes scanned it critically. "I didn't want to make it grim, you know? That's why I put the flowers on there."

"It's perfect. Can you do all these things?"

"All except the self-defense," Joyce said.

"Didn't Mitch have a gun?"

She nodded. "Mitch and Eddie used to hunt these woods together when they were kids, but I never even fired it. Besides, I'm not sure I'm talking about guns."

"What are you talking about? Hand-to-hand combat?"

"I don't know what I'm talking about yet. I don't want to start teaching people to kill each other, but a lot of these women are involved with men who hit them as part of the regular routine. It's so ordinary, nobody even talks about it until somebody gets beaten so bad she has to go to the hospital. Then the whole discussion focuses on what she did to set him off like that." Joyce turned the paper sideways to read my note in the margin. "Why'd you change it?"

"Too long," I said. "Too political. Nobody uses words like *shackles*, Comrade. This is the nineties, remember?"

Joyce made a face at me. "Ungrateful wretches."

I told you she will say that old-time stuff in conversation like it's the latest thing.

"We changed the world for you and what do you do?"

"We fuck it up," I said. "Big time."

She studied the list again. "Did I leave anything out?"

I leaned over to check the list again, then took it and wrote these five additions off the top of my head as subsets of the basic sex education component:

1. Don't fuck men you don't like.
2. Bring your own birth control.
3. Practice safe sex every time.
4. If it's hurting you, it shouldn't be exciting him.
5. Don't fake—demonstrate.

I slid the page back across the table to Joyce, who read it quickly.

"Why not love?"

"Why not love what?"

"Why not, don't fuck men you don't *love?*"

Spoken like a woman who was lucky enough to meet the true love of her life when she was fifteen.

"Because love is too rare to make it a condition for sex. You could spend your life waiting, celibate and evil."

"Maybe it's worth waiting for," Joyce said, and she wasn't being smug. She really couldn't imagine having sex with anybody you didn't love.

"Maybe," I said, "but as a practical solution, it's right up there with *just say no to drugs.*"

She nodded. "What if they're lesbians?"

"Then they don't have to worry about it," I said. "They won't be fucking any men, period."

"But should they be fucking *women* they don't like?"

I hadn't thought about it. *Why would they?* Women fucked men they didn't like for all kinds of reasons—money, safety, protection, purely sexual release, ambition. Did the same stuff apply to women? I didn't know, but I figured until I did, it'd be safer to just say:

Don't fuck people you don't like.

Joyce noted the change. She nodded agreement through two, three, and four and grinned at the last one.

"Does number five mean what I think it means?"

"It means if he's not doing the things that make you feel good, it may be that he just doesn't know what they are and would benefit greatly from being told." I thought about Eddie. "Or *shown*."

Joyce looked at me. "You're not going to start talking dirty to your big sister, are you?"

"I hope you won't be using uptight words like *dirty* when you're talking about all this to the sisters of the Circus," I said, teasing.

"Not a chance," Joyce said. "I wasn't always a widow."

"I know." I rolled my eyes remembering listening to the muffled sounds of pleasurable exchange coming from Joyce and Mitch's room when I was growing up. They were newlyweds when Mama died and the honeymoon was still in progress when I left and moved to Detroit. When I was about twelve and my adolescent hormones were truly raging, I remember getting up to go to the bathroom and hearing their lovemaking so distinctly as I passed their bedroom door that I hurried back to bed and discovered masturbation. It was probably one of the most intense solo sexual experiences I've ever had, but that's when I moved my room downstairs where it is now. I knew I was out of line. Some things are supposed to be private.

"I think you're right about the statement of purpose, too," Joyce said, putting the papers in a folder labeled *Sewing Circus.* "I'll make the changes and maybe you'll look at it again for me?"

Of course I would. I really felt the possibilities of what Joyce was trying to do for the first time and I had to admit it was sort of exciting to be a part of it. I was looking for a new gig anyway and even though it was only temporary, this one did not require me to fool with anybody's hair or fry up a chicken sandwich to go. There was no big reason to rush my ass off to San Francisco. Things here were clicking along at a very interesting pace and I am a firm believer in the bit of old Negro wisdom that says: *if it ain't broke, don't fix it.*

• 2

eddie went by to sit with Johnny Mack for a while and then came by our place afterward with an idea. Eddie has known Mack all his life and he wanted to make sure he was okay and offer to look in on him on a more regular schedule. It was hard for a lot of these old men to ask for help or to accept it when it was offered. They had been so strong so long, and all of a sudden they couldn't hardly get to the grocery store. It scared them first and then it made them angry, a typical black male pattern, if you think about it. Brothers tend to be more familiar with anger than any of their other emotions, so if you leave them to their own devices, that's usually where they'll go. It can start out as fear, or confusion, or sorrow, or hurt feelings, but nine times out of ten, it's going to come out on the other end *mad.* Sometimes you can talk them out of it if you catch it on the front end, but the process requires lightning reflexes, infinite patience, and nerves of steel. Sort of exhausting as a lifetime commitment.

But old Mack was beyond anger. He was just *through.* He had worked at the post office all of his life, supported his wife, raised his children, and scraped together enough money to buy a house on Idlewild Lake so they could take his reliable federal pension and retire in peace. Now his children all lived in the city, his wife had died in her sleep, lying beside him the way she had done every single night of their fifty-two-year marriage, and he didn't feel safe in his own house anymore. He was disappointed and exhausted, and when Eddie sat down beside him in the living room, the empty space on the doily-covered table where his television used to sit was just proof that things weren't the way they used to be.

Eddie said when he offered to come by a couple of times a week, Mack snorted.

"You figure you'd a been stopping by here at two o'clock in the morning, do you?"

It was a rhetorical question, of course, and the old man waved off Eddie's suggestions for improved security measures.

"None of that matters. If they want it bad enough to beat me in my own bed to get it, they can have it. All of it!"

He told Eddie he had called his son and told him he was ready to move into the Baptist Home, which is what his kids had been lobbying in favor of for months. He had resisted because he knew what it meant. Nobody ever moves *out* of the old folks' home.

"The thing I'm going to miss is how it used to be," he told Eddie, looking out across the lake. "This used to be a place where Negroes acted like they had some sense. You could leave your door unlocked all summer and your place empty all winter once the snow started and nobody would touch a thing. Now these young boys got no respect. They'd just as soon kill me as look at me."

The anger was returning, but it was just a flash.

"I'm too old to teach them any better," he said. "So it's time for me to go. I'm going to put the house on the market on Monday. If you know anybody who wants it, let me know. I'll give them a good price."

Eddie said he would and headed straight this way. He's been thinking about the Sewing Circus just like we have. We all know Joyce can't keep having the meetings at the house. It's not big enough. It's cozy to have a crowd around the kitchen table, but it gets to be a problem when there are so many people only half of them can be in any room at a time. What Joyce is dreaming needs a place to spread out. Eddie thinks Johnny Mack's place might be a possibility. He only wants ten thousand dollars for it if the buyer can pay cash, and it's got three acres of land with sun enough for a huge garden and unobstructed lakefront access.

Joyce was concerned about the small rooms, but Eddie said he could knock out most of the walls and make a common room big enough to hold fifty people seated if it had to. He said he didn't have any money to put in, but he could do all the renovations himself and that would save us a lot.

I could see Joyce was really excited about the idea. I could practically hear her brain trying to figure out how to get the money together. I listened as she asked Eddie for estimates on the cost of this or that, and he sounded as enthusiastic as I felt. My mind started doing budgets, too. I had my real estate windfall to work with and as I sat there listening to them cutting costs here and making do there, that money started burning a hole in my pocket. San Francisco seemed more and more like somebody else's dream.

I felt more alive here than I had for years. I had my sister, the lover of my dreams, a role as part of a long-term project that excited me, and a big-eyed, baldheaded baby girl to take on my morning walks. I was meditating morning and evening, walking three miles a day, and I hadn't had anything stronger than a glass of wine with dinner in a month. It was my *choice* that had brought me back here, and for the first time, it really felt like home.

I sat down beside Joyce and looked at the pad where she was scribbling figures. I took the pencil and put a check mark next to where she had written: *Mack's property, $10,000.*

"I can take care of the house," I said.

She looked at me. "What?"

"I have enough to buy it," I said. What the hell? I had enough to live for two years without having to get paid by anybody but my own bank account, but that didn't mean I couldn't get a job if I really needed one. I can always open a salon if I have to. Nobody ever went broke making sisters' hair look good. Besides, quiet as it's kept, I wasn't really in a position to get hung up on planning that far in advance.

I didn't say all that to Joyce and Eddie, of course. We all have regular conversations in all our various combinations about my health—current state of, prognosis, and options. I know they talk about it when I'm not around, just like they do when they talk to me one on one, but I don't encourage a lot of discussion about dying. I figure there will be plenty of time for that later.

"Are you sure?" Joyce whispered. Her eyes were already shining, but she wanted me to say it again.

"I'm sure," I said, a little embarrassed at how they were looking at me. I had never been in a position to give anybody enough money to do something really important.

Joyce leaned over and hugged me so hard I almost fell out of the chair. Eddie was on the other side pumping my hand like I'd just promised him my vote and looking like he wanted to kiss me, but didn't want to be inappropriate. So I kissed both of them and we all sort of danced around the kitchen like maniacs, loving each other and savoring the moment like the rare, sweet thing it was.

No wonder old Rockefeller and the boys give away so much money. *It felt great.*

• 3

eddie and i finally got Joyce to agree to keep a shotgun in the house. She still hates the idea, so we're going to keep it in the closet in my room. I'm downstairs, so I'd be the one who could get to the problem first anyway. It also puts the gun in a room far from Imani. Joyce kept quoting all these awful statistics about how many kids are killed in gun accidents in their own homes. I assured her that each and every one of these children was older than two months and almost certainly walking at the time. She looked skeptical, so I promised to find another place to put it when Imani started crawling, which won't be for another four or five months on the outside.

Once we got that straight, Eddie showed us how to clean it, how to load it, and the basic safety stuff about how to carry it without pointing it at anybody. Then we each fired it a couple of times so we could feel the kick and hear the noise so it wouldn't surprise us. After that, I cleaned it again by myself, loaded it, put the safety on, and propped it up in the corner of the closet.

The first couple of days, it was like having a pile of plutonium in the room with me. I was so aware of the gun being there, I felt like it was *glowing*. I got up a couple of times, opened the closet door, and just looked at it sitting there. I was glad we had it, but it still made me feel weird.

I never could have imagined needing to have a gun in Idlewild. The whole time I was growing up, we never even locked the door. But it's dangerous to pretend. That was then and this is most definitely now.

When Joyce was trying to make up her mind, she said, "I would never shoot somebody over a television set." She was sitting in the rocking chair feeding Imani.

"Would you shoot somebody over Imani?" Eddie said, cool as shit, knowing Joyce would do *anything* for Imani.

Joyce ran her hand gently over Imani's head and looked at Eddie.

"You win," she said.

Eddie put his hand on her shoulder lightly. "I'll win if you never have to use it."

• 4

once we decided what to do, everything was easy. Mack was really happy we were going to buy his house. It was a continuity that he needed right then. We helped him pack up all the things he wanted to take with him, and Joyce volunteered to ship whatever he couldn't carry easily. Eddie helped coordinate travel arrangements with Mack's very grateful son and drove with him to the airport on the designated day of departure.

Joyce and I stayed at the house. I was boxing up his incredible collection of paperbacks when Joyce discovered a shoe box full of old photographs he'd been searching for unsuccessfully all morning.

"Look at these," she said, spreading them out on the coffee table.

Almost all of the pictures were taken in Idlewild during its vacation-paradise heyday. There were barbecues on the patio, highballs by the lake, and dinner dances at the Lot Owners Club House. There were smiling women striking the classic one-hand-on-hip, one-hand-behind-the-head pose of bathing beauties through the ages. There were amateur anglers holding up strings of bluegills and gardeners showing off baskets of oversized summer tomatoes. There were a lot of pictures of Mr. and Mrs. Mack while their boys were growing into manhood and later, of their grandchildren.

In every shot, the black folks looked rested, relaxed, and proud to be exactly where they were. They exuded the confidence of people who know the house note will be mailed on time and the car payments are always up-to-date.

"The good old days," I said, tying up a stack of twenty-five detective novels with the white string old people always save in their kitchen drawers.

"I wish I knew what happened to all that," Joyce said, replacing the pictures and labeling the box to send to Mack in Detroit.

"The factories closed," I said. "You been to Detroit lately? Nobody's working."

"It's not that simple."

"Yes, it is," I said, scooping up a stack of cowboy sagas.

"You think if all the girls in the Circus were working, their lives would be that different?" she said.

"I think if *any* of them were working, their lives would be that different."

Joyce was quiet for a minute. "Then we have to figure

167

that out, too," she said, like she was adding unemployment to her list along with teenage pregnancy, domestic violence, crack, and AIDS. I told you Joyce was an action girl. Big sister was definitely on the move.

• 5

me and joyce walked halfway around the lake this morning. She's so busy with Imani and the Circus, sometimes I have to drag her out to walk, but it's worth it. She's lost some weight already and is starting to look like her old self. We took a big stick for unruly dogs, but all the ones we saw looked at us like we were crazy and kept on minding their own business.

We did pass by a great big rottweiler that we hoped was chained and who looked to be asleep.

"You just keep on sleeping," Joyce said under her breath like if he woke up, that was going to be his ass.

I almost had a heart attack trying not to laugh out loud. I didn't want to disturb him and have to count on Joyce to back up those wolf tickets she'd been selling.

Eddie had come by early just as I was starting out alone and he offered to stay with Imani, who was still sleeping, so Joyce could go too. When we got back, he was sitting on the top step, holding Imani against his shoulder and patting her back gently to encourage a burp. He even had a cloth diaper over his shoulder for any mishaps.

"You're getting good at this," I said, suddenly wishing we could have had a kid together. Eddie had a lot of *daddy stuff* he'd never had a chance to give anybody.

"You're getting good at that," he said, indicating the sweat I'd worked up walking. He assured Joyce that Imani had eaten and he had the empty bottle to prove it, so we went in to make a quick change and reconvened in the kitchen, as usual.

Eddie had been working on the plans for renovating

Mack's house. We had finally gotten everything cleared out and cleaned up and he wanted to get started on the inside. Joyce had told him generally how she saw things and given him a copy of Ten Things Every Free Woman Should Know so he could see the kinds of activities she was planning. He came back with drawings and descriptions for a flexible space that could be modified depending on what was required.

He wanted to knock out most of the walls and add a couple of skylights in the nursery area, which could be closed off completely so activity noise wouldn't interrupt naps or bedtime when things ran long. He suggested a new stove and refrigerator since Mack's were pretty well shot and a garden area running across the full front of the house. Mrs. Mack had been an enthusiastic gardener and the sun in that spot guaranteed bumper crops of green beans, squash, tomatoes, and collards.

He said the whole thing could be done easily within the budget we had set since the electricity and plumbing were in pretty good shape. Joyce was really excited and we were still poring over the drawings when the mailman turned his truck up into the yard and jumped out with a special-delivery letter for Joyce. She signed for it and came back in to tear it open.

She started reading and frowned. "What the hell?"

Eddie and I looked up to see what was the matter, and Joyce sat down heavily and held the letter out to me.

"She has lost her natural mind," Joyce said. "The woman is completely out of control."

Eddie read over my shoulder.

Dear Mrs. Mitchell:

It is with regret that I write to let you know that your request for a change of venue for the female youth activity known as the Sewing Circus must be tabled until certain questions can be cleared up to the satisfaction of our staff as well as the consultant panel which initially reviewed your grant. Although I initially indicated to you that the grant was to support your activity and was not site-specific, grave allegations have now been made by Mrs. Geraldine Anderson, who reportedly observed some activities at a recent session that are well beyond the scope of activities funded by this department and certainly not in line with the proposal you submitted to us for funding consideration.

In order to convey to you the seriousness of our concerns, let me quote the specific charge from Mrs. Anderson's letter to us:

"Upon arriving at the church fellowship hall, to my surprise and horror, I saw Mrs. Mitchell teaching a group of young women techniques for sexually stimulating men by using hot dogs mounted on a stick. It was as if I had stumbled upon a class for concubines! Mrs. Mitchell's defiant refusal to explain her activities to the Good Reverend's satisfaction has resulted in her being banned from conducting any more of these shocking sessions at the New Light Baptist Church. My husband and I both felt that it was our responsibility to alert you before any more state funds are allocated for such sinful purposes."

I will, of course, look forward to your full and complete response to these charges at your earliest convenience.

> Yours sincerely,
> Talbot Ames, Deputy
> Commissioner for Youth
> Programs, State of Michigan

• 6

joyce spent the day on the phone to the state capitol in Lansing. The reception she was getting from people who had praised her program just a few months ago was skittish at best. The conservative Christians around here have got everybody so scared of doing anything controversial that one indignant letter from an angry voter is cause for concern. When the person is a minister's wife and sends copies to everybody from elected officials to newspaper editors and garden club presidents, alarm bells go off and any bureaucrat worthy of the name immediately activates the time-honored process of covering his ass.

Joyce was trying to exercise some kind of damage control before the ass covering shifted into high gear. Once that happened, the possibility of getting a straight answer from anybody about anything was about as good as having a whole winter up here with no snow. In other words, not a chance.

By the end of the day, Joyce figured the only thing to do was go to Lansing in the morning and meet with whoever she could find face-to-face and tell them what really happened. She also wrote a letter refuting Gerry's version of the events in question and printed out enough copies on her computer to personally distribute them to everybody on Gerry's list who she could find. She figured that would take her all day and into the evening, so she'd stay overnight and come back the next morning.

I walked over to Eddie's to tell him the plan and he told me he had taken a carpentry job in Ludington that he could finish in two days if he left early and stayed overnight, so he was leaving in the morning, too. Eddie was a careful craftsman and he had all the carpentry work he wanted. People who worked with him always recommended him to other people, so he had jobs lined up as far in advance as he wanted to take them. He hadn't gone on an overnight job in a while and I realized I was going to miss him, even for one night.

"I'll miss you, too," he said, pulling me over close to him and blowing out the candles so we could leave the windows uncovered while we made love.

Eddie and I decided not to try oral sex. Both of us agreed that the taste of latex is too much to deal with. We can try it later if we want to, but right now we're going to let it slide. I never could figure out how to hold a dental dam in front of everything that has to be covered and still have any fun. It just ain't the same thing at all.

What I'm really liking a lot is all the touching we do. When you can't do the stuff you've always done, you have to get creative, and we sure do that. Eddie knows a lot about sensual massage and he can do things by stroking my calves that most men couldn't do with full and complete access to every orifice I've got.

Something else I really like is that Eddie and Joyce already loved each other unconditionally, so there wasn't any of the weirdness that usually comes when you're integrating somebody new into your family. We're all so close now, it's almost incestuous.

After we made love and he was getting ready to walk me back to Joyce's, he put his arms around me and nuzzled against my neck.

"If anybody ever asks you," he said, "you tell them Eddie Jefferson loves him some Ava Johnson. You hear me, girl? Tell them I love me some Ava."

That was the first time I spent the night.

• 7

i had never kept Imani by myself. I fed her and changed her and bathed her and burped her and she continued to be my best walking partner, but this was our first overnighter.

"So how am I doing?" I asked, wrapping her in a big towel and patting her dry after an uneventful bath. She looked at me with what I chose to interpret as approval while I put lotion on her arms and legs, cornstarch on her bottom, and wiped her newly pierced ears with alcohol.

Imani came home from her last visit to the pediatrician with tiny gold earrings. So many mothers wanted pierced ears for their girl babies, and before the doctor started doing it with a one-step gun, they'd do it themselves with a needle and thread and risk injuring or infecting the baby, who probably didn't care about earrings one way or the other but didn't get a vote yet.

Joyce hadn't even thought about it, and since she was legally still a temporary mother at this point, she probably didn't have the right to do it, but when the doctor pronounced Imani right on schedule for six weeks and asked if she wanted the baby's ears pierced, Joyce said sure.

I wiped each little bitty earlobe front and back and gently turned the earrings so they would heal correctly. The gold shone against her rosy brown complexion. She had enough hair now so that her head was covered in soft black fuzz. She had gained weight, too, and her little spindly arms and legs had rounded out nicely.

She hadn't done any of the terrible things they warned us she might, and Joyce immediately took that to be evidence that crack babies are being unfairly maligned and can be rescued and rehabilitated through the power of love. To me, it's apples and oranges. A lot of crack babies are angry and unhappy and damaged and probably real hard to handle. On the other hand, real love and consistent sweetness can bring out the best in anybody no matter how knocked around you've been. It was kind of sad, though, to think that the only thing that can save these babies is the one thing they usually can't get anywhere close to. When I looked at Imani, I was glad we had gotten one to higher ground anyway.

"All right, miss," I said, kissing her stomach and breathing in that well-oiled, powdery smell that surrounds babies who are being raised right. "Time for bed."

I gave her a bottle and watched her struggle unsuccessfully to keep her eyes open. She finished her milk, burped loudly, sighed, and slept. It was a perfect moment and I just sat there looking at her for a few minutes. Maybe it was better for her not to be able to tell me the journey she took to get here. From what I already knew, it's a miracle she made it through at all, but she damn sure did.

Thank you, Jesus/Buddah/Mother/Father/God, whoever or whatever you are. You done good.

• 8

the sound of the car in the yard woke me. Joyce and Eddie weren't due back until tomorrow and it was still deep night from the pitch black outside the window. I had fallen asleep with Imani in my arms at sunset without turning on any lights and the house was dark, inside and out. Nobody blew the horn, but they didn't turn the motor off either. I went over to the window, knowing that in the dark I could see out better than they could see in, and pulled back the curtain.

There in the yard was the Good Reverend's Cadillac. Behind the wheel was Tyrone. The passenger door opened and Frank got out, pulling his girlfriend after him.

"Stop, Frankie," she said. "This shit ain't funny. Let's go!"

"Ain't nobody home," Frank said. "You see any light on in this muthafucka? You see any cars around? You see any, Ty?"

He gestured dramatically and Tyrone laughed.

"Naw, man. I don't see shit."

"Let's go, Frankie," she said again. "This shit ain't funny, okay?"

"You say you wanna see where the bitch live, right? This where she live."

My heart was beating so hard, I was afraid I'd wake Imani. What the hell were they doing here? The clock on the desk said 10:30 P.M., but they sounded like they were already pretty drunk.

"Okay, this is where she live, awright? Let's go!"

Frank grabbed her arm. "Why don't you go on up and say hello?" He started toward the steps, pulling her along behind him.

"I thought you said ain't nobody home," she said, struggling against him.

He stopped abruptly and jerked her up against his

chest. He had a half-empty beer bottle in his other hand, but he had no problem pinning her thin arms behind her back.

"You callin' me a liar?"

"Ow, Frankie! You hurtin' me! Stop it now!"

I walked down the hall as fast as I could, laid Imani down in the center of my bed, put pillows around her so she wouldn't fall off, and opened the closet door. I heard Eddie's voice in my head: *Would you shoot somebody over Imani?*

No problem, I thought. These kids are drunk and probably been smoking crack, too. I wondered where Gerry and the Rev thought their car was. I picked up the shotgun and walked back to the window.

Frank and the girl were now locked in an embrace. She was bent backwards over the hood of the car, her legs wrapped around his waist. Over his shoulder, I could see her head thrown back, eyes squeezed shut. Frank's pants were around his knees and he was thrusting himself into the girl harder with every stroke.

Frank had left the car door open and the inside light illuminated Tyrone's face as he gaped at the couple through the windshield like he was enjoying an X-rated, drive-in movie.

I closed my eyes, but I could hear Frank clearly.

"Yeah, bitch, come on, bitch. You such a bad-ass, shit-talking bitch, what you got to say now?"

"Take it all, baby," she said, panting. "This ain't nobody pussy but your pussy. Take all of it!"

Frank slowed down and looked through the glass at Tyrone. "You want some of this, Ty?" he said.

The girl sat up. "What you talkin' about, nigga? You can't be givin' me to him just like that!"

"What did you just say?" Frank said, still moving against her. "Whose pussy is it?"

She didn't say anything and he reached up and grabbed her hair, pulled her neck back hard.

"Ow, Frankie! Stop it now!"

His voice was low, ominous. "I said, whose pussy is it, bitch?"

She struggled briefly, then surrendered. "Your pussy," she said. "It's your pussy."

"Goddamn right," he said, stepping back and pulling up his pants so suddenly she would have stumbled to the ground if he hadn't caught her. "Now, get your ass back in that car and give my boy some of *my* pussy before you make me mad, you stupid bitch." And he pushed her inside the car, slammed the door, reached down to rescue his beer, and sucked it hungrily.

He leaned down to look in the window and laughed. "You the man, Ty! Ride that bitch, brother! That's how she like it. Up the ass and shit!"

From inside the car, there was silence. Frank stood up and tipped his head back to drain the last of the beer, but he had already finished it. I hoped he'd want another one bad enough to head for wherever it was they got it from, but I underestimated the random nature of his anger. Looking around for somebody to blame for this sudden lack of available alcohol, his eyes fell on our picture window. It must have struck him as a worthy way to vent because he hurled the empty bottle through it with enough force to spray glass half-way across the room.

I stepped back quickly to avoid the fragments and took the safety off the shotgun. I could hear the panic outside immediately.

"Shit, man," Tyrone said. "What the fuck you doin', man? You crazy? Get in, man! Hurry up! What if they got a alarm and shit? Come on!"

I heard the car door slam and the gravel flying as Tyrone gunned the motor and took off.

I waited to be sure they were really gone and then went back to check on Imani. She was lying there in the middle of the bed where I'd left her, awake as hell, but she wasn't crying.

I put the safety back on, put the gun back in the closet carefully, and closed the door.

It wasn't until I picked up Imani that I realized my hands were shaking, not with fear but with frustration. I wasn't afraid I was going to have to shoot Frank. I was sorry I hadn't had an excuse.

• 9

eddie got back just before noon. When I told him what happened, his face went gray. He just sat there with his arm around me and Imani, not saying anything. I could feel him breathing real slow, but his arm felt like a brick around my neck. I told him the sheriff had already come by to look at the damage. I was going to wait until Joyce got back and then go into town and formally press charges.

"You don't have to do that," Eddie said.

I was surprised. "Don't you think we should?"

"I can take care of it."

"What do you mean?" I said, but I knew exactly what he meant.

He looked at me.

"He's a kid." I couldn't believe I was making a case for leniency in regard to Frank, but something in Eddie's voice, in his face, made me know what we were talking about was a permanent solution.

Eddie shook his head. "He's going to push it and push it until he kills somebody who isn't even a part of the game he's playing."

He took a deep breath. "I have taken people out because the army told me I had to so that the country could feel safe. I've taken people out because some coke dealer told me to so *he* could feel safe. I'm not going to let some hardhead come at my family so *they* don't feel safe. What kind of man would that make me?"

I had never had anybody offer to kill somebody for me and it scared me a little. It wasn't a bad feeling; just *new*. All the women I know talk about how black men prey on us. Almost nobody speaks on how well they protect us from anything, including themselves. Most of us don't have much experience with that side of their natures. Eddie sounded like how I thought black men probably used to sound talking about how to handle attacks by the Klan and other renegade white folks. Did the rules change when the predator wasn't a group of white men with hoods, but a black kid who could have been my little brother? I wasn't sure.

"I need to talk to Joyce before you do anything," I said. "This should be the *three* of us deciding, okay?"

He made me wait a minute, but then he smiled and shook his head. "Black women are the only women in the world who make you wait until they decide whether or not they're worth protecting."

"It's a new experience for us," I said. "We need time to get used to it."

"You want time," he said. "I want solutions."

"People in hell want vodka and tonic," I said.

That made him laugh. "I thought they wanted ice water."

"Shows how behind the times you are," I said, loving his smile. "I missed you."

He kissed my eyelids and put his hand on my cheek. I leaned into his warm palm and closed my eyes.

"You okay?" he said softly.

"Can you hold both of us at the same time?" I said, and he picked me and Imani up and sat there on the porch steps with us cradled in his arms like it was the most natural thing in the world for him to do on a Tuesday morning in the middle of the Great North Woods. I could hear the steady rhythm of his heart and I don't think I've ever felt safer in my life.

when joyce pulled up, she saw the window and freaked out so bad she almost drove through it. While I told her what happened, she just kept holding Imani real tight and shaking her head and saying, "I can't believe it. I just can't believe it."

When I finished, she hugged me and said: "I'm so glad you didn't have to use that gun."

I didn't say anything. There was no point in letting Joyce in on my realization of how much I had wanted to waste Frank. Especially in light of the discussion Eddie wanted to have about what he thought was an appropriate response. She'd think she left us a bunch of meditating wanna-be Buddhists and returned to find Murder, Incorporated.

I appreciated the immediacy of Eddie's offer, but I didn't think I was ready to order an execution because the kid was a crack-smoking, woman-hating asshole who threw a bottle through our front window. I wasn't sure the danger he represented was best met by becoming even more violent than he was. I hoped it wasn't, anyway.

Eddie kept asking me what I thought was going to be the thing that turned Frank's life around. The thing that transformed him from predator to productive citizen, and I couldn't think of anything. I tried to trot out the same old tired answers, but Eddie wasn't having it.

Graduating from high school? That was a joke. They were barely learning how to read and write. Going to college? Not a chance. No grades. No money. No motivation. A good job? Doing what? Where? There weren't any jobs for miles.

"He could join the army," I said, knowing how lame it sounded even to me.

Eddie grinned. "And see the world?"

I hated to admit it, even to myself, *especially* to myself, but he was right. Frank was gone. Destroyed. Tyrone probably was, too, in spite of his grandmother's grip on him. There was no place for them and they knew it at some deep level where all the bullshit messages about how bright their futures could be if they just applied themselves were filed away. They knew the real deal was about drugs and jail and mean, unsafe sex and more death in the neighborhoods than there had been in Vietnam. And they were *pissed*. Across-the-board *pissed*. But they're still our kids, so what the hell are we supposed to do?

When Eddie made his proposition to Joyce, she looked at him like he was losing his mind. He had repaired the window and we were sitting in the living room admiring his handiwork when Joyce said she guessed we better go fill out the report with the sheriff. That's when Eddie repeated his delicately phrased offer to *take care of it*.

"It's not fair," she said after giving him a minute to take it back. "He didn't kill anybody."

They looked at each other for a long minute and then Joyce reached out and took his hand. "Nobody even got hurt."

"Do we have to wait for that?" Eddie said quietly.

"We have to wait for more than a broken window."

"Okay," he said. He leaned over and hugged Joyce. "But say the word and youngblood is history."

"He might be history around here anyway," Joyce said. "He's still on probation. If he gets in any trouble, he has to go back to Detroit and serve his time in juvenile."

"Buys time, but it doesn't solve the problem," Eddie said, volunteering to drive us in to the sheriff's office.

Joyce rode in the back with Imani in her car seat. I rode up front with Eddie and we held hands like teenagers used to do. When I turned on the radio, they were playing "Get Ready." Eddie cranked it up as loud as it would go, and in light of all that had happened in the last twenty-four hours, I thought the Temptations would forgive us for adding three very off-key lead singers to their sublime quintet. I knew they would. If anybody ever understood the power of a love song better than those five fine brothers, you can't prove it by me. And the truth of the matter is, if we can't love each other, none of it makes any sense anyway.

• 11

i gave a complete statement and swore out a complaint. The sheriff, a weary-looking brother whose mind was obviously already enjoying his first year of retirement, looked at the three of us standing there full of righteous indignation, sighed, and said since they didn't actually try to get inside the house, the most serious charge he could probably bring was malicious mischief. He also said since they were only sixteen and nobody got hurt, they'd probably only get a fine and a reprimand when a judge finally heard the case.

When Joyce asked about the possibility of Frank being sent back to Detroit, the sheriff dug an official-looking letter out of the stack on his desk and handed it to her. It was a notice from the juvenile court that Frank had successfully completed the terms of his probation. It was dated a week ago.

"Bad timing," I said.

We all felt it. If Frank had been rehabilitated during his time up here, we had truly missed the transformation. Joyce handed the sheriff back Frank's freedom papers and asked him for a suggestion as to how we should proceed. She wasn't looking anywhere near Eddie, who had on his *I-told-you-I-can-take-care-of-it* face. The sheriff said if we wanted to have a conference with *the boys* (the way he said it made them sound like the kind of wayward scamps with hearts of gold that used to populate Hollywood movies like *Boys Town*), he could call all the principals together in his office in a couple of days and make it clear that if anything like this happened again, there would be serious consequences.

Eddie's plan was sounding better and better, but Joyce agreed to the meeting and they scheduled it for Friday.

"What's the point?" I said as we headed home.

"I want to look at them," she said quietly. "I want to know if I can see it in their faces."

Eddie didn't say anything and neither did I. We didn't have to ask her what *it* was. Joyce was still hoping to appeal to their consciences, but the only way that's possible is if the person doing the bad shit has some guilt, or some remorse, or even some vague feeling that the stuff they're doing may be wrong. But Frank and Tyrone didn't give a damn, about us, about themselves, about anything. So it doesn't matter how hard Joyce looks in their faces. All she's going to see is one big blank.

• 12

eddie has been working on Mack's place. Joyce wants to get it ready for a grand opening in September, so he's only got six weeks. When I went over there this afternoon on my walk, he was standing in the middle of what had been the living room. There was plaster dust all over the place and it had settled on his hair and his eyebrows so that they were almost all white. I had a flash of what he would look like once his dreads went gray and I hoped I'd be around long enough to see it.

He had a mask on over his nose and mouth, but the way his eyes crinkled up when he saw me, I could tell he was smiling. He stepped out of the pile, pulled the mask down, and kissed me. I liked that about Eddie. He always kissed me when we first saw each other and he always kissed me when we said good-bye. He was affectionate without being possessive, a rare and wonderful combination.

"What do you think?" he said, indicating the ruined room behind him.

"I think it's going to be great," I said, surprised at how

much bigger the space inside the house looked with most of the interior walls down. "How'd you know which ones you could take down without all of it falling?"

He shrugged. "I didn't. I just knock them down, cover my head, and hope for the best."

I was shocked until I realized he was teasing me. "Right," I said. "That sounds like how you usually do things. A regular fly-by-the-seat-of-the-pants kind of guy."

He grabbed a broom and started sweeping the debris into a neat pile. "Let me get this up and we can have some tea, if you've got time."

"How're you going to make tea in here?" I said, looking at the empty space where he'd already taken out the stove and refrigerator.

He finished sweeping, put the broom down, and walked over to his truck. He reached in and when I saw what he brought out, I had to smile and admit it to myself: *I liked his whole act.*

"You always bring your tea to work in a tea cozy?" I said.

"Only when I'm expecting company."

"And what made you expect company?"

"I got a lady friend who is crazy about my . . . tea," he said, with just enough pause and implication to make me blush. He spread out an old, green army blanket on the grass and poured for both of us. It was almost sunset and the sky was turning pearl gray above the lake. We just sipped our tea and watched the water, listened to the birds and the waves lapping against the dock.

Eddie and I still spent a lot of time together without saying much, but it felt like we were talking the whole time. At first it made me nervous. I was so used to hiding behind words that the silence made me feel more exposed than being naked. I was always trying to figure out what he was thinking and worrying about what to say next, but the more we are together, the more I don't even think about that stuff. I know whatever I feel is what I feel. Whatever I say is what I say. Everything else is just a game I don't have time to play anymore.

"I'm thinking maybe I'll teach a karate class once things get going," Eddie said.

"At the Circus?"

He nodded. "These hardheads are out of control. It might be a way to get to some of them before they're too far out to haul them back in."

I knew Joyce had been trying to figure out how she could do some activities for boys. Mitch used to coach a youth basketball team, but without him, she had really concentrated on the girls.

"You know what I said the other day?"

"About taking care of it?" I said.

"I figure if I'm prepared to take these young brothers out for acting a fool, I should have tried everything else first, and I haven't. Nobody learns how to be a man by watching TV and listening to their homeboys."

"Can you make them all act just like you?"

He grinned at me. "I don't know if everybody would find that idea as appealing as you do."

"That's because everybody isn't as smart as I am."

"Is that it?"

"That's part of it."

"What's the other part?"

"They've never made love with you, so their information is incomplete," I said. "And you know what else?"

"What?" he said, leaning back on his elbows.

"It's going to stay that way." And I kissed him.

"How come I had to wait so long for you?" he said, reaching up to pull me across his chest.

"I had to grow up first."

"Me, too," he said.

"So are we grown now?" I whispered into his hair.

"We're getting there," he said. "And you know what they say."

"What do they say?" I pulled back to look into his face

and he rubbed his hands across my head the way I like to do to Imani.

"Getting there is half the fun."

I laughed and leaned into his hands like cats do when you scratch between their ears.

"Well," I said. "They sure got that right."

• 13

"how much do you want to bet Frank and Mattie don't show?" Joyce said as we arrived at Sheriff Gates' office and were directed to a mediation room down the hall. A bored-looking woman sitting in front of a dusty computer said the sheriff was on the phone and would join us in a minute.

"The Reverend probably won't be here either," I said. "If the Holy Spirit calls, he has to answer."

"Maybe it'll call Gerry this time," Joyce said.

No chance. When we opened the door to the dingy little room, Gerry and Tyrone were already there. Gerry was sitting stiffly on a battered yellow plastic couch that would probably take the skin off the backs of your bare legs if you sat on it on a hot day, and Tyrone, dressed in his Sunday suit and tie, was wandering around looking for a way to disappear.

"Hello, Gerry," Joyce said as we sat down on an identical and equally battered couch against the far wall. "Tyrone."

Tyrone looked at his grandmother, and when she didn't make a sound, he didn't either. Joyce sighed.

"Look, Gerry, I think we need to put our differences aside and think about what's best for Tyrone, don't you?"

"Tyrone cannot be blamed for falling victim to your schemes." Even Gerry's hairdo was trembling with righteous indignation.

What was she so mad about? Last time I checked, we were the victims. I was sorry now that Eddie hadn't come with us. There was no way I was going to be able to describe to him how truly weird this whole scene was getting.

"What schemes?" Joyce said. "If you're talking about the Sewing Circus—"

"You brought it up," Gerry interrupted. "*I* didn't."

"This doesn't have anything to do with that," Joyce said. "And you know it."

Gerry sniffed and turned away. "I don't know anything of the sort. *Tyrone!* Come and sit down."

He slouched over and slumped down in the far corner of the couch as far away from his grandmother as he could get.

"Sit up, son!"

The harshness of her voice seemed to pull him up like a puppet with a string at the back of his neck.

"Fine," Joyce said. "Let's wait for the sheriff and you can tell him all about it."

"That is exactly what I intend to do."

What I intended to do was go to a pay phone, call Eddie, and ask him if his offer was still good for Frank and could I please add one crazy-ass old lady to the mix, but that would be wrong and certainly less than sisterly. I tried to meditate, but I'm not that good yet, so we all just sat there looking at each other until Sheriff Gates finally came in, trying to look official and concerned. He took a seat in the only chair between our two camps and frowned at all of us like we were bad kids who had been sent to the principal's office. He reached into his pocket and took out a well-creased piece of notebook paper, which he unfolded laboriously, read over carefully, and then looked up at us again.

"Where are Frank Richards and his guardian?"

We all just looked at him. Nobody was prepared to speculate. The sheriff refolded his paper and sighed.

"Well, we'll just go on without them for right now. Do all of you know each other?"

We had to admit that we did.

"Good," the sheriff said. "And we all know why we're here?"

I think he assumed we all agreed we were there to talk about Frank and Tyrone coming to the house drunk and tossing a beer bottle through the front window. The question mark was just his way of being polite, but Gerry took him at his word.

"I would like to have that clarified," she said.

The sheriff was confused. "Have what clarified?"

"The purpose of this hearing."

"It's not really a hearing," the sheriff started to explain, but Gerry interrupted him.

"Then what is it?"

The sheriff sighed and looked at Joyce like it was her fault for taking him up on his suggestion that we all meet in the first place.

"Mrs. Anderson, I appreciate you coming here this afternoon."

Joyce looked at him and raised her eyebrows.

"And you too, Mrs. Mitchell, and . . ." He looked at me and decided the effort to remember my name was just too great. "All of you." He clasped his large, soft hands over his even larger, softer belly, sighed again, and rocked forward in his chair trying to look stern.

"I think we can all agree that what we're trying to figure out is what is best for these young men."

Joyce cleared her throat. "Before we do that, what I am trying to do is find out why they threw a beer bottle through my front window and what they and their guardians intend to do about it."

"That about sums it up, I guess," Sheriff Gates said. "I told Mrs. Mitchell that since they're still juveniles, the court would probably slap a fine on them for malicious mischief and assess the cost of the damages."

"I'm prepared to pay for the damages to the window

today to clear my grandson's record," Gerry said. "Although under the circumstances, I think a fine is out of the question."

Joyce's voice was calm but cold. "And what circumstances are those?"

Gerry whirled suddenly and looked Joyce in the face for the first time. "Ask your sister," she hissed, pointing a trembling finger in my direction.

"Me?"

"Oh, don't act like you don't know what I'm talking about," Gerry said, clutching her white straw bag against her stomach like a shield.

"I have no idea," I said, amazed at so much venom directed my way.

"Mrs. Anderson," the sheriff said, looking at least as confused as I felt. "What are you talking about?"

Gerry took a deep breath and drew herself up as tall as she could without standing. "They should not have done what they did. Tyrone knows better." She glared at him. "And the Good Reverend and I have agreed to play a more active role with young Frank so he, too, can be guided along a righteous path. But young boys have forever been at the mercy of women like her!"

"Oh, hell no!" I stood without knowing I was going to or where I was going once I did. I knew one thing, though. I had no interest in whatever this crazy woman was talking about, and if I never saw either of the *the boys* again, it would be too soon.

"You see," Gerry crowed, triumphant. "She can't stand to hear the truth spoken aloud. She knows what really happened that night."

"What really happened," I said, "was that your grandson and his friends drove up in my yard in your car and lost their minds!"

Joyce stood up and put her arm around my waist. She was so mad I could feel her shaking.

"She invited them!" Gerry spit out the words in our direction.

"Invited them?" the sheriff said. This time the question mark was for real.

"She told them it was a young people's meeting."

Gerry was looking at me intently like she thought I was going to break down and confess to the bullshit like they always do at the end of *Perry Mason.* I was trying to remember if I'd ever stood any closer to a person who was obviously a raving lunatic.

"She told them there would be punch and cookies . . ."

"They were already beer-drunk," I said. "I don't think they had any interest in punch and cookies."

"And neither did she." Gerry switched her focus to the sheriff.

I could hardly hear Joyce ask the question. "Just what do you think my sister was interested in, Gerry?"

Gerry pursed her lips. "Ask her if you aren't afraid to hear the truth."

Joyce walked over until she was standing right in front of Gerry. "The truth? The truth is that these two young brothers came to my house drunk. They had sex with the mother of Frank's child inside and outside of your Cadillac, and when Frank got tired of watching, he threw a bottle through my front window because he couldn't think of anything better to do."

Gerry sputtered and tried to get to her feet, but Joyce was standing so close up on her and the couch was so low that she couldn't get her balance. Joyce didn't move.

"If they told you anything else, anything else at all, they're liars and you and the Good Reverend are fools."

Gerry leaped to her feet.

"Hold on now." The sheriff finally found his voice. "Just hold on! Everybody just relax!"

All I could hear was my own heart beating. I wondered whose idea it was to put this spin on things. I have to admit, I've been accused of a lot of things in my life, most of which I was probably guilty of doing, but this was a first. Coming on to kids has never been my style.

"Everybody sit down," Sheriff Gates said, and when nobody moved, he said it again, loud enough to break the spell created by Gerry's inane accusation. We all sat back down without taking our eyes off each other. The sheriff looked at Gerry. You could tell this was the kind of morning he hated, when he actually had to confront a problem and decide what to do about it.

"Mrs. Anderson, this is the first I have heard of anybody inviting the boys over that night, and it is a pretty serious accusation."

"Ask her!" Gerry pointed at me again. Joyce leaned forward to respond, but Sheriff Gates held up his hand for silence.

"I'm asking you," he said. "What do you mean she invited them?"

"My grandson was in town having a soda with his friends while I did some errands and I ran into her in the drugstore."

She said it like my name was too nasty a word to pass her lips.

"We had a difference of opinion on my responsibility for my grandson's safety and welfare, and when she left the store, she saw a chance to defy me even further."

"*Defy you?*" I wonder if that was before or after Frank decided I had *death pussy*.

"Please! We'll get your side of the story in a minute." Sheriff Gates held up that silence hand again, but now it just pissed me off.

"*My side of the story?* There is no *story!*" I said. "I watched them break the window. I was there! The baby was there! What *story?*"

Sheriff Gates looked pained. "I have to hear all parties," he said. "Please?"

I sat back beside Joyce. We looked at each other. If that harassment outside the drugstore could be described as an invitation for punch and cookies, who knew what might happen next? We didn't have to wait long to find out.

"Then what?" Sheriff Gates said to Gerry, who was waiting to finish her fairy tale.

"The young people had been to the movies and they decided to stop by and see if any of their other friends had decided to attend, but when they got there—" Gerry cleared her throat "—there weren't any other children there—"

"Except a sleeping infant, of course," I said.

She ignored me. "So Tyrone did a foolish thing. They should have gone home right then, but they didn't do that, did you, Tyrone?"

Tyrone shook his head without removing his eyes from a spot on the floor in front of him. Gerry patted his hand encouragingly and he jerked away from her as if her touch burned him.

"Tyrone wanted to thank her for the invitation and apologize for arriving so late, so he knocked on the door and she came out in her . . . her . . ."

This was giving me a headache. I wondered what kind of Frederick's of Hollywood getup she was going to say I greeted them in. Probably a leather bustier and some crotchless panties.

"In her nightgown!" Gerry closed her eyes at the thought.

"Come on," I couldn't resist saying. "If I'm seducing teenagers, wouldn't I at least wear a black negligee?"

"Go on, Mrs. Anderson," the sheriff said, sounding skeptical.

"She waved at the children waiting in the car and asked Tyrone to come in so she could give him some cookies to take home, and when he did, she . . ." Gerry closed her eyes again, reached over, and grabbed Tyrone's hand before he could jerk it away. "She tried to kiss my boy!"

The sheriff looked at me, then at Gerry, then at Tyrone.

"Did she touch you?" the sheriff said to Tyrone.

"Naw."

"Did anybody touch you?"

"Naw."

"What did you do then?"

Tyrone shrugged. "I went outside and got in the car. When I told my buddy it wasn't no party like she promised, he got mad and that's why he threw the bottle."

That's when I started laughing. I didn't mean to, but it was either laugh or cry, and tears were not an option. I believed Eddie about the lessons being everywhere if you just took time to look for them, but I'll be damned if I could see one in the middle of this madness. I felt Joyce's arm tighten around me, squeezing me a little so I'd stop laughing, but I was scared to stop. I figured if I stopped laughing, I was going to go off on Gerry and that fat fool of a sheriff and that grinning little weasel, Tyrone.

I finally got myself together and took a deep breath. Joyce was still holding on to me. She spoke to the sheriff, but she was looking straight at Gerry. "So where does that leave us?"

Sheriff Gates looked at Gerry. He was tired, but he wasn't stupid. He knew she was lying, but he was obligated to ask the official question.

"Mrs. Anderson, are you prepared to file a formal complaint?"

Gerry shook her head slowly. "That is not my intention. I don't want to put my grandson through a public spectacle. He's been through enough."

I started laughing again, but I squashed it pretty quick. I felt like I was headed for hysteria.

"Then what do you want?" The sheriff was getting tired of the game, whatever it was.

"I want them to agree to leave my grandson and the other children of this town alone."

Bingo! Joyce was right. This was still tied to the Sewing

Circus. Nobody's giving out grants for youth work to some-body's who's harboring an attempted child molester.

"Then you have to swear out a complaint against her."

"Why? I've already told you what happened. Isn't that enough?"

"I'm just the sheriff. Corrupting a minor is a very seri-ous offense, Mrs. Anderson. There will have to be a trial if you press charges."

"A trial?" Gerry sounded surprised and even a little frightened. What did she expect? That she could say that shit and the sheriff would slap my wrists and send me home to sin no more?

"I don't want . . . I don't want Tyrone to have to go through a trial. An experience like that can mark a child for life."

The sheriff shrugged and sat back. He hadn't believed her story, although I could tell he was titillated by it, with his tired ass. "Then we got no place to go."

"Yes we do," Joyce said. "I want to pursue my com-plaint for damages and any fine that can be levied for mali-cious mischief."

"Like I told you, Mrs. Mitchell, the judge will probably just throw it out."

"I don't care."

"Fine." The sheriff made a note on his pocket paper. "Anything else?"

Joyce stood up and I stood up right with her. She pointed at Gerry and her hand was steady as a rock. "If I hear one word of this ridiculous story anywhere in this town, or read any part of it in letters to anybody outside this town, I'll sue you and the Good Reverend for slander. Then we will have a trial for sure."

We started out, but Joyce turned at the door and looked back at Gerry. She spoke slowly and clearly like she wanted to be sure Gerry didn't miss anything. "You should be ashamed."

Gerry struggled up off the couch and followed us out into the hallway.

"Just keep walking," Joyce said. "I'm through with all this madness."

"Been through," I said.

"If there is shame to bear, it is on your shoulders, not mine!" Gerry's voice called after us, and when we just kept walking, one final insult. *"Harlot!"*

I added that to my list of firsts for the day. I had never been called a harlot before either.

Joyce backed the car out so fast and wild I thought she was going to hit the side of the building. Neither of us said anything for a while, then Joyce said, "I'm sorry, sweetie. Are you okay?"

I looked at Joyce's tight, angry face. "It's all your fault," I said.

"How do you figure that?" Joyce said.

"What was she supposed to think after she caught you with those jumbo hot dogs? She probably figured this slut thing runs in the family."

Joyce laughed a little bit then and shook her head. She slowed the car down until she was actually taking the curves on all four wheels.

"I almost didn't have enough sisterhood to make it through that one," Joyce said. "And where the hell was the Rev?"

"Probably talking to the Holy Ghost about me," I said. "Asking for guidance on what to do."

"Did you see her face when we were leaving?" Joyce said. "She looked crazy!"

"She *is* crazy," I said.

"And dangerous," Joyce said, pulling into our yard.

"Why dangerous?" I said.

"Anybody carrying around that many lies and that much anger is dangerous."

"This can't all be about the Sewing Circus," I said.

"I don't know what it's about," Joyce said. "But whatever it is, I don't think it's over."

i washed eddie's hair this morning. I liked every part of Eddie's house, but I think the bathroom was the part I liked the best. A lot of people think of the bathroom as a practical place *only*. They don't care what it looks like, what the vibe is, because all they intend to do is maintain their basic hygiene requirements and answer calls of nature. Not Eddie. His bathroom was a tropical rain forest. He had painted the walls pale green and installed a couple of skylights for the plants that were *everywhere*, hanging, sitting in pots, curling around the edges of the basin.

It was a big room. He'd knocked out a couple of walls to expand it, and he had an old-fashioned claw-footed tub big enough to slide down in up to your chin and not slop water over the sides. I loved it. I feel so peaceful and safe there, it didn't even freak me out when I told him about the stuff Gerry was saying about me.

He couldn't believe it either, but he agreed with Joyce that she's probably not through with us yet. His locks are so thick they took a whole bottle of conditioner, but they look wonderful. They smell great, too. I remember I had this fantasy about a lover with serious dreads, but as in any fantasy worthy of the name, the maintenance is overlooked in favor of the sepia-toned, slow-motion sequences where he leans over you, his hair forming a private curtain behind which you explore the full realm of sensual pleasure. But then one of my clients took a lover whose dreads were almost down to his knees, and she said you can't just be rolling around in bed with that much hair casually. *You got to deal with it.*

Eddie's hair wasn't long enough to be a problem yet, and *dealing with it* was a constant source of pleasure and innovation. The first time I saw him swimming with that hair loose and spread out around his head like sunbeams, I wished I were a painter so I could get it down on canvas for future reference.

While I was blow-drying, I wondered aloud how long his hair would be if it was relaxed. Eddie said he thought saying you were *relaxing* hair when you put chemicals or a hot comb in it was weird. Why would the hair be more *relaxed* once you took it out of its natural life into a whole nother thing?

I asked him if that was some more Buddhist stuff. He just laughed and said that as far as he knew, most serious Buddhists shaved their heads so they didn't have to spend a whole lot of time worrying about their hair one way or another. Good thing there're not more black Buddhists. They'd be hell on hairdressers.

• 15

aretha called last night from Interlochen. She learned how to do the breaststroke, finished a sketch called *The Face of It*, which she promised to bring home to show us at the end of the summer, and made friends with a Native American girl from North Dakota. She's done so well in her lab classes, they already told her if she keeps on like this, she has a good chance at a scholarship for next year.

We cheered so loud Imani probably thought we had finally gone crazy for real.

Just before we hung up, she said, "Ava?"

"Yes?"

"Guess what."

"What?" I said, loving all the things I heard in her voice.

"Everybody loves my hair. They want to know who cuts it for me."

I laughed with her.

"Thanks," she said.

"No problem." But I loved hearing it.

In the midst of all that craziness with Gerry, Aretha is the best reminder of why Joyce had started the Sewing Circus in the first place. No matter how much I complain about having to help, I'm real proud of what Joyce is doing—what *we're* doing. I think Mitch would like it too.

• 10

i didn't think this was a good idea, but I couldn't talk Joyce out of it and I didn't want her to go alone, so here we were, walking up to Gerry's house to see if we could get a straight answer from her about what was going on. The television was on inside, so Joyce knocked on the door. We could hear voices and some rustling around, then just the television again. Joyce knocked harder and then we heard footsteps and Tyrone opened the door and stood there in his underwear, scratching his stomach.

"Is your grandmother at home, Tyrone?" Joyce said.

I wanted to grab him in a headlock and force him to take back the bullshit he'd said in the sheriff's office, but I had promised Joyce I would be a supportive but silent presence, so I didn't.

He looked at us like we were complete strangers, yawned, and shook his head. "Naw."

"How about your grandfather?"

He left us standing there, went back inside the house, and knocked on the first closed door.

"Yes, son?" The Good Reverend's voice sounded muffled, but unctuous as ever.

"Somebody's here to see you," Tyrone said, and sat back down on the couch. He was watching cartoons, and the outraged sputterings of Daffy Duck were the only sound in the room.

197

"I'm at work on next Sunday's message, son," the Rev said through the door. "Tell them to come back another time."

Tyrone ignored that completely. Scratching and watching seemed to be the limit of functions he could perform at the same time. Joyce and I looked at each other. Tyrone in his Skivvies was not something I had ever hoped to see, especially after our recent exchange of stories regarding my inability to restrain myself when confronted with his overwhelming sexual presence. I was ready to go, but Joyce stepped inside and walked up to the closed door.

"Reverend Anderson?" she said, knocking on it hard enough to elicit a frown from Tyrone, who was obviously a serious Looney Tunes fan and did not like his Bugs Bunny viewing disrupted. "This is Joyce Mitchell out here. I need to talk to you."

There was a long pause, during which Bugs Bunny concocted an elaborate setup to make a fool of Elmer Fudd, then the Rev said, "I'm busy right now," and I heard the slur for the first time. Joyce heard it too.

"He's drunk," Joyce whispered to me, although she didn't need to. Tyrone was incapable of the kind of attentive inattention it takes to eavesdrop effectively.

Through the door she said: "This can't wait, Rev."

Another pause. Elmer Fudd earned his paycheck by stumbling effortlessly into the trap Bugs had set for him and the Rev finally opened up the door.

He was so drunk he could hardly stand up. His eyes were bloodshot, his lids were at half-mast, and the smell of bourbon was so strong on him that you could get a contact high just standing too close. His tie was twisted around sideways and his shirt looked like he'd slept in it. He staggered toward us, swayed a step, put out his hand and patted Joyce's shoulder in a move that was meant to be fatherly and reassuring, but wasn't even close.

"Of course you can't wait, my sisters. The Lord sent you here for answers, for guidance, and as his servant, I am charged with . . . I am charged with . . ." Seeming to hear the TV for the first time, he turned to Tyrone and frowned. "What are you doing, son? What are you *doing?*"

Tyrone never took his eyes off the screen. "I'm watching TV. What does it look like I'm doing?"

I had seen Tyrone defy his grandmother in subtle ways, but nothing like this. It was clear who was in charge at Gerry's house. No wonder the Rev wasn't seen around much during the week. She probably had all she could do to get him sobered up for Sunday morning.

The Rev looked confused. "Your clothes, son!" His voice was wheedling as if he were trying to convince a cranky two-year-old that it was time for a nap. "Go put some pants on."

Tyrone stood up and turned off the television. He looked at his grandfather for the first time, stretched to his full height, and made a noise that was a cross between a snicker and a snort.

"Oh," he said, "now it's time to put the pants *on,* huh? Make up your mind, why don't you?"

His grandfather's eyes followed him as he swaggered off down the hall with an expression of exasperation and something else I couldn't identify and decided I didn't want to. The Rev was too drunk to give us a straight answer about anything, and Tyrone wasn't about to try. When he slammed the bedroom door behind him, the Rev turned back to us.

"Please," he said, blowing bourbon in our direction. "Have a seat. I'm sorry about Tyrone. He's going through one of those . . ." His voice trailed off helplessly. He had no idea what he had started out to say.

"Phases?" Joyce offered.

"Exactly," said the Rev, smiling and nodding with drunken gratitude. "He's going through a *phase.*"

"I think it's more than that," Joyce said. "I think he needs professional help."

The Rev looked confused again, then he smiled like

drunks tend to do when they think they're going to put one over on you.

"Well, then the blessing is, he can get that help from his grandfather who loves him."

It was real clear to me that this guy was not only drunk, he was delusional. Him helping Tyrone was like Mattie raising Frank. *A joke.*

Rev leaned toward us like he was speaking confidentially. "I know about our boys." He nodded and looked around to be sure we were alone. "I know how to guide and direct them away from the path of Satan and into the arms of Christ Jesus."

I wondered if he even knew about the story Tyrone and Gerry had concocted for the sheriff.

"Reverend Anderson," Joyce said. "I was hoping you'd be able to be at the meeting at Sheriff Gates' office yesterday."

He frowned like he was trying to remember that long ago. "Sheriff Gates?"

"Your wife was there and . . ."

Suddenly the Rev's face darkened and he scowled at Joyce like he'd just caught her in a lie, but he couldn't get hold of exactly what lie it was, so he did what drunks always do: he went *left*. Through the Jack Daniel's fog in which he was floating, the mention of his wife held out the first recognizable port in a storm, and like a drowning man, he grabbed it and went for broke.

"My wife," he said, and his voice trembled with drunken emotion even while his tongue stumbled over the words. "My wife is a living saint. Her spirit is too big for this . . . this place." He was getting more indignant by the second. "She has looked evil in the eye, *unblinking.* She has propped me up on every weak and leaning side and it is her voice alone, lifted in praise, that can soften God's heart toward the lowly sinner!"

He stood and walked unsteadily toward the window. "When the Devil tested me, when he had me in his clutches, breathing his hot breath into my face, my wife reached out and took my hand. Her faith opened the jaws of the beast and pulled me through, praise the Lord!" he said, throwing up his hands and almost losing his balance. He grabbed the arm of the nearest chair and lowered himself carefully into it. His eyes struggled to focus on us, then he smiled and spoke as if offering us the sweetest gift he could find.

"She can pray with you," he whispered. "The Lord still listens to her voice even though his ears are closed to me."

I was curious. "Why?" I said. "Why are his ears closed to you?"

He looked at me and shook his head sadly. "I strayed from the path. I was tempted and tested and I failed the Lord. Until I prove myself worthy, my cries will be in vain, although I pray without ceasing."

I was amazed to see tears running down his face.

"Without ceasing!"

Joyce stood up to go. This was clearly hopeless, but I held up my hand to stop her. He wanted to tell us something and I sure wanted to hear it.

"What did you do," I said, "to make the Lord so mad?"

His head jerked up and he looked suddenly wary. He wagged a drunken finger at me. "No, no, no," he said. "She warned me of you! Of both of you! She warned me that when you came, you would not be alone. That a dark messenger would be at your side. But I see his cloven hoof! I smell his awful sweat and hear the roar of his eternal fire, but I hold to my God! I hold fast to my God!"

Then he slipped out of the chair and fell to his knees on the rug, closed his eyes, and began to mumble frantically into his tightly clasped hands. I don't even think he saw us leaving.

From the room down the hall, I could hear the muffled honk of the Roadrunner and the explosion earmarked for Wil E. Coyote.

• 17

i went over to Mack's old place to do some painting and it's not *Mack's old place* anymore. It's something *new*. Eddie finished all the drywall and inside repairs, so we're giving everything a couple of coats of basic white. Joyce isn't sure what she wants it to look like eventually. She's talking about murals and communal collages and hanging photographs of everybody all over the place, but it changes every day, so Eddie figured we can just put down a basic covering and she can decide later.

When he asked me if I wanted to do some painting, I told him up front that home improvements aren't really my thing. Even when I moved into an apartment that needed a little touching up around the edges, I'd buy the beer, pick up some chicken wings, and recruit from among my gentlemen friends a few who considered themselves to be *handy*, as opposed to the ones who leaned toward white linen suits in the summer months and regarded household repairs as a way for some other brother to make a few honest dollars.

I asked one of the ones from column B to help me move once in a moment when money was tight and all the handy guys were otherwise engaged. The brother showed up with a bottle of Dom Perignon, an eighteen-foot U-Haul, and three huge Morehouse students with big shoulders, boundless energy, and the enthusiasm an unexpected couple hundred bucks can bring on Saturday afternoon. Easiest move I ever made.

Another reason I usually don't do crew is that most men can't explain a simple task to you without going overboard and becoming obnoxious clones of their half-witted seventh-grade shop teacher. But working with Eddie was different. He got me set up with a half gallon of the whitest paint I've ever seen and a new roller, filled the deep end of the shiny new paint pan, and left me to my own devices. He was in the kitchen and since everything was open now, I could see him. Every once in a while he'd smile my way, but mostly he was working the way he did everything, like there was nothing else he'd rather be doing in this world.

Eddie had a gift for *focus*. When we made love, I always felt like his mind was on whatever he was doing with me at that very moment, not off somewhere checking the stock reports, or wondering if he could still catch the second half of the game, or even speeding through the preliminaries as quickly as possible so he could get to the main event. Every part was as pleasurable to him as every other part.

That's why he could drive me crazy rubbing the soles of my feet, or kissing the palms of my hands. At any given moment I felt like all of the energy in his body was in complete connection with all of the energy in mine, physical, mental, emotional, sexual, spiritual. The man knew how to be *present*.

Sometimes, at first, I used to just lie in his arms and cry afterward. I couldn't believe how good I felt. He was touching parts of me that I hadn't even known were there, much less that they were capable of the kind of rolling waves of pure pleasure that were now a regular part of our exchanges. When I tried to explain to him why I was crying, the closest I could come to describing the feeling was just absolute relief that I could finally give somebody all that sweet stuff I'd been saving up for so long.

I didn't realize I had stopped painting and was staring until I looked up and saw Eddie grinning at me.

"Me, too," he said.

I knew he was pretty good at reading my mind, but I also knew it was important not to let him get too cocky about it. As close as I am to Eddie, it's only a short step from mind reading to mind control, and I had no interest in gong there.

"Me, too, *what*?" I said, testing him.

He put down his paintbrush, walked over to me, laid my roller back in the pan, and kissed me for what felt like about half an hour. He was holding me so tight, I felt like those Hollywood movie girls who always swoon at the end of a close-up kiss from the conquering hero.

By the time we came up for air, I figured he had answered the question to my satisfaction. He must have thought so, too, because now he had a question of his own.

"Ava?" He leaned back to look at me without taking his arms from around my waist.

"Yes?"

"Will you marry me?"

• 18

i was so freaked out when Eddie proposed that I just stuttered something at him about having to be by myself for a minute and headed out the front door back to Joyce's. I'm sure he was surprised, but he didn't try to stop me. What I *really* needed was a drink, but I'm so damn pure these days, there isn't even any damn vodka at the damn house! Maybe I ought to call the Rev. I'll bet he's got a taste of something that takes the edges off.

I was walking so fast, I sounded like a bear crashing through the woods. I took the long way because I wasn't sure if Joyce was home or not, but I knew I needed to calm my ass down before I was ready for people.

I can't believe it. I've been waiting all my life to find what I've got with Eddie and when it finally arrives, I'm a walking time bomb. I wanted a life with Eddie so bad it made my bones ache, but what did I have to offer him? A honeymoon full of night sweats? A future full of ugliness and pain and stink?

In the movies, people die of AIDS in a nice clean bed with their family around and a discreet respirator humming softly in the background. In real life, they die with diapers full of bloody diarrhea and purple Kaposi's lesions on their faces and lungs full of phlegm and bodies full of bedsores. I know *fair* isn't in it, but *goddam!*

•

I haven't done flashbacks in ages, but now, suddenly, my mind was clicking through a photo montage of all the men who could have been *the one.* The nasty one. The infected one. The lying, bisexual one. The intravenous dope fiend one. I wanted somebody to blame besides me. Somebody else to be mad at. Somebody else to hold responsible for the crime of my own stupidity and carelessness.

But there wasn't anybody to blame. There was just me, wanting time that wasn't promised, missing moments I hadn't even lived through yet, turning away from this day because I couldn't be sure about the next one. I was doing just fine being in the damn moment, being grateful for every sunrise, all that bullshit. But Eddie's words made me greedy for *more. More* time. *More* love. *More* sweetness. I didn't want anything to change. I wanted everything to stay just the way it was right now so I could wrap it around me tight enough to keep me from flying into a million scared, screaming pieces.

I have to tell Eddie no. The whole idea is crazy. He's pretending worse than I am. Hoping that if we stand up together and promise to love each other forever, we can stop time. But we can't, any more than Joyce can make me all better by running up another pair of blue plaid curtains.

Or maybe it's worse than that. Maybe he just feels sorry for me. The thought made me feel like I was going to throw up. Maybe he's prepared to help Joyce take care of me when things get really bad and he figured being married to me might make it easier. Or maybe he just wanted to make sure I didn't go to my grave an unmarried woman.

This is making me crazy! I never should have come here for the whole summer. I should have stopped by, made Joyce pack up, and headed us both toward San Francisco Bay as fast as we could get there. *But I didn't.* I hung around pretending and got caught up in my own daydream. Now it was just going to be that much harder to wake the fuck up and smell the coffee.

• 19

as soon as I saw Mattie step out of that social worker's car, I knew there was going to be trouble. She had combed her hair and put on what looked like a brand-new pale blue sundress. She was smirking a little like people who aren't real bright always do when they think they've got the jump on somebody smarter.

The social worker was the same sister who brought Imani to us that first day. I couldn't remember her name, but she looked miserable and nervous, which was not a good sign. I stepped out on the porch since Imani was asleep in the living room and I didn't want whatever conversation this was going to be to wake her.

"Ava, right?" The social worker extended her hand like they always do. "I'm Janice Randle, Joyce's friend from Children's Services?"

I nodded. "Joyce isn't here right now." She was due back any minute, but I wasn't raised to tell everything I know. Janice glanced at Mattie, who rolled her eyes and looked at her watch like any delay might throw off her schedule.

"I ain't got all day."

Janice looked at her own watch. "Do you know when she'll be back?"

"I'm not sure," I said. "If you have something else she needs to sign, I can make sure she gets it."

Mattie folded her arms and shifted from one foot to the other. "We gonna have to do this another time," she said. "I told you, I got someplace I gotta be."

"All right, all right." Janice spoke sharply to Mattie, and I realized how nervous she really was. People talk smart to social workers all the time and they're trained to take it. Whatever was going on clearly was working my girl's last nerve.

"What's the problem?" I said, hoping she would tell me the truth, even though legally I was only a bit player.

Janice sighed. "We've got a little bit of a situation here," she said.

"What kind of situation?"

"I'd rather talk to Joyce first before we go into all the details."

"Suit yourself. I'll ask her to call you when she gets back," I said just as Joyce pulled into the yard.

She looked at the three of us, then got out of the car and looked at me for some kind of sign about what was going on.

"Janice says we've got a situation to deal with and Mattie says she's got someplace else to go." Now she knew everything I knew.

Joyce turned directly to Janice and smiled. "Hey, Jan. A situation? Is it an outside situation or can you come in and sit down?"

"I'm sorry," Janice said, ushering Mattie in ahead of her. "Of course we can sit down. How're you doing?"

"Fine," Joyce said. "How you doing, Mattie?"

Mattie just shrugged and picked at the chipped polish on her fingernails. "I'm doin'."

"What's the situation?"

Janice took a deep breath. "The family wants the baby back."

"Imani?" Joyce's eyes went black. The tone in her voice sucked the warm air from the room and replaced it with ice. Mattie sat up and looked nervously at the door. Janice extended a hand toward Joyce, but drew it back before she made contact. "What are you talking about?"

"Mattie says she's ready to take the baby back home now."

"Back *home?*"

"Your custody is only temporary, Joyce. You know we talked about this."

"I filed the papers for permanent custody. They told

me there wouldn't be a problem with it. She's thriving here and you know it."

"But she ain't your kid, is she?" Mattie said, real nasty.

Joyce looked at her and then back to Janice. "Have you been to her house?"

Janice nodded. "It doesn't matter."

"Doesn't matter?"

"They weren't denied custody. They were never even accused of being unfit. They chose to give up custody temporarily. They can change their minds anytime they want to."

Mattie smirked at Joyce. "See? You shouldn't believe all that bad shit you heard about me, 'scuse my French. I'm turning my life around."

"She's a crack-head," Joyce said as calm as if she'd just said good morning. "Her brother is a violent, woman-hating hoodlum, and neither one of them has even bothered to come and see Imani since we brought her home. They don't even know her name."

"You a lie," Mattie said. "I'm a call her Frankie. After my baby brother. What you think about that?"

"Jan, you can't be serious," Joyce said.

Janice nodded and pulled out some papers, handed them across the table to Joyce, who looked at them and back at her friend.

"Listen, Joyce, they dropped this one on me this morning. It's wrong. Somebody must have pulled strings to have the order issued that fast. I have to transfer her this afternoon, but we can file papers today and get a hearing first thing next week so she can be returned to—"

Mattie poked Janice in the arm like they were girls on a school yard.

"Hey," she said. "You 'spose to be on my side."

"I'm on Imani's side."

"Her name *Frankie*."

Joyce looked at Mattie. "Why the hell are you doing this?"

"You didn't want trouble, you shouldn't have put the cops on my brother!" Mattie said.

"Is that what this is about?"

"Naw, this ain't what this is about," Mattie said. "This is about you takin' my sister's kid and not tellin' me about the money."

"What money?" Janice and Joyce spoke at the same time.

Mattie looked sly. "Don't she get money for keepin' the kid?"

"All foster parents get money, but—"

"Well, if anybody's 'spose to be gettin' paid off her, it should be me."

"You're her *family*," Janice said wearily. "You might not even be eligible for—"

"She say we will be 'cause we got hardship."

"She *who?*" Joyce said.

Mattie turned her attention back to her nails. "That ain't none of your business, is it? All you gotta do is pack up that baby's shit and let me get on up outta here. This ain't no soap opera, so we ain't gotta drag it out all day. Let's go!"

"Now?" Joyce looked at Janice, who nodded and waved helplessly at the official papers.

"I know we can get a hearing if we—"

Joyce no longer had time for Janice, who seemed to have no solutions and no suggestions.

"Look, Mattie," Joyce said. "You can have the money. I don't want it. I'll send you the check every month and you don't even have to keep the baby at all."

Mattie laughed. "That's just what she said you would say."

"Who are you talking about?"

"Miz Anderson, who you think? She said it was her Christian duty to help me get what's coming to me."

I sat down. *Damn!* Gerry again? What was she trying to do now?

"She said you all not fit to be raisin' no baby." She

looked at me. "It ain't healthy with what you got. So she gonna pay me double what they payin' you to be sure Frankie get brought up someplace where she ain't gonna get sick like her dumb-ass mama."

Joyce looked at Janice like *you see what I mean?* Janice looked away.

"Don't take this personal, Jan," Joyce said quietly, "but before I'll let you carry Imani out of here, I'll blow both your brains out."

Mattie jumped up. "I ain't scared of you!"

"You should be."

"Joyce, wait!" Janice was pleading, hands extended in front of her like Joyce had already aimed a .357 Magnum in her direction. "This isn't the way to do it! If you don't give her to me, they'll send the sheriff with me tomorrow."

"Then that's what they're going to have to do," Joyce said.

"They'll still take her."

"They'll have to find her first," Joyce said, cool as shit.

"I'm outta here," Mattie said, heading for the door.

I opened it for her and she rolled her eyes at me as she stomped down the back steps in her platform sandals.

Janice put her hands on Joyce's shoulders. "Listen to me, girl! You're going to get custody as sure as I'm standing here, but if you run with her, you'll be a kidnapper with no rights and you'll never get her back."

Joyce turned away and I could see the tears on her face.

"Not today, okay?" She turned to Janice. "Let me get her things together and . . . tomorrow you can take her."

Janice hesitated.

"Please, Jan."

"Okay. No tricks though, Joyce, all right?"

"Did you know Gerry Anderson had a hand in this?"

Janice shook her head. "No, but I should have. It's not like Mattie had a sudden surge of maternal feelings." She glanced at Mattie waiting in the car. "I'd better go on."

Joyce didn't move. She seemed lost in her own thoughts. Janice squeezed her hand once and headed for the door.

"Jan?"

Janice hesitated.

"Thanks."

"No problem."

I watched them pull out and turned back to Joyce, who was gone. I knew where she was, sitting in the rocking chair holding Imani, smiling and cooing like things had never been better.

"Joyce?" I said, and when she looked up at me, I knew we were at war. "Tell me what you need for me to do."

• 20

i called eddie and the three of us sat up half the night trying to figure things out. Joyce talked to her lawyer, who reminded her that the kind of temporary custody that she had brought with it almost no rights when it comes to any conflict with the family. The fact that Gerry was, in effect, bribing Mattie to take the baby had no legal effect on things at all.

Joyce wanted to demand hearings, interview witnesses, prove what she knew about Mattie and what her house was like, all of which was fine and could be done, but it was going to take time. The lawyer agreed with Janice that a hearing would almost certainly result in Imani's return, but none could be scheduled before Monday, which would mean Imani would be spending the weekend at Mattie's.

At first Joyce refused to consider it. She had seen inside Mattie's house and we all knew what Frank was like, but the alternative seemed more than risky. How far could Joyce get on the run with a two-month-old baby, even with me and Eddie aiding and abetting every step of the way? Even worse, Janice was right. There was no way Joyce would ever get custody if she kidnapped Imani before the legal process had a chance to kick in.

It was a terrible discussion and even though the three of us sounded all sane and mature, I could feel the panic rising as we realized the box we were in, even if it was only temporary.

Around midnight, we had said everything we could think of to say. Imani had been asleep for hours, but Joyce never put her down. Finally, after we just sat there in silence for about five minutes, Joyce said, "I'm going to let them take her for this one weekend, but I'm going to go over there in my car every day and sit outside to make sure nothing happens to her, and on Monday, if they don't give me a hearing and hand me back my baby, I'm going to go over to Mattie's house and get her." She looked at us. "After that, we'll take it one day at a time."

"I'll sit with you," I said.

"And if you need to go inside, just give me the word," Eddie said.

Joyce looked down at Imani in her arms. "Once we get this straight, Gerry Anderson has a lot of explaining to do."

I keep trying to tell Joyce every evil thing can't explain itself. In Gerry's case, I think the truth is buried under so much screaming bullshit, she doesn't have a clue herself, but something in us touched off every alarm the woman's got. We thought we were arguing about a youth center, but that ain't even in it. Gerry's fighting for her life.

• 21

i dreamed that me and Eddie made love without any latex. Skin to skin. Inside and out. When I woke up, the dream taste of him was still in my mouth.

september

• 1

i woke up this morning and the sheets were soaked through. I immediately started rationalizing about it being summertime, hot weather and all, but that's all bullshit. I know exactly what it is: *night sweats*. it's my first real, live, full-blown, straight-ahead, no-denyin'-it, even-if-you-tryin'-it AIDS symptom.

It scared me so bad to realize and admit it that I felt weak. Faint, even. I would have lain back down, but the damn bed was all damp and clammy because I hadn't changed it yet. Then I wanted to burn the sheets and start popping Nodoz so I could sit up all night instead of going to sleep and risking it happening all over again.

I was thinking all kinds of crazy shit, pacing up and down. I'm surprised Joyce didn't hear me. I think a part of me probably wanted her to hear so she'd come in and give me a plausible explanation for what my body was doing that didn't have anything to do with AIDS. *Girl, pleez! It was so hot in this house last night, I got up and changed my own sheets twice!*

But that's the problem with *knowing*. It takes away the possibility of pretending. Which is what I have been busy doing ever since I got here. Pretending that the Sewing Circus can change the world. Pretending we can rescue Imani. Pretending this place is so far away from the scene of the crime that the consequences can't catch me. Pretending I've got time to fall in love.

• 2

janice wasn't kidding. When she pulled up this afternoon with Mattie, Sheriff Gates pulled in right behind her. He didn't get out of his car, although he did raise a weary hand at us out the window. I guess he was hoping his presence would be enough to keep us under control.

Eddie and me stood on either side of Joyce when she came out with Imani and a small suitcase. Joyce had a list of child-care things she hoped Mattie would take the time to read, but I knew there was no chance of that happening. I was counting on Imani being strong enough now to survive a couple of really fucked-up days even if all they remembered to do was change her every now and then and feed her when she cried. Except that she never cried. Joyce always said she couldn't figure out if Imani was a really, really good baby, or if she was just trying to stay out of the way.

Eddie strapped the infant seat into the car and Joyce buckled Imani in. We had already kissed her about a million times and assured her everything was going to be okay, but Joyce kissed her again and whispered something to her and then she stood up and stepped back from the car. Janice got in behind the wheel and Mattie climbed in beside her and lit a cigarette without even glancing at Imani.

"I'll drop them off and come back for you so we can get the hearing papers filed today," Janice said.

Joyce nodded. She never took her eyes off Imani. I hoped Imani couldn't see the worry in her smile as clearly as I did. Knowing her, she probably did, but from where I was standing, she just looked confused.

We stood there and watched them pull out, Sheriff Gates right behind them. I looked at Joyce and she wiped her eyes and shook her head.

"If anything happens to her—"

I interrupted her. "*It won't*. Come on. Let's get the documents we need for the hearing request so we'll be ready when Janice gets back."

That was what Joyce needed. Something to *do*. Otherwise she wasn't going to make it through what I knew was going to be a very long weekend.

• 3

me and joyce spent the next two days parked a couple of hundred yards from Mattie's front door. The houses on both sides were boarded-up empty, so we made sure we were on somebody else's property and then we just sat there. We were close enough to hear Imani if she cried, but so far, everything had been cool. Good thing, too. I don't think Joyce could have taken it if she had.

Eddie came up periodically so we could go pee and get something to eat and he took the midnight-to-sunrise shift so we could get some sleep. Frank came and went a lot and there was a regular stream of bug-eyed crack addicts who only slowed down long enough to make sure we weren't cops and then ignored us. There is nothing so single-minded as a crack addict on the way to get high. If we could apply all that energy to something more constructive, we'd be free by now.

Everything had been happening so fast that I hadn't really been alone with Eddie since he proposed, which was fine with me. My brain and my heart were already on overload, but on Sunday afternoon he brought a message to Joyce from her lawyer, who needed to talk about the hearing on Monday. He offered to stay with me and handed Joyce the keys to the truck. She looked at the house, which was quiet, and back at me and Eddie.

"If you hear anything weird—"

I stopped her. "Go talk to the lawyer. We got it covered."

217

"It's already Sunday," Eddie said. "If they haven't acted a fool by now, they probably aren't going to."

"One hour," Joyce said. I think she felt like as long as she was there giving them the hard eye, nothing bad could happen to Imani. "I'll be back in an hour and I'll bring some sandwiches."

"Coffee," I said. She nodded and was gone.

Eddie and I looked at each other. "Want to stretch your legs?" he said.

I hesitated.

"We won't go far."

"Okay."

Walking up the road was probably easier than sitting beside him in the car. He put his arm around my shoulders.

"How are you doing?"

"I been better."

"She'll be okay," he said, glancing back at the house as Mattie opened the front door and looked to see if Joyce's car was still there. When she saw me and Eddie, she turned around and went back inside, slamming the door behind her as loud as she could. A few seconds later, the sound of a bass-heavy rap record poured out of the windows.

"She'll be okay," Eddie said again.

"What's the lesson?" I said.

"You can't know the meaning of the lesson until class is over."

"And when will that be?"

"When Imani is back home with Joyce and you're not scared to look me in the eye anymore."

Of course, he was right. I was looking at the trees, the rocks in the road, the boarded-up house next to Mattie's, the puffs of white clouds floating in that vacationer's-paradise blue sky.

"Two for the price of one?" I said, trying to play it off.

We had made it back to the car. The music was pretty loud, but we would have been able to hear anything out of the ordinary without much trouble. Still, I didn't want to take any chances, so I leaned against the hood. He did, too.

"I've thought a lot about what you asked me," I said.

"Me, too."

"I guess this isn't really the time to talk about it."

"I think it's the best time," he said.

That sort of made me mad. It probably wouldn't have ordinarily, but I was looking for any excuse to get angry so I wouldn't feel so crazy telling him no way could I promise him forever when I might not make it to Christmas. When he said that, so calm and serene and shit, I wanted to scream at him, but I just said, "The best time for who?"

"For us."

"And why is that?" I said, real nasty. "Because you say so?"

He turned toward me and touched my cheek with his fingertips. "Do you love me?"

I nodded, not trusting my voice to retain the required nastiness.

He smiled at me. "And I love you. What you used to be. What you are. What you're going to be."

"I'm sick, Eddie," I said, wanting to feel his name in my mouth even in the middle of all this craziness. "What I'm going to be is sicker."

"I know that," he said. "I can take care of you when—"

"I don't want you to nurse me." I heard my voice quivering all over the place.

"Is that what I've been doing?"

"Give it time," I said, and turned away from him. "Give it time."

He put his hands on my shoulders and turned me back around. "I promise to help you do whatever you want to do when the time comes for all that. There is nothing you can show me, nothing you can ask me to do, that will ever make me turn away from you. *Nothing*."

I leaned into his chest and closed my eyes. "I'm so scared," I said. "Sometimes I just get so scared."

He pulled me closer and his lips brushed against my ear.

"It starts here," he said. "All the strength and all the courage and all the peace we're ever going to need starts right here with me loving you, just like this. And you loving me, just like this."

He kissed the top of my head and I could feel his hair tickling my neck.

"I'm not here to watch you die," he said softly. "I'm here to help you live."

I looked up into his face and it looked like *home*, and all of a sudden, standing there keeping watch outside of that madhouse, I felt like I almost *understood*. What was important and what was not. What was worth the time and effort and what was just a bunch of bullshit. And the more I looked at Eddie looking back at me, the more it was starting to make sense. Not all of it, but a little. Just a little, and at this point, that was all I needed.

"You remember those tunnels I told you about?" he said, touching my cheek.

I nodded.

"Well, that's what we're building, too, except they're different from the ones I saw in 'Nam. You know why?"

"Why?" I said, not caring that I felt tears on my face.

"Because," he said, "those were for war. What we're building are tunnels of love."

• 4

by the time Joyce got back, two more cars had come and gone, and the rap music had gone into overdrive. I wondered if any of the young brothers whose voices demanded such a dizzying range of sexual favors in the most aggressive possible way ever got the desired response from the objects of their lustful affections. I had my doubts. Anybody who can't ask for it any better than that probably won't know what to do with it when you hand it to him.

Eddie and I had agreed to talk more about marriage between the two of us before we said anything to Joyce. I knew I wanted to be with him as long as I could, but I also knew I've never made a decision in a crisis that I didn't live to regret once the moment passed.

Joyce had good news from her lawyer, who knew somebody who knew somebody who knew somebody with some clout. The hearing had been scheduled for nine A.M. Monday morning. If everything went the way it was supposed to, Imani would be home before noon tomorrow. Joyce looked as relieved as I felt. When Eddie volunteered to stay longer so she could take a break, Joyce didn't even think about it. If she could have gotten away with camping out on Mattie's front porch, she would have. Eddie kissed me good-bye, hugged Joyce, and promised to be back at midnight.

When we settled back down in the front seat, I poured a cup of fresh coffee from the thermos she had brought, and Joyce leaned back and closed her eyes. The music playing in the house was another presence in the car with us. You could *feel* the beat inside your body.

"I wish they would turn it down," Joyce said. "What if we can't hear her if she needs us?"

"The windows are open," I said. "We'll hear her."

"I'd like to walk up in there right now, grab Imani, and run like hell."

"Plan A," I said. "We tossed it in favor of Plan B. Remember?"

"Do you think she's okay?"

"I'm sure she is." I still had Eddie's confidence draped around my shoulders like a Spanish shawl.

"I'm going to figure out how to make peace with Gerry," Joyce said.

"You didn't start the war, did you?"

Joyce shrugged without sitting up, but she opened her eyes. "I don't care. This woman is crazy enough about something that she's prepared to accuse you of molesting a kid and

221

give Imani to a crack addict to make sure I don't challenge her and her drunken husband. Well, they can have it, whatever *it* is. I'm going to stay so far away from them, they'll forget they ever knew me."

I opened my mouth to agree with Joyce when she held up her hand.

Listen!"

At first I didn't hear anything, but then, down under all that bass, I heard Imani crying. Inside the house, Frank heard it, too.

"Shut that bitch up, goddammit! I'm not tellin' your ass again!"

Mattie shouted something back at him that we couldn't hear, but his answer came through loud and clear.

"Don't think I won't! I ain't scared of them bitches! Kung Fu neither. *Fuck 'em!"*

We looked at each other. We were here for this moment, but now it was here and we weren't exactly sure what to do about it. Imani's cry was becoming a breathless wail, then we heard the sound of glass breaking and the music stopped. Imani did, too.

Joyce and I practically fell out of the car. We hit the ground running and started knocking on the door and ringing the bell. Imani started screaming inside the house and Joyce kicked the door so hard it cracked. The music started up again even louder and Mattie jerked the door open just enough for Joyce to get her foot in it.

"Get the fuck out of my house," Mattie shrieked. We could hear Imani crying so hard she was gasping. Joyce reached in and grabbed a piece of Mattie's blouse, pulling her toward us outside on the porch.

"If you don't open this goddam door, I'm going to—"

The door opened so fast, Joyce stumbled and I grabbed for her, but she leaned into the fall and tried to duck by Frank, who reached out and snatched her back without taking his eyes off me.

"Where the fuck you think you goin'?" He was very high and very pissed off.

"Give me my baby!"

"She ain't your baby," Mattie hollered. "You ain't got no baby!"

"Give her to me now!" Joyce shouted.

Frank looked at her and twisted his face into a terrible smile.

"She's asleep," he said as if we couldn't hear her crying. "Now, get the fuck out of my face."

He was pushing us easily out of the doorway, and Imani's sobs from somewhere back inside the house were desperate and terrified. I tried to look around Frank and Mattie to see if I could see her, but what I saw was old Mack's black-and-white, rabbit-eared TV sitting on a table in the living room.

Joyce started begging. "Don't do this," she said, her nails clawing at Frank's sleeve. "Please, please, don't do this!"

"Do what?" he said, brushing Joyce off as if she were a child. "I ain't doin' nothin'. If I was doin' somethin', I'd be flashin' this, awright?" He reached in his pocket and waved a nine-millimeter pistol in Joyce's face. "But I ain't did that. I ain't did shit."

"Please." Tears were running down Joyce's face and I was trying to calculate the odds against us if we rushed them. *"Please."*

"You're trespassing," Frank said. "Get going. Especially *you*." He leaned forward and nudged my shoulder with the gun. It looked huge and so did Frank. "I don't want none of what you got."

"Come on, Joyce," I said, not knowing anymore if I was more afraid for Imani or for us. I half dragged, half carried her back to the car, but when I tried to push her in the passenger side, she wouldn't go. She gripped the side of the car and held on.

"Goddammit, Joyce," I whispered. "That fool is still on

the porch waiting for us to get in this car. What good will it
do Imani if he shoots us?"

"I can't leave her here." Joyce was sobbing.

"Just get in the car," I said. "When he goes inside, we
can figure out what to do."

That made sense to her because she let go and jumped
in the car. I ran around to the driver's side, started it up, and
took off. In the rearview mirror I saw Frank put the gun back
in his pocket and go inside. I made sure we rounded the first
curve so they couldn't see us and then pulled over to the side
of the road. Joyce wasn't crying anymore. Now she was defiant, and since I was the only one there, she aimed it at me.

"I've lost two babies," she said, opening her lips but
not her teeth. "I'm not giving up another one."

"He's got a gun," I said. "We need some help."

"*We've* got a gun." The shotgun was still standing in
the corner of the closet in my room. I could tell by the way
she said it that she wished we had it with us. I did, too, even
though the idea of actually using it made me feel cold and
queasy. I wondered if Frank had ever shot anybody.

"I'll go get it," I said, before I knew I was going to say
anything. But it was out there now and Joyce was looking at
me like I was in charge. "You go back and watch the house,"
I said. "Don't let them see you."

"I won't."

"I'll be right back."

Joyce nodded, opened the car door, and headed back
toward the house. I watched her and wondered what the hell
we were doing. I drove to the main road with every intention
of turning right toward our house, but where I went was left,
straight to Eddie's.

• 5

the rest of the ride is a blur. So is whatever I told Eddie. So is the ride back to Mattie's house until we pulled up in the yard. Then everything slows way down the way it does in a bad dream.

The red lights of the ambulance. The paramedic rushing out with Imani on a tiny stretcher with an oxygen mask over her whole face. Joyce with frantic eyes running behind them, leaping into the ambulance before they think to question her right to be there, turning her ruined face to tell me that Frank broke the baby's legs before the attendant slams the door and they race off into the night, sirens blaring, lights flashing, and we are left standing there, trying to understand.

But no explanation is possible. Frank and Mattie are gone.

• 6

when me and Eddie finally got back from the hospital, the sun was coming up. Joyce had checked into a motel across the street from the medical center to grab a few hours sleep until they brought Imani to a postop room where Joyce could sit with her, which is what Joyce intended to do. Mattie and Frank were still missing, and Joyce wasn't taking any chances. I was supposed to stick by the phone in case anybody called with news.

The three of us had spent the night in the windowless emergency room, talking to doctors, giving statements to cops, comforting each other, praying for Imani, trying to piece together what happened.

When I pulled off toward Eddie's, Joyce had headed back to the house, trying to stay out of sight, but as soon as she rounded the curve in the road, she could hear Mattie screaming.

"Are you crazy? What did you do?"

Frank shouted back, "She fell, okay? The bitch *fell!* Why you screamin' at me?"

Joyce ran around to the back of the house and the door wasn't locked. Mattie sounded hysterical.

"She hurt bad, nigga. Do somethin'!"

"Nobody tole you to bring the bitch up in here in the first place," Frank said.

Joyce saw the telephone on the kitchen wall and dialed the number at the hospital without caring if they heard her. She thought Frank was going to kill her when he ran around the corner and saw her shouting into the phone, so she screamed at the dispatcher to send the cops, too, because there was a man threatening her with a gun. He grabbed the phone, ripped it out of the socket, and sent it flying across the room so hard it shattered when it hit the far wall. Then he snatched the gun out of his pocket, cocked it, and pointed it at Joyce's head.

Mattie was still screaming. Joyce looked at Frank and she said right then she stopped being scared. She didn't care what he did to her. If he was going to shoot her, that's what he was going to have to do, but he was going to have to do it on her way to Imani.

"Why you keep fuckin' with me, huh?" he said. "You think you made of steel or some shit?"

"Get out of my way," she told Frank, and took a step toward him.

"She called the cops, fool!" Mattie was tugging at his arm. "We gotta go, man. We gotta get the fuck out of here!"

Frank glanced at her and back to Joyce, who took another step in his direction.

"Let's go, Frank!" Mattie grabbed her purse, swept a

counter full of crack paraphernalia into a drawer like any cop worth the badge wouldn't find it in his sleep. "Cops, man! Let's go!"

Frank seemed to hear his sister for the first time. He looked at Joyce and lowered the gun slowly.

"You ain't seen the last of me, bitch," he said. "Count on that shit."

Then they both headed for the door and Joyce ran to find Imani.

When she did, she almost lost it. Imani was lying on her stomach on a blanket spread out on the bare floor. She wasn't moving and at first Joyce thought they had killed her, but when she put her hand on her back, she could feel Imani breathing. That's when she saw her legs. They were splayed out at weird angles they never would have found on their own and dark bruises were already forming where Frank had twisted them so hard he broke the bones. Imani had passed out.

It took Joyce a long time to say all this because she was crying and shaking so bad she almost couldn't talk. When she saw what he had done, she was afraid to move Imani because she didn't want to make the injuries any worse. So she covered her up with part of the blanket and just sat there with her, praying that the ambulance would get there quickly, and it did.

By early this morning, they had operated on Imani's legs, set the broken bones, and put two tiny casts on her. The left leg was broken at the thigh, and the right one just below the knee. Both ankles were severely strained, but neither one was broken. The X rays hadn't shown any other internal injuries and the doctor said she had probably passed out from pain and shock when her legs were hurt and not from any blows to the head.

Joyce was sitting there, listening intently to the doctor, but she was squeezing my hand so hard I wanted to pry her fingers loose, but I didn't. She needed somebody to hold on to and that somebody was me.

The truth of it was, we couldn't get close enough to

suit me. I knew I could have lost both of them tonight—Joyce and Imani. Frank had been moving in the wrong direction so fast, we hadn't been able to figure out how to head him off before it was too late. I knew it was a miracle that he hadn't shot everybody in the house, including his sister.

The doctor told Joyce that Imani was going to be pretty doped up for the next couple of days and she was going to need therapy for her legs once the casts came off, but that she was a strong baby and would probably make a complete recovery.

"If we're lucky," he said, "she won't even have much of a limp."

• 7

since we were too keyed up to go inside, me and Eddie walked down to the dock and laid out full length side by side in the sunshine. It was still early and the breeze off the water was fresh and cool. The birds were singing, the water was lapping at the shore, and there were black-eyed Susan's and Queen Anne's lace growing up the sandy slope to the house. It seemed impossible that Frank could have done what he did in a world that felt as sweet as this one.

I used to feel like I had a pretty accurate picture of what we were like, us black folks. I knew we weren't perfect, but I still hoped we weren't terminally fucked up, even though sometimes the evidence to the contrary is so overwhelming, it's hard to avoid that conclusion.

I had met enough good brothers—a small number, but *enough*—not to think all black men were unworthy of my time and affections. I had been around white folks long enough to know they weren't as smart as they thought they were, but a whole lot meaner than they admitted to being. I knew how to make a living, get where I needed to go, and balance my checkbook, but none of it made any sense anymore.

I thought there was a limit we would reach. A cutoff. A damn bottom line. We used to almost brag about it. There were certain crimes we considered ourselves incapable of committing. When we would read in the paper that somebody had stabbed their mother to death or raped a two-year-old, we would shake our heads and cluck our tongues and turn the page because we *knew* it wasn't one of us.

Not anymore. We do it all, mostly to each other, and when we get caught and the six-o clock news shows us in our bright orange prison coveralls with our hands cuffed behind us and lint in our hair, we don't look sorry. We don't even look scared. What we look is *bored*.

"What was he thinking about?" I said to Eddie, whose fingertips were just touching mine where our hands lay between us on the dock's weathered boards.

"It doesn't matter," he said.

"Doesn't matter? How can it not matter?"

Eddie sat up and squinted out across the sunlit lake. "I watched a brother in 'Nam rape a pregnant woman," he said. "When she aborted before he was finished with her, he slit her throat and stomped the baby's head. What was he thinking?"

"I don't know." I didn't have a clue.

"I don't either, but I don't have to know. I don't think it matters anymore. What matters is what he did, and what Frank did, and what we're going to do about it."

That's when I knew he was going to go look for Frank and Mattie. We both figured they hadn't gone far. They were too scared and too high and too broke.

"The way I figure it, they're probably scuffling around trying to raise some cash," Eddie said. "Once they do that, they'll head for Detroit or Chicago and we'll lose them."

He was right about that. There were so many people wanted for so much evil shit in the city, some young fiend breaking a baby's legs in some little town a couple of hundred miles up the road wasn't going to get anybody to send out an all-points bulletin.

"What are you going to do?"

"I'm going to find them and make sure they stay put long enough for the police to come."

"How are you going to do that?" I was trying to sound cool, but he was making me really nervous.

He smiled at me. "I used to do this for a living," he said. "Don't worry."

"I'll worry."

"Aren't you already worried?"

He had me there. "Maybe they'll just go on to the city, like you said."

He shrugged. "And maybe they won't." He stood up and reached down for my hand. I let him help me up and put my arms around his neck.

"I don't get a vote on this, do I?"

He shook his head and kissed me. "I can't love you if I can't protect you."

We walked back up into the yard. "You still got the shotgun, right?"

I nodded.

"Loaded?"

"Loaded."

"Good," he said. "I don't see them coming back here, but if they show, do what you have to do. Don't take chances."

"I won't," I said, feeling like we were at war, and maybe we were.

"I'll take a look around town and see what I can see. You okay?"

"I'm okay," I said, and kissed him again before he swung up into the truck and started the motor.

"Eddie?"

"What, baby?" He reached out for my hand through the window.

"I thought all the warriors were dead or crazy."

"Just biding our time," he said. "Just biding our time."

I watched him until he was gone, then went inside and locked the door.

• 8

i don't know how much rest Joyce got. She called right after Eddie left to see if we'd heard anything from the police, who were supposed to be looking for Frank. I told her no, but that Eddie was out trying to see what he could find out, too. Then she called to tell me that Imani was now in a private room and the nurse was going to let her stay there as much as she wanted. I asked how Imani was doing and there was such a long pause before she answered, I knew she was crying.

"Oh, Ava," she finally whispered. "She's so tiny. She's got tubes everywhere."

"The doctor said she was strong," I reminded her. "She's going to be fine."

"I never should have let them take her, even for a minute."

I knew trying to talk Joyce out of feeling guilty was going to be impossible until Imani opened her eyes and Joyce could hold her and feed her and rub her legs to help their healing. Joyce was waiting for Imani to wake up so she could apologize and promise that nothing bad was ever going to happen again. I wanted to tell Joyce it wasn't her fault. That all you can ever do is try and make the best choice based on what you know. Promising that everything is going to be okay is just asking for trouble no matter how much you want it to be true.

But all that could wait until later. In offering advice, sincerity is worth a lot, but timing is everything.

"She's going to be fine," I said again. "I'll call you if Eddie turns up something. Don't worry."

"*Right*," she said.

"Okay. Don't worry a lot."

"Better."

She promised to call me later, but the phone rang almost as soon as I hung it up.

"Worry central," I said, figuring Joyce had forgotten to tell me something.

"Pardon me?" The strange voice on the other end sounded confused. "I'm trying to reach Joyce Mitchell."

"She's not here right now," I said. "This is her sister, Ava Johnson. Can I help you?"

"Is your sister the Joyce Mitchell who's running the youth program at the church?"

"The program isn't affiliated with the church anymore," I said.

"Thank God!" The relief in her voice was so intense, it surprised me.

"Who is this?" I said.

"I have some information for your sister."

"About what?" I said. In light of the events of the last forty-eight hours, I felt a healthy suspicion of strangers on the telephone was in order.

"About Reverend and Mrs. Anderson. I was a member of their church in Chicago."

She was visiting her aunt not far away. I gave her directions to the house and put on a fresh pot of coffee. I figured the nap I'd been headed for could wait a little while. This sister sounded like a woman with a story to tell, and I was damn sure ready to listen.

• 9

susan hughes was driving her aunt's old blue Chrysler and she rocked it to a stop in the yard like she was still getting the feel of the brakes. When she got out of the car, she stopped for a minute and looked at the lake with real affection. I wondered if she had come here as a kid, too. People who haven't been here for a while are always surprised at how beautiful it still is. They forget that the reason people stopped coming wasn't because the place stopped being pretty, but because too many folks found the idea of an all-black paradise to be a contradiction in terms. It was sort of like that Groucho Marx joke about not wanting to be a part of any club that would have us as a member. Reminded me of people moving to Atlanta because it's supposed to be *the black Mecca* and then running to buy a house in an all-white suburb.

She accepted my offer of a cup of coffee and we sat down in the living room. She looked to be about my age, even though she was stylishly dressed in an outfit made for someone fifteen years younger.

"I read about your sister's program in the Lake County paper," she said. "My aunt has back issues for a year stacked beside the coffee table like she's really going to get around to reading them all one day. I was going through them to prove to her she wasn't going to miss anything if she went on and threw them out and I saw this picture."

She reached in her purse and took out the folded page she'd taken from the paper. There was a lot of religious news about revivals and homecomings and bake sales, and right in the middle, a photograph of Joyce, the Good Reverend, and Gerry standing in a group of about ten of Joyce's Sewing Circus regulars holding up their babies and grinning like somebody had told them to smile and say *money*. The caption said: *Expanded Nursery Program First Step in Youth Outreach Initiative.*

Joyce had shown me the picture and laughed about how pissed off Gerry had been and how nervous the Rev was about having his picture taken, but the photographer had shown them the assignment sheet where it specifically called for the minister to appear in the shot. As far as the photographer was concerned, that settled it.

"I guess Reverend Anderson was nervous," Susan Hughes said. "After what he did, he ought to be in jail. That's why I was glad when you told me your sister had moved her program away from him. Better be safe than sorry."

She said that like she had just thought it for the first time. She looked at the picture thoughtfully and then frowned. "Is it just for girls?"

"So far," I said, wondering when she was going to tell me what she was talking about. "Once we get our own place open, there'll be activities for boys, too."

She nodded vigorously. "Good for you. These young brothers need all the help they can get. I have a son myself."

She reached for her wallet and flipped through credit cards to a school photograph of a boy who looked to be about thirteen. He was looking seriously into the camera like whatever he had interrupted to come and take a picture was waiting for him to get back to it.

"Corey," she said, touching his cheek with her fingertip delicately like even his likeness might reject such a blatant display of motherly affection. "He'll be fourteen in August."

She put the photograph carefully back into her wallet. "He's really why I called your sister when I saw that picture. I started not to bother her, or you." She sounded apologetic. "But then I thought how much difference it would have made if somebody had called any of us. Just to warn us, you know?"

"I don't know," I said, putting my coffee down and turning toward her sitting beside me on the couch. "Why don't you start at the beginning and tell me everything you think we need to know."

"All right," she said. "I will."

• 10

by the time Susan Hughes left the house, I had typed up what she told me on Joyce's computer, printed out five copies for her to sign, and decided I needed to find Eddie. I thanked Susan for coming to tell me what she knew and went to take a quick shower and change clothes before going into town.

I turned on the shower as hard and hot as I could stand it and stood there breathing in the steam and going over what I'd just heard. Now everything made sense. Gerry had no choice about getting rid of youth activities. That was the only reason the Rev wasn't behind bars.

It seems young Corey Hughes, a member of the Rev's Youth Corps for Christ in Chicago, had complained to his father that Reverend Anderson kept trying to touch him and hug him after he told the Rev to quit. His father went immediately to the Deacon Board to demand an investigation. The deacons, basking in the glow of all the positive publicity and new members the well-publicized youth program had generated, instead made discreet inquiries among the other parents, who spoke to their sons and soon discovered that the Good Reverend had not only been trying to touch other boys, he had also invited them to take naps with him on a cot in the church nursery and offered them money to visit with him at the parsonage while his wife was away.

Whether or not any of them responded to his invitations was open to question, but the evidence was so compelling, the church fathers had no choice but to respond aggressively. They called the Rev in and told him that several of the parents were prepared to bring charges. They dismissed him from their pulpit, effective immediately, and asked him what he had to say for himself.

That, said Susan Hughes, is when Gerry stood up. She pleaded for her husband's reputation as if she were pleading for his life. She lowered her eyes and blamed the Devil, reminding them that Satan always tempted most sorely the one most loved by God. She wept and recounted the history of the last ten years she and the Rev had spent tirelessly building that church from a struggling congregation with a sanctuary that was falling down around their ears into a thriving hub of activity that spilled over from the sanctuary into the streets.

In a quiet conclusion, she whispered what the consequences would certainly be to the church's reputation and future viability if this story was allowed to pass beyond these walls.

At the end of Gerry's plea, she requested that the one without sin among them cast the first stone, and sat down beside the shuddering, weeping wreck of the Rev to await their decision. She didn't have to wait long. The deacons had a quick caucus during which they decided that discretion was the better part of valor. They agreed to pay tuition at any Illinois public college for any victims in return for their pledges of silence, and they agreed not to press charges against the Rev if he left town, promised to get therapy, and refocused his energies away from any youth ministry for the next five years it would take for him to reach retirement and receive a pension.

Someone had heard that one of their smallest churches was looking for a pastor to minister to a congregation made up mostly of retirees. Gerry closed her eyes and thanked the Lord for all his tender mercies, the Rev cleaned out his office, and Susan Hughes' husband made the deal with the Deacon Board that would send their son to college and told her to forget about it.

"But then I saw that picture of them and it all came back," she said. "They made it sound like there was nobody up here anymore but people my aunt's age, but that isn't true. I don't want him to be able to do what he was doing anymore. Not to one more child!"

I thanked Susan Hughes for taking the time to come by and she got up to go, then I remembered another question I thought she might be able to answer.

"Do you know what happened to Tyrone's mother?"

She turned toward me and shivered as if to shake off a bad memory.

"AIDS."

I finished my shower and got dressed quickly. I folded a copy of Susan's statement into an envelope and tucked it into my purse. I needed to show this shit to Eddie *now*. I knew this was part of the lesson. I just didn't know which part.

• 11

i hadn't been in town fifteen minutes when I saw Gerry coming out of the drugstore. I guess the Lord does work in mysterious ways. She hadn't seen me when I pulled up beside her and stopped. The last time we had been together, she was accusing me of seducing Tyrone. I wondered if she'd heard about Imani yet. I double-parked so she couldn't pull away without talking to me and got out of the car.

She looked surprised to see me and I think a little afraid. I walked over to her so we were standing face-to-face. She shrank back a little, looking guilty as hell, and reached out her hand like she was going to touch me.

"I was sorry to hear about the baby."

So she did know what had happened, but her fake condolences were the last thing on my mind.

"Stop lying," I said. "I know everything."

She looked confused and wary. "What do you mean? Everything about what?"

I reached in my purse and extended the white envelope. "About the Good Reverend. About the Youth Corps for Christ. About Corey Hughes. About you, Gerry. I know all about you."

When I said that about the Youth Corps, she snatched the envelope from my hand, but then she tried to regroup fast.

"I don't know what you're talking about," she said.

"Sure you do," I said, leaning against her car. "Read it."

"I'm on my way to take some medicine to Sister McNeil," she said, trying to reach around me and open the door. "I don't have time."

"Sure you do."

•

She realized I wasn't going anywhere and a quick look around showed us to be the only ones on the street.

"Go ahead."

She tore open the envelope slowly and unfolded the one-page statement. Her eyes scanned it and all the air seemed to go out of her body. Everything drooped.

"Why are you doing this?" she said, refolding the letter slowly without looking at me.

"That's the same question we kept asking you, remember?"

"The Good Reverend is—"

"Save it," I cut her off. "He's anything but good."

"What do you want?" she whispered.

"I want to help you pack," I said.

"Please." She grabbed my wrist and squeezed it. "Let me explain. It's not what you think."

"Okay," I said. "What is it, then?"

"Not here," she said, looking around quickly to be sure we were still alone.

"Where?"

"The church office. I have to drop off these pills and then I'll be there. It won't take but fifteen minutes."

I started to tell her I'd follow her just to be on the safe side, but where was she going to go? I figured while she dropped off the medicine, I'd take one fast turn down Main Street to see if I could find Eddie and then head on over to the church. Nothing was going to change that fast, and whatever lie she spent the next fifteen minutes concocting didn't mean a damn thing. I had proof.

"I'll wait ten minutes," I said. "Then I'm going straight to the newspaper."

"The newspaper?" She looked at me and her eyes were begging me to understand, but I wasn't having it. "I'm sorry," she said.

"Me, too," I said. "Don't be late."

And she wasn't.

november

• epilogue

we didn't plan to have a big wedding. It started off with just me and Eddie, Sister Judith and Bill and Joyce and Imani, at the house. But of course, we had to invite Aretha, who got special permission to come home from Interlochen before the Christmas break, and then Joyce announced it at the Sewing Circus and they all took that to be an invitation and started shopping for new outfits and figuring out how to organize the child care and who was going to bring what to feed everybody and calling the oldsters to see who needed a ride and that was that.

Bill said Sister Judith doesn't know how to do a wedding anyway unless there's a hundred people dancing in the aisles. She said she knew exactly *how*. The question was, *why would she?* If you can't dance in the aisles for love, when the hell can you dance in the aisles?

My feelings exactly once I realized there was nothing I could do to stop the wave rolling toward us with such sweet determination. Besides, after everything that happened this summer, we all deserved a party.

Two months ago, celebration was the last thing on anybody's mind. Imani was still in the hospital. The trials hadn't even started. The church was in chaos. Gerry had to take the Rev back to Chicago and have him committed. Once we confronted him with the Corey Hughes story, he retreated for good into some dark corner of his mind where all he was required to do was sit where you put him and rock back and forth until you put him somewhere else. Gerry rejoined her old church and prayed for her husband's forgiveness.

The police picked up Frank and Mattie on the highway less than fifty miles away, headed for Chicago with the gun lying on the seat between them and no alibis. Tyrone's partici-

241

pation in the robberies earned him a two-year stint in juvenile, which puts him behind bars until his eighteenth birthday.

All that seems like a bad dream now. Imani's casts came off last week and she kicked her legs in the air all day like they were the most beautiful things she'd ever seen. She just figured out how to turn over, and the first time she gave a little twist and flipped from her back to her stomach, she laughed out loud. So did we.

As quiet as she was at first, now she's making up for lost time. She coos and babbles and laughs all day long and Joyce talks right back to her. Sometimes I sit on the porch and listen to them while Joyce is cooking dinner, and I swear, they understand each other.

We got our grant from the state back, too, once everything came out, and I'm helping Joyce work on some other proposals so we can keep the Circus going the way it's supposed to go. I knew when I told Joyce she could put me to work, I was in trouble. Now she says she can't imagine trying to do this without me.

We've started going to church again, too. I still like the music, and Sister Judith never talks about the lake of fire, but it's not really about the religion to me. It's just that the church is still the place where the most people get together regularly, and that's worth a lot. Eddie doesn't come yet, but we're working on him.

When Sister Judith got here, the first thing she did was come and talk to Joyce about the Circus and offer her back the fellowship hall space if she wanted it. By that time, though, Eddie had almost finished the renovations on Mack's house and we were headed for our grand opening.

Sister Judith had been sent here by the Baptists, but she'd been in San Francisco for five years, so she had a New Age overlay that appealed to me. When she prayed, she said *Mother/Father God* just like Joyce, and the robes she wore on Sunday were accented with strips of Kente cloth. Her husband, Bill, was a teacher and a poet who shared Eddie's passion for

Motown music and sang bass in the choir because he thought he sounded like Melvin Franklin.

I was a little nervous when they first got here. Even though they had spent a couple of summers here as kids and said they always wanted to come back to live, they seemed too good to be true. Why would anybody leave a city like San Francisco to come to Idlewild?

When I put the question to Sister Judith directly, she looked surprised.

"San Francisco never really belonged to me. Not like this place does. There's something about it. How it started. How it used to be, and how it fell apart. I want to see if we can fix it."

I still must have looked a little skeptical.

"You came here from Atlanta, right?"

I nodded. It seemed a million years and a million miles from Peachtree Street.

"The *black Mecca?*" She rolled her eyes.

I laughed. "So they say."

"Then what are you doing here?"

Watching the sun rise, I wanted to say. *Walking in the woods. Falling in love. Raising a child. Helping my sister. Protecting my family. Living my life.*

"Planning my wedding," is what I said.

We decided to have it the same night we officially opened the Circus. At sunset we all crowded into the house and Joyce stood up front with Imani on her hip and said how happy she was and proud of what they had done and how she knew Mitch's spirit was proud, too, and she lit a candle.

Patrice and Tomika spoke on behalf of the women who had started the nursery which became the Sewing Circus and lit their candles from the flame Joyce was holding.

Then one of Mack's friends spoke on behalf of the old-sters and thanked God they felt safe in their homes again and said how much they all appreciated the young people (any-body under fifty was young to them) checking on them when

the robberies were happening and how they especially appreciated that they kept on with it now that everything was okay
just because everybody enjoyed the contact.

Then a couple of other people said how it felt a little
like the old days to have everybody there together like we
were and Sister Judith said a prayer to *Mother/Father God* and
asked the group to make a circle around me and Eddie so we
could look each other in the eye and promise to go the
distance.

Joyce stood by me, Aretha held Imani, who was cooing
like a dove, and Bill stood up with Eddie, and Sister Judith
asked and we answered and the candles were the only light
around us and for just a second, when Eddie reached out for
my hand, I felt myself wanting to stay in this moment forever
because nothing was ever going to be this perfect or this complete again.

But then, right in the middle of Sister Judith saying
something about our hearts becoming one with the heart of
the universe, Eddie leaned over and kissed me like we were
alone in that room, and right then, right there, I didn't care
what came next. Whatever it was, I knew it would be all right,
or it *wouldn't* be all right, but it would be part of the same
unbroken line we were all walking in, which is, of course, the
real lesson, and about as much perfection as I could stand
without crying right there in front of everybody, which is, of
course, what I did. Then it was done, *official*, and the party
could begin in earnest.

And it did. And we danced too wild, and we sang too
long, and we hugged too hard, and kissed too sweet, and
threw back our heads and howled just as loud as we wanted
to howl, because by now we were all old enough to know that
what looks like *crazy* on an ordinary day looks a lot like *love*
if you catch it in the moonlight.